**Praise for Anna Bennett's
Debutante Diaries series**

The Duke Is But a Dream

"The pace of their story is steady and the flow is smooth, with plenty of chemistry and passion . . . A deeply satisfying tale of love persevering despite social constraints."
—*Publishers Weekly*

"In this story of finding yourself, it's the family the central characters create together that's the most satisfying discovery of all."
—*BookPage*

"Again she creates relatable heroines similar in force and tone to those created by her sister historical romance authors Tessa Dare and Sophie Jordan."
—*Booklist*

"A wonderful read, one that is hard to put down."
—*Affaire de Coeur*

"Anna Bennett is a fantastic storyteller . . . A delight of a read with characters you will love and subplots that add to the fascinating tale of old memories, new beginnings, and a happily-ever-after that made me smile."
—*Fresh Fiction*

"A finely crafted historical romance novel and a wonderfully entertaining read from cover to cover."
—*Midwest Book Review*

First Earl I See Tonight

"Will win readers' hearts."
—*RT Book Reviews*

"Sexy, clever . . . will bring smiles to its readers."
— *Publishers Weekly* (starred review)

Praise for the Wayward Wallflower series

The Rogue Is Back in Town

"Fans of Regency romance authors Eloisa James, Tessa Dare, and Mary Jo Putney will go wild for the final installment of Bennett's Wayward Wallflowers trilogy."
— *Booklist* (starred review)

"Smart and sassy romance . . . simply a joy!"
— *RT Book Reviews* (A Top Pick)

"A standout historical romance novel . . . truly delightful."
— *Romancing the Bookworm*

"Bennett's gift for writing a page-turner of a plot is on full display . . . a solid Regency story of true love."
— *Kirkus Reviews*

"Entertaining . . . [offers] plenty to satisfy Regency fans."
— *Publishers Weekly*

I Dared the Duke

"Sharply drawn characters, clever dialogue, simmering sensuality, and a dash of mystery make this well-crafted Regency thoroughly delightful."
— *Library Journal*

"Readers will enjoy this sassy Regency take on the classic *Beauty and the Beast* tale." — *Booklist*

When You Wish Upon a Rogue

ANNA BENNETT

St. Martin's Paperbacks

This is a work of fiction. All of the characters, organizations, and events portrayed in this novel are either products of the author's imagination or are used fictitiously.

First published in the United States by St. Martin's Paperbacks, an imprint of St. Martin's Publishing Group.

WHEN YOU WISH UPON A ROGUE

Copyright © 2020 by Anna Bennett.

All rights reserved.

For information, address St. Martin's Publishing Group, 120 Broadway, New York, NY 10271.

www.stmartins.com

ISBN: 978-1-250-19950-8

Our books may be purchased in bulk for promotional, educational, or business use. Please contact your local bookseller or the Macmillan Corporate and Premium Sales Department at 1-800-221-7945, ext. 5442, or by email at MacmillanSpecialMarkets@macmillan.com.

Printed in the United States of America

St. Martin's Paperbacks edition / June 2020

10 9 8 7 6 5 4 3 2 1

For Molly

Chapter 1

At precisely eight o'clock, Miss Sophie Kendall strode to the head of the long, rough-hewn table in the back room of Madam Laurent's dress shop and gazed at the women gathered around. They perched on chairs two rows deep, their expectant faces framed by satin-trimmed hats, simple straw bonnets, and white ruffled caps.

This particular moment—just before Sophie spoke, when she felt every pair of eyes trained upon her—was always the most exhilarating. She drew in a deep breath, savoring the flutter in her belly for one more exquisite second.

At last, she flashed a wide, sincere smile at the eclectic group of women and launched into her greeting. "Thank you, ladies, for attending this meeting of our secret society, in which devotees of The Debutante's Revenge column explore sensitive topics such as courting, desire, intimacy, and love. Welcome," she said, pausing slightly for dramatic effect, "to the Debutante Underground." The room erupted in jubilant cheers and enthusiastic applause before quieting again.

Sophie continued, her expression a bit soberer as she stared at the assembly—their largest to date. "Some of you are new to our ranks, and we are delighted to have you here. However, we do insist that every participant abide by a strict set of rules, which we review at the beginning of each meeting.

"Rule number one," she began, reciting from memory. "The Debutante Underground shall not be discussed outside these walls. Indeed, as far as the rest of London is concerned, *it does not exist.*"

In response, the women chanted, "Hear, hear."

"Rule number two," Sophie intoned. "Anonymity is paramount. We use only given names here—no surnames, no titles. If you should happen to see a fellow member as you stroll down the street, you shall not acknowledge her unless you are acquainted through other means."

"Hear, hear," the women chorused.

"Rule number three: Discussions are to be held in the strictest of confidences. While our goal is to enlighten each other regarding subjects that are typically taboo, no personal details related in the course of our conversations here may be shared."

"Hear, hear."

"And last," Sophie said, "rule number four: We shall always speak the truth, the best we know it."

"Hear, hear," the women said solemnly.

"Now then," Sophie said, clasping her hands together. "We will begin, as always, by reading the latest column." She held up that morning's edition of the *London Hearsay*, folded open to The Debutante's Revenge and its accompanying sketch—a gorgeous vignette of a gentleman nuzzling the neck of a woman wearing a smile that could only be described as *satisfied*. Indeed, the besotted expressions on the couple's faces made Sophie's chest ache. She shook off the familiar yearning and cleared her throat. "Sarah, would you like to do the honors?"

The pretty, auburn-haired young widow, still in half

mourning, nodded eagerly. She stood and read aloud from her own copy of the newspaper:

> *Dear Debutantes,*
> *A gentleman's ability to please a woman has*
> *less to do with his sexual prowess than with his*
> *attentive nature.*
>
> *If you wish to know whether a man will be a*
> *skilled lover, look for small, thoughtful gestures.*
> *Perhaps he insists you eat the last slice of cake*
> *or holds his jacket above your head to shield you*
> *from the rain. Maybe he picks you a bouquet of*
> *wildflowers or refrains from interrupting you while*
> *you finish the chapter you're reading.*
>
> *A man who happily puts your needs above his*
> *own is likely to be a generous and ardent lover—*
> *and that is the very best kind.*

Several of the ladies fanned themselves; others sighed. For the space of several breaths, no one spoke; then Mrs. Abigail Sully, the witty, if weary, mother of three young children, piped up. "I'd settle for a man who changes nappies."

"I'd settle for a man who took the time to remove his boots before climbing into my bed," an older woman said mirthfully.

And before long, the women waded into a discussion that was sometimes playful, sometimes wistful, but always forthright and supportive. While they helped themselves to tea and scones, Sophie slowly retreated to her usual corner, where she could observe the proceedings to her heart's content.

These meetings were the best part of her week, aside from visits with her friends Fiona and Lily. Fiona was the talented artist behind the sketches that accompanied the wildly popular Debutante's Revenge column; Lily was the inspired authoress. The covert project had originated when their close-knit trio—Fiona, Lily, and Sophie—made a pact to faithfully keep journals about their experiences as they entered the marriage mart and fell in love. Over a year had passed since they'd first toasted to the debutante diaries, and so much had changed since then—for everyone but Sophie.

Fiona had married a dashing earl who adored her. Not long after, Lily had made a love match with a brooding duke. The diaries had morphed into the anonymous column all of London was talking about, and the column, in turn, had spawned the secret society.

Of their trio, only Sophie was still unmarried.

But if her parents had their way, she wouldn't be for long. Her father had squandered his modest fortune, leaving the family in rather dire straits. Sophie's sweet, meek mother refused to acknowledge Papa's habit of drinking to excess. Last week, when he'd passed out at the dinner table, landing face-first in a plate of roast beef and gravy, Mama rushed to his aid and exclaimed that he'd obviously been working himself far too hard. Sophie and her older sister, Mary, had blinked at each other across the table and refrained from comment, for Mama wouldn't tolerate a hint of criticism directed at Papa.

But even Mama knew they couldn't continue on as they were. One of her daughters needed to marry well—and fast. Given that Mary was the oldest, the burden would have fallen on her if she hadn't nearly succumbed to scarlet fever as a child.

Even now, fear gripped Sophie's heart as she remembered the morning she'd stood helplessly in the doorway of her sister's darkened room. Papa had sobbed and Mama had knelt beside the bed, her voice hoarse as she whispered the same prayer over and over: that her daughter might live to see her twelfth birthday.

Miraculously, Mary had.

In the months that followed, Mary had slowly recovered, thank heaven. But even now she remained frail and peaked, which meant her parents were taking no chances where her health was concerned. No invigorating walks, no horseback riding, no crowded balls . . . and no opportunity to meet single gentlemen.

Leaving the family's fate squarely in Sophie's hands.

She wasn't opposed to the idea of marrying. On the contrary, she craved a deep and lasting connection to another person. She longed for someone to talk to at breakfast each morning and someone to lie next to each night. But she'd always harbored romantic notions of falling in love before becoming engaged. Unfortunately, marrying for love was a luxury that she and her family quite literally could not afford.

So Papa and Mama had determined that she should wed Lord Singleton at the end of the season. She and the handsome, well-to-do marquess weren't officially betrothed yet. The last time he'd come to call, Sophie had locked herself in her bedchamber and pleaded a headache. On the occasion before that, she'd slipped out the back door and gone on a two-hour stroll through the woods. The mild case of poison oak she'd contracted had been a small price to pay.

She knew she was behaving poorly and didn't intend to shirk her duty to her family forever. She only wanted the rest of this season to herself.

One more season to continue hosting meetings of the Debutante Underground.

One more season to dance and flirt with dashing gentlemen.

One more season to feel young and free.

Sophie dragged her thoughts back to the meeting in progress and watched an earl's shy daughter—recently betrothed to a portly older man—furrow her brow during a rather explicit conversation about wedding night disappointments. But then another woman smiled fondly as she recounted the story of how her husband once took extra jobs at the docks just so that he could buy her a pretty hair comb—an extravagance they could ill afford. As usual, the women balanced their negative stories with uplifting ones, painting a picture that Sophie hoped was realistic and fair to both sexes.

Some women asked questions related to the evening's topic, and others chimed in with their own experiences and advice. A few women simply listened raptly, soaking in the knowledge and camaraderie.

Time passed quickly, and when Sophie checked the old clock wedged between spools of thread and a basket of frippery on one of the workroom's shelves, she realized they'd been meeting for almost two hours. Reluctantly, she left her spot at the back and made her way, once more, to the head of the table.

She waited for a pause in the conversation, then shot an apologetic glance at the women. "I'm afraid it's time for us to bring our meeting to a close. On behalf of everyone, I'd like to express my thanks to Cecile"—she inclined her head toward Madam Laurent—"for allowing us to convene here again this week. I wanted to let you all know that I'm working on securing a larger space and hope to have some news in that regard by next week's meeting."

A murmur of approval and excitement swelled inside the room, and Sophie's belly twisted. She couldn't continue to impose on Madam Laurent week after week, and their group had clearly outgrown the back room of her dress shop—a few of the women had to share chairs and others had to stand. But Sophie had yet to find a suitable alternate location—something large and centrally located, with an inconspicuous entrance.

She pasted on a cheerful expression and continued. "Please, be safe as you return to your homes, and be mindful of the rules stated earlier, especially the first: the Debutante Underground shall not be discussed outside these walls. Until next time, good night."

Several of the women embraced before filing out, a few at a time, so as not to create a throng on the pavement outside the shop. Meanwhile, Sophie began the process of setting the workspace back to rights. Dishes were washed, furniture was moved, and sewing projects were carefully returned to their former places. Ivy, one of the shop's hardworking seamstresses, insisted on staying and helping Sophie after everyone else had left.

"Thank you," Sophie said, handing Ivy the box with a few leftover scones. "Please, take these home and enjoy them."

Ivy grinned. "My youngest brother will devour them before I can remove my bonnet." As she reached for her shawl on a hook by the door, she asked, "Where's the new meeting location that you're considering?"

Sophie frowned as she buttoned her pelisse. "I'm still looking for the ideal place. Some friends have generously offered to host at their private residences, but I'd prefer something closer to shops and businesses—in an area where most of the members are comfortable coming and going. It doesn't need to be anything elegant. Just a bit bigger than this, with seating for three or four dozen of us."

Ivy tapped a finger to her lips, thoughtful. "There's a

vacant building down the block. Madam Laurent said it used to be occupied by a tailor's shop, but they shut their doors a year ago. She's considering expanding to that space if business continues to be brisk for another season or two. But until then, perhaps you could ask the owner if he'd allow you to use it. After all, it's just sitting there, unoccupied."

Sophie wrinkled her nose. "I dislike the notion of asking a stranger—especially if he's the curious type. He's certain to inquire about the nature of our meeting. What on earth would I tell him?"

Ivy arched a mischievous brow. "That it's a Bible study group?"

Sophie chuckled. "I fear that's stretching the truth a bit too far."

"Fine," Ivy said, with a *suit-yourself* shrug. "You're fond of gardening, are you not?"

Sophie nodded vigorously. Plants were her first love— her passion long before the Debutante Underground had come into existence.

"So," Ivy continued, "you could tell the owner you chair a weekly meeting of the Ladies' Botanical Society."

Not a bad idea. Not at all. Except—"I hate to dissemble more than I have to." Even as Sophie said it, she could picture Fiona and Lily rolling their eyes at her. Telling her that she was allowed a minor transgression every now and then. Urging her to focus less on following the rules and more on following her heart.

"Well," Ivy drawled as she opened the door and pulled a key out of her pocket, "you do have another option."

"What's that?" Sophie stepped outside into the alley behind the shop and waited while the seamstress locked the door.

"You could simply skip the part about asking the owner's permission."

"What?" Sophie cocked her head. "Are you suggesting that we use the space without asking?"

"If we're able to find a way in," Ivy said, pointing at a bottle-green door in a brick building half a block down the street, "I don't see why not. After all, it's just sitting there, empty, day after day. It's not as though we'd be pilfering anything or leaving a mess behind. Knowing you, you'd leave the place tidier than you found it."

"Yes, but I'm not sure that's the point."

Ivy rolled her eyes. "Good night, Sophie. I'll see you next week." The young seamstress sauntered down the alley, shaking her head with good-natured regret—as though she should have known better than to think Sophie Kendall had a daring bone in her body.

And something inside Sophie snapped. She called out, "You know, Ivy, I believe I *shall* consider the old tailor's shop as an option."

"I'm glad to hear it," Ivy replied in a kindly if vaguely disbelieving tone. "Be careful as you make your way home."

Home? Dash it all, Sophie wasn't *going* home. She was off to have herself a peek at the tailor's shop—and, if it proved suitable, the future meeting place of the Debutante Underground.

Before she could lose her nerve, she marched down the dark, dank alley, lifting her skirts to avoid a few lily-pad-sized puddles that shone in the moonlight. As she approached the green door, she glanced up and down the narrow lane, confirming no one was about. Ivy had already turned the corner, leaving Sophie alone, if one discounted the mice skittering in and out of the drainpipe behind her.

The chipped paint on the door revealed that it had once been a lighter color—gray, perhaps. A small, faded metal plate nailed to the brick on one side read "B. D. Peabody, Tailor." Mullioned windows covered the top half of the door, but the panes were smudged with grime and dust, preventing her from seeing inside.

Vexed, she rifled through her reticule, pulled out her handkerchief, and vigorously rubbed at the center pane—gasping as the door swung open.

Gads. She hadn't imagined it would be unlocked, much less unlatched. The faint scents of leather and cigars wafted through the door opening, but the interior was cloaked in shadows, still and quiet.

She placed her hand on the doorknob and hesitated. She hadn't *planned* on breaking and entering into a vacant building this evening, but now that she was there, one foot already over the threshold, why shouldn't she scout out the location? It would certainly save her the trouble of a return trip during the week, and she could only concoct so many excuses for leaving the house before Mama became suspicious.

One quick glance around the inside would tell her if the building was a viable meeting place. Half of her hoped it was filled with trash and rat dung, so she'd be able to close the door firmly behind her and walk away. Only one way to find out.

She pushed the door open and took a tentative step inside. "Hullo?" she called, praying no response was forthcoming. If anyone *did* reply, she intended to dash outside and be two blocks away before they could reach the door. "Is anyone here?"

Emboldened by the continued silence, she took two more steps inside and paused, giving her eyes time to adjust to the inky darkness. She could make out a few large shapes in the center of the room—furniture, most likely—and a long counter along the far wall.

Already she could see the potential here—room for at least fifty women, an easily accessible back entrance, and even some seating. She'd need to inspect it during the day to be sure, but—

The air at her back moved unexpectedly, sending a chill over her skin. The courage she'd felt moments ago drained through her slippers. Deciding she'd had more than enough adventure for one night, she gulped and took a step backward. She reached behind her, feeling for the wall or the doorjamb, but as she did, the swath of moonlight that had painted the floor a pale yellow shrunk to a thin ribbon before being swallowed up by darkness.

The door slammed shut with a bang that made her heart buck like a spooked foal. She leaped halfway to the ceiling and let out a cry before she managed to find her voice. "Who's there?" she asked, wishing she sounded more assured and in command. Less terrified to the point of casting up her accounts.

"If you don't mind," came the exceedingly dry, hauntingly deep, eminently masculine voice, "*I'll* ask the questions here."

Chapter 2

Henry Reese, Earl of Warshire, dropped his cheroot and ground it under his boot heel before making a slow, appraising circle around the intruder—a woman, if he wasn't mistaken. He scrubbed his eyelids with the backs of his hands and blinked to make sure she wasn't some sort of hallucination. Sometimes, when he'd gone for a week without any sleep to speak of, his brain deceived him. But she seemed real enough.

Even in the dark, Reese could see her trembling like a rabbit hiding from a fox on the prowl. And yet, she raised her chin—a subtle act of defiance that was admirable, if ultimately futile.

No, this woman was not his usual sort of vision. The grotesque monsters lurking in the corners of his admittedly warped mind were made not of flesh but of pain and terror. Their bony fingers had clawed at his soul and wrung it out until it was nothing but a shriveled casing.

But the woman standing before him was slender, and the tendrils of hair that peeked out of her bonnet appeared to be fair—white gold. While there was no denying that she'd broken into his building, she smelled like the earth and wildflowers and springtime.

In a tone that brooked no argument, he said, "Do not move."

He strode to the large picture window at the front of the building and yanked open the heavy, mite-filled drapes, bathing the room in pale moonlight. When he faced the intruder again, she gazed at him warily and clutched a pink reticule tightly in one hand. The gown she wore was the color of freshly sprouted grass, and the soft muslin clung to her willowy frame.

"What are you doing here in my building?" he asked, fairly certain that a lie was about to spout forth from her mouth.

She licked her lips nervously. "Actually, I wasn't intending to come inside. I only wanted to peer in the window."

Reese narrowed his eyes and let his gaze travel slowly around the room. "You were window shopping," he said, not bothering to mask his skepticism. "Simply strolling down an alley late at night, looking for a new waistcoat? Maybe a cravat or two?"

"No," she said, frowning. "Of course not. I'd heard that the shop was vacant and thought it might make a suitable location for my . . . that is, I . . ." She clamped her mouth shut before taking a breath and starting again—with more confidence. "I thought I might rent the space."

He arched a brow, intrigued—and, perhaps, secretly pleased that she'd managed to surprise him.

"I'm Miss Kendall," she said, thrusting a gloved hand toward him. "You must be Mr. Peabody."

Reese kept his face impassive and reached for her hand. Curled his fingers around her palm. Held on a bit longer than was strictly necessary. "A pleasure," he growled, not bothering to tell her that Mr. Peabody, the elderly tailor, had turned up his toes over a year ago.

"Are you a shop owner, Miss Kendall?" He walked to the smooth, old oak counter and lit the lamp there.

She hesitated. "No."

When she didn't elaborate, he sank into one of a pair of large leather armchairs and waved a hand at the other. "Care to sit?"

She gulped and hazarded a look at the worn seat before perching on the edge. "I must apologize for intruding. I didn't expect the door to be unlocked, and when it swung open, I . . ."

"Decided to give yourself a tour?" he provided.

"Something like that."

He reached for the snifter on the table next to him and took a swallow of brandy before offering the glass to her. "Care for a drink?"

She recoiled as if he'd offered a vial of venom. "No, thank you."

"Well, feel free to look around. There's a work area and storage room at the rear." Reese had been killing time back there when he heard the door creak open and ventured out to investigate.

She remained seated as she said, "If you don't mind me asking, what were you doing here at this time of the evening? It's awfully late to be working."

A lie hovered on his tongue, but he swallowed it and told the truth—or, at least, part of it. "I come here when I'm restless. When I feel the need to escape my house." There was nothing worse than lying in bed, drowning in colorless shadows and unnatural silence while his body and mind battled for control. Every part of his physical being longed for sleep. Craved it like an addict needs opium. But his mind lived in fear of the moment he drifted off—when he relinquished control of his thoughts to the foulest of demons. They sat on their haunches, ready to charge into the void, swamping and suffocating him. He shuddered but pretended to merely shift in his seat.

"I see," she said simply—and something in her perceptive blue eyes suggested that she *did* understand.

He cleared his throat, leaned back, and stretched his legs. "As I was saying, you're welcome to inspect the shop if you're curious."

She shook her head and straightened her spine. "I've seen enough. Your building will suit my purposes perfectly."

Reese chuckled. "I'm afraid this place isn't available to let."

Miss Kendall's face crumpled. "Why not?"

"As I've already explained," he said slowly, "I use it."

"But you haven't even heard me out," she countered. "I only require the use of the room one evening each week—and I'm willing to pay a fair sum."

"How much?" Lord knew he could use the money, but the real reason he asked was because the amount she offered would provide a useful measuring stick. Give him an idea of how badly she wanted to rent the space—and what she could afford.

She paused, probably unaware that her forehead crinkled. "What do you think would be reasonable?"

The slight tremor in her voice said she was just shy of desperate—and that her coffers were nowhere near full. But she wanted to know his price.

He rubbed the stubble on his chin, idly wondering when he'd last shaved. When one rarely slept, the days melted together like pats of butter on a hot skillet. "If I were willing to let out my building for one evening a week—which I've already indicated I'm not—I'd have to charge ten pounds."

"Per month?" she asked hopefully.

"Per week."

"I see." For an interminable, golden moment, she searched his face, then stood regretfully. "If I thought you might reconsider, I might attempt to negotiate, but I can see that you're quite . . ." She paused, searching for a word.

"Pigheaded?" he provided. "Mulish?"

The grim line of her mouth softened into a half smile. "I was going to say 'adamant.'"

"Of course you were," he said smoothly. "But pigheaded fits better."

"Thank you for your time." Her eyes shone with a kindness that was damned disconcerting. Especially since he hadn't been particularly charming. In the short time since she'd arrived, he'd done nothing but swill brandy, behave like a boor, and crush her dream of renting his building. To top everything off, he must look like he'd staggered out of a pub just before closing time. He dragged a hand through his hair, which was already standing on end. And he had no bloody idea where he'd left his jacket or cravat.

He supposed he should say something gracious, maybe walk her to the door. But he didn't want her to go. Didn't want to be alone with his dark thoughts and insidious visions. So he continued to sit there morosely, the portrait of an arse.

She took a step toward the door, then turned back. "May I ask you something else?"

He shrugged as though he were indifferent. But on the inside, he was more like a stray dog, embarrassingly starved for a scrap of attention or compassion. "Ask away."

She tilted her head and frowned. "When was the last time you slept?"

"Last night," he answered reflexively. It was true enough—he'd drifted off on the sofa in his study for nearly an hour before bolting upright, drenched in sweat and shaking like he'd gone for a midwinter swim in the Thames. Afterward he'd immediately vowed to avoid shutting his eyes again for at least a week.

She leveled an assessing gaze in his direction before asking, "How *long* did you sleep?"

He thrust himself out of the chair, crossed his arms, and paced the ancient wood floor in front of the counter. "I don't see why that's any of your concern, Miss Kendall."

"You're right," she replied—with more gentleness than he deserved. "It wasn't my intention to pry. But my mother is prone to sleeplessness, and I recognized some of the signs."

He muttered a curse. Why should he give a damn that this young woman, a complete stranger to him, had just lumped him in the same category with her dear mama? "And what are the telltale signs?" he asked, his tone dry as dust. "What gave me away?"

To her credit, she didn't shrink in the least. "The shadows beneath your eyes, the slight tremor of your hands, and a general state of . . ." She hesitated, again perusing her mind for the correct word.

"Irritability?" he offered. "Cantankerousness?"

"I was going to say 'anxiousness,' but your suggestions are also apropos." Her words might have stung, if not for the playful twinkle in her eyes. A bit more soberly she added, "A lack of sleep can take its toll on a person."

He shrugged as though he had only the vaguest sense of what she was talking about. As if his life weren't a wasteland of paralysis and remorse. The last thing he wanted from Miss Kendall was pity.

She pursed her lips in consternation, then looked up

at him and beamed. Her wide, genuine smile was almost blinding, and he recoiled from the unexpected brilliance like a man emerging from a dark cave at high noon.

Oblivious to the effect she had on him, she began rummaging through her reticule. "I may have something in here that will help." At last, she withdrew a small pouch and held it up, triumphant. "Here we are."

"What is that?" he asked, not bothering to hide his cynicism.

She held the herbs an inch below her nose and closed her eyes as she inhaled deeply. "Valerian root for your tea. It's a remedy for sleeplessness." She naïvely thrust the dainty muslin pouch into his hands like it was the antidote to all that ailed him. She couldn't possibly know that he was way beyond help—so far beyond it that he might as well have been in another realm.

Reese sniffed the herbs and found them pleasantly earthy and fragrant. Idly wondered whether Miss Kendall's skin would smell the same and simultaneously chastised himself for the errant thought.

"I don't drink tea," he said curtly, handing the pouch back to her.

She looked appropriately appalled. "Well then," she said slowly, as if still coming to grips with this diabolical confession, "I suppose you could sprinkle some in your soup." She held out the pouch with a brooking-no-argument expression. The same stern face his own nanny had used when she expected him to swallow a spoonful of castor oil—except that Miss Kendall was approximately one hundred times more lovely.

"I appreciate your concern." He shoved his hands in his pockets so she couldn't force the bloody herbs into his palms again. "However, I have no use for quackery."

She narrowed her eyes at that—as if he'd issued a

challenge. She tucked the pouch under her elbow and began tugging at the fingers of her gloves, pulling them off. The sight conjured all sorts of wicked thoughts, which only proved how demented he was.

"Have you a kitchen, Mr. Peabody?" she asked briskly.

Reese blinked. "Here? No. There's a small stove in the back room."

"That will do," she said brightly.

He trailed after her as she strode past him, toward the room in the rear of the shop where he'd been lurking before she'd arrived. He'd lit a fire in the stove a few hours earlier, and when Miss Kendall spotted a kettle on a shelf above it, she turned toward him and arched a mildly accusatory brow.

"I don't use it," he said.

She continued to stare at him while she lifted the kettle and smiled smugly when she felt water sloshing inside.

"I *rarely* use it," he amended, shrugging.

With an entrancing combination of grace and efficiency, she placed the tin kettle on the stove, rinsed out a chipped teapot, and polished a dimpled strainer. Reese sank into an armchair and watched, grateful for the distraction and—to his amazement—her company. For there were very few people he could tolerate for more than five minutes, and even fewer people who could tolerate *him*.

While Miss Kendall waited for the water to heat, she moved about the room humming softly as she fluffed the pillows on a threadbare settee, organized the random pieces of crockery and dishware on the shelf, and stacked a week's worth of old newspapers in a neat pile beside his chair.

Once the room was mostly in order, she leaned over a small potted plant that looked like ivy but probably wasn't and began tenderly plucking off its brown, shriveled leaves. Reese snorted to himself, thinking she'd have more luck resuscitating Marie Antoinette. "Why are you tidying up?" he asked.

Her long, graceful fingers froze, and her gaze slid toward his. "Because it's *un*tidy."

"But it's not your duty to clean."

She frowned at the gossamer layer of dust on the table holding the pot. "Apparently, it's no one's duty." The comment would have sounded snide coming from most people, but Miss Kendall managed to make it sound like a compliment. "Besides, it's more pleasant to pass the time in surroundings that are serene and free of clutter," she said.

Reese grunted. He could row to the center of a glass-surfaced lake on a windless day. He could meditate in the middle of a peaceful, ancient forest. No amount of tranquility on the outside would ever calm the tempest raging inside him. But Miss Kendall wouldn't understand his particular brand of misery. What could a vibrant, beautiful young woman know of war and terror and shame?

When the teakettle began to whistle, she reluctantly left the plant she tended and set about preparing two cups of tea.

"I told you I don't drink tea," he said, acutely aware that he sounded like a crotchety old curmudgeon.

"You did." She deftly poured, then handed him the larger of the two cups. "I'm hoping that you'll indulge me and try a taste. I'll even join you, just to prove that there's no hemlock or eye of newt mixed in." She perched daintily on a wooden stool, lifted a cup to her pink lips, and tilted her head. "Not bad, but you may prefer to add a lump of sugar."

"Absolutely not," he said gruffly. "Wouldn't want to mask the flavor of toad and newt."

She raised her teacup, amusement shining in her eyes. "Cheers, Mr. Peabody."

Shit. He'd forgotten she didn't know who he was. But it didn't matter. "Cheers, Miss Kendall," he said, before taking a drink of the earthy, potent, but oddly soothing tea.

They sat and sipped their tea in comfortable silence for a while, and when she offered to pour him some more, he agreed—just so she might stay a little longer.

When she rose to clean her cup and the teapot, he stood, but she waved him back into his chair. "Finish it up," she urged. "And if you nod off, don't worry about me. I'll let myself out."

He chuckled at that. "I won't fall asleep," he said confidently. "And the hour's grown late. You should permit me to walk you home or secure you a hackney cab."

"That's not necessary," she said, "but thank you."

He opened his mouth to insist, but thought better of it and contented himself with watching while she ran a dishcloth over the small table where the plant sat, lifting the pot to dust beneath it. Then she retrieved the cooled teakettle and carefully poured water into the thirsty, cracked soil. The sickly plant only had three yellowish leaves left on it, but it looked grateful nonetheless, perking up under her ministrations.

"You have a green thumb," he said, his voice sounding unexpectedly groggy to his own ears. "Do you enjoy gardening?"

Her face took on a dreamy, ethereal quality. "Very much so. There's nothing more satisfying than watching a garden grow and change and thrive."

"I can think of a few things more satisfying," he said, half-amused, half in awe.

"Plants give us food, medicine, and beauty," she said. "For me, they also bring a sense of peace—a tangible connection to nature. A feeling that I'm part of something bigger." She paused and shook her head. "I've never told anyone that before."

"I'm glad you told me," he said sincerely. It seemed important that he knew one true and important thing about her—before she walked out of his door and his life, never to return again.

"And now," she said playfully, "I think you should tell me something about yourself. Just so that we are even."

"Fair enough." He swallowed the last drops of his tea as he searched his mind for something to tell her. Something true and important, like she'd told him. Something that wouldn't send her running for the hills or scare the devil out of her. "The only time I feel free is when I'm riding my horse. Not trotting around town or through the park but galloping across wide-open fields and jumping over rushing streams. When the wind licks at my face and billows my coat behind me. That's when I can forget, briefly, who I am and what I've done."

Jesus, he hadn't meant to say the last part out loud. But he didn't regret it. Miss Kendall deserved to know that much. Deserved to know he was unworthy of spending time with someone like her.

But if his words gave her pause, she gave no indication of it. She merely continued to fawn over the plant as she said, "Then I'm glad you have your riding. We all need an escape now and again."

He wondered what *she* needed to escape from. Fear, drudgery, fate? It was on the tip of his tongue to ask, but it seemed his brain and mouth weren't working in tandem. So he sank back into his chair and allowed himself a rare moment of relaxation. His eyelids twitched, and though he strained to keep them open, they fell with the inevitability of a stage curtain at the end of act two.

He could still hear the whisper of Miss Kendall's skirt as she moved around the room. Her scent—the same as a field after an April shower—tickled his nose. Her soft humming, unexpectedly sultry, seeped beneath his skin and calmed his soul.

As sleep grabbed his boots and inexorably pulled him under, he had two distinct thoughts.

The first was that Miss Kendall would soon be gone—a very good thing, given the ugliness that was sure to ensue.

The second was that he would never see her again. And *that* was a damned shame.

Chapter 3

"How was the meeting last night?" Fiona asked, glancing up from her sketchpad, where she'd outlined a couple standing beneath a garden trellis. Even in its unfinished state, Sophie could see that the drawing was destined to be one of her favorites. The way the gentleman held the woman's hand was so tender—almost reverent. Flowering vines trailed all around them as they leaned toward each other, their lips only a breath apart.

Sophie gave a wistful sigh and walked to the window of the lovely studio where she, Fiona, and Lily met every Saturday morning to conduct business related to The Debutante's Revenge. The studio, located in Fiona's house, reflected the passions of all three women. Fiona's breathtaking paintings graced the walls; Lily's exquisite desk—a gift from her besotted duke—flanked shelves filled with novels, poems, and other inspiration; and Sophie's lush plants sprouted and blossomed in every nook and cranny, adding beauty and softness to the elegance.

"The meeting went very well," Sophie reported happily. "The members adored your sketch and Lily's latest column. Both sparked a great deal of lively conversation."

Lily blew a dark curl away from her face, set her pen on the desk blotter, and leaned back in her chair, her green eyes gleaming with curiosity. "Tell us more," she urged. "What do your members wish to know? What topics capture their fancy?"

Sophie paced the length of the studio slowly, carefully considering her answer. She'd founded the Debutante Underground so that devotees of the column would have a place to discuss the column and other topics of interest to them—especially the ones that were deemed unsuitable for genteel drawing rooms. As such, the meetings were an excellent source of ideas for future columns, but Sophie was very careful not to violate her own guidelines—particularly those ensuring anonymity and forbidding the sharing of personal details. Fortunately, Fiona and Lily respected her adherence to the rules and never pressed her to share more than she felt she could. They could have attended themselves, of course, but perhaps they sensed that Sophie needed the meetings to be her domain—her unique contribution to their project.

"The women agreed wholeheartedly that a generous spirit is an important quality in a lover," Sophie began. "But some of them wondered how to nurture that quality in their current partners. Others wished to learn how to be more generous lovers themselves."

"Interesting," Lily said. She picked up her pen, dipped the nib in her inkpot, and began scribbling notes. "Perhaps I should write about the importance of explicitly communicating one's desires."

"An excellent idea," Fiona chimed in. "Honest communication is key to every aspect of a relationship."

"Agreed," Lily said firmly. "In next week's column, I'll advise women to tell their partners what they desire—both in the bed and outside of it."

There was a time, not so long ago, when such forthright talk would have made Sophie blush to the roots of her hair.

But she now realized that carnal pleasure was as natural as a seed sprouting in the sun. It was nothing to be ashamed of, but rather, something to appreciate—even celebrate. The Debutante's Revenge had opened the door to an enticing, passionate new world.

So far, for Sophie, that world existed only in sketches and words. She'd yet to experience the thrill of a lingering kiss or a sensual touch. But she intended to—maybe before she was married to Lord Singleton.

While Lily continued writing, Fiona said, "I noticed you returned from your meeting much later than usual."

In the months since the Debutante Underground began, Sophie had taken to spending Friday evenings at Fiona and Gray's house and staying overnight. The routine spared Sophie from having to explain where she was going every week and also provided time for the three friends to work on the column the next morning. Fortunately, Sophie, Lily, and Fiona had grown up together, and Mama was inordinately fond of the entire Hartley family—so she didn't object to the arrangement in the slightest.

"Forgive me if I worried you last night," Sophie said. "After the meeting I stopped by a vacant building near the dress shop to see if it would make a suitable alternative location."

Fiona arched a strawberry-blond brow. "And would it?"

"It would . . ." Sophie mentally debated telling her friends about Mr. Peabody. She'd thought of him often since leaving him snoring softly in his chair.

The harsh lines of his face had softened as he slept, and his tightly coiled muscles had relaxed. If he'd been dangerously handsome stalking about the tailor's shop, he'd been doubly so as he dreamed, with his long legs sprawled in front of him and his full lips parted. She'd turned down the lantern and carefully placed a blanket across his lap before gathering her things and tiptoeing out of the shop's back door. If anyone in the world could understand her odd attraction to a relative stranger, Sophie was sure that Fiona and Lily would.

But part of her feared that talking about her evening with Mr. Peabody would strip away the magic, make it feel strange or trite. So she decided to keep him solely to herself. "Unfortunately," she continued, "the building isn't available for let." She shrugged as though it were nothing but a mild disappointment. "I'll find something else."

"The offer to hold the meeting here still stands," Fiona said kindly, "but I know you'd prefer a spot that's more centrally located."

Sophie smiled gratefully. "Yes, dozens of people strolling up to your front door would attract undue attention, I'm afraid."

"Would you like us to help you secure a location?" Lily offered. "If money is an obstacle, we'd be more than happy to cover the rent. It's the least we can do."

"Thank you," Sophie said sincerely. "You're both so generous. But I'm going to attempt to do this on my own— if only to prove to myself that I can."

"Of course you can," Fiona said encouragingly. "We have complete confidence in you. But in the meantime, if you should find yourself in a bind, please know you can count on us."

"I know," Sophie said, thankful. "I've always been able to depend on you. Indeed, I'm not certain I would have survived our years at Miss Haywinkle's without you."

"You have that backward," Lily said with a chuckle. "*I* was the one who was forever being called into the headmistress's office. *You* were the one taking first honors in every subject."

"We had such grand dreams back then," Sophie said,

almost overcome with longing to return to the days when anything seemed possible. Swallowing the lump in her throat, she glanced at the clock on the mantel and shot her friends a regretful look. "I promised Mama I'd return home by early afternoon. I should go."

Fiona gave a playful pout. "Our time together always passes too quickly."

"Always," Sophie agreed. "But perhaps I'll see you both at Lady Rufflebum's ball Wednesday evening?"

"Gray and I will be there," Fiona said brightly.

"Nash and I are going too." Lily looked up from her journal and waved her pen like a flag. "Soph, you should wear the emerald silk to the ball!" She and Fiona had given Sophie the gorgeous gown as a birthday gift several weeks ago. Sophie had planned to save it for a special occasion, but the season would be over before she knew it, and opportunities were running out. Soon she'd be officially betrothed to a man she didn't love, and shortly after that, she'd become his wife. She suppressed a shiver and reminded herself that a loveless marriage was a small price to pay for her family's security.

"Perhaps I *will* wear the green gown," Sophie mused. "Let us hope that the shocking display of décolletage doesn't cause Lady Rufflebum to faint straightaway." She gave her friends a wink before collecting her portmanteau and saying goodbye. Fiona and Lily proceeded to hug and fuss over her like she was embarking on an expedition to Egypt instead of walking a few blocks across town.

A half hour later, Sophie breezed through the front door of her family's townhouse, hung her bonnet on its peg, and peered into the hallway looking glass, smoothing several tendrils of hair behind her ears. "Hullo," she called out. "I'm home, Mama."

Her mother emerged from the drawing room doors at the top of the stairs and waved at Sophie excitedly. "You have an unexpected visitor, darling."

Sophie's belly somersaulted at the announcement. Mama's pink cheeks and shining eyes left no doubt that the visitor in question was a gentleman, and Sophie couldn't help but wonder if Mr. Peabody had come to call. It was the height of foolishness to suspect it—and even *more* foolish to hope for it—but her body thrummed at the mere possibility that he might be sitting in her drawing room.

"Who is it?" Sophie asked in a stage whisper.

Mama merely smiled and met her halfway down the stairs, grabbing her arm so she could hurry her up to the landing. "You look lovely," Mama assured her. "The brisk walk home has given you a fetching glow. Let me take your portmanteau so you may join your guest in the drawing room without delay. I've already rung for tea."

Sophie planted her feet outside the drawing room door and faced her mother. "You're not going to tell me who's in there?"

"Go see for yourself," Mama said, giving Sophie a surprisingly strong shove toward the door.

Sophie stepped into the drawing room and spotted her gentleman caller lounging on their slightly shabby settee, his back to her. His broad shoulders, clad in an expertly tailored jacket, were visible above the settee's curved back, and his muscular arms spanned its length as if staking out his territory.

Drat. Lord Singleton had finally succeeded in cornering her.

She looked longingly over her shoulder at the door but knew she couldn't avoid the marquess this time. "Good afternoon, Lord Singleton," she said, trying valiantly to mask her lack of enthusiasm. "What a pleasant surprise."

He quickly scrambled to his feet, took her hand, and bowed over it. "I assure you, the pleasure is all mine, Miss Kendall."

Sophie resisted the impulse to snatch her hand away. The marquess was well-mannered, impressively fit, dark haired, and clean-shaven. Attractive by most standards . . . just not hers.

When she could politely withdraw her hand, she waved at the settee, encouraging him to sit. She poured a cup of tea, handed it to Lord Singleton, and pretended to be oblivious to his chagrined expression when she sat in the chair opposite him rather than joining him on the settee.

"I spoke to your father again last night," he said smoothly. "He's eager for you and I to . . . move forward. As am I."

Sophie's tea gurgled in her belly. This conversation was the primary reason she hadn't wanted to be alone with the marquess. "I see no need to rush into anything, my lord."

"No one could accuse us of rushing." He blew out a long breath, clearly frustrated. "Your father led me to believe that you were amenable to the arrangement. If you've changed your mind . . ."

Sophie shook her head. "I haven't." She wouldn't shirk her duty to her family, no matter how much she might like to. "However, I thought perhaps we could wait a few more months before making anything official."

"Two months," he said firmly.

Her traitorous teacup trembled on its saucer. "I beg your pardon?"

"I'm willing to wait two months—and then we will announce our betrothal."

Sophie's mouth went dry. "We can discuss the timing and the other particulars toward the end of season," she

hedged. The mere thought of adhering to a timeline, setting a definitive date, made panic bubble at the back of her
throat.

"Two months," he repeated as if he hadn't heard her,
"should be sufficient. It's longer than I'd hoped, but we'll
use the time to become better acquainted and marry as
soon as the banns are read. With any luck, you'll be with
child by Christmas."

Sophie choked on a swallow of tea. Barely managed to
keep from spraying it across the table onto the marquess's
pristine waistcoat. She smothered her mouth with her napkin, hacking and coughing until tears spilled down her
cheeks.

Lord Singleton leaned forward, clearly distressed and
unsure what to do. "Forgive me," he said. "I didn't mean
to upset you."

She blotted her eyes with the corner of her napkin and
shook her head. "I'm fine. Your comment simply took me
by surprise." The truth was that she couldn't imagine any
of it—not the betrothal, the wedding, and most *definitely*
not the wedding night. An involuntary shudder enveloped
her body.

Though she'd met Lord Singleton almost a year ago,
he was still a relative stranger—who was already anticipating procreating with her. She fanned herself with her
napkin.

"Your mother tells me you're planning to attend Lady
Rufflebum's ball," he said, oozing a specific strain of
charm—one she seemed to be immune to. "I do hope
you'll allow me to claim you for the first set."

Sophie pasted on a smile and graciously agreed. It felt
like she was taking the first momentous step toward saving her family from financial and social ruin.

But she couldn't help wishing that saving her family didn't mean sacrificing her own future. Like yellowing leaves on the brink of a brutal winter, her dreams were about to shrivel and die.

Chapter 4

Lurking behind the hedges outside Lady Rufflebum's ballroom and trying to avoid amorous couples on the terrace had to be a new low—even for Reese.

His valet, Gordon, had tried to cajole Reese into attending the ball as a guest. But that would have required him to wear an evening jacket and to walk through the front door and to be generally . . . civil.

Which was really asking a bit too much.

Reese was desperate to speak with Miss Kendall, however, and *that* was the reason he was currently peering over a bush beneath a window, peeking into the ballroom like a common criminal. At Reese's behest, Gordon had made some discreet inquiries among the staff at her family's residence and determined that Miss Kendall would likely attend the Rufflebum ball. There were no guarantees, of course, but it wasn't as though Reese's calendar were full.

The one thing he had plenty of—an endless supply, really—was waking hours. And therein lay the problem.

The last time he'd slept more than a couple of hours was five nights ago—on the evening he met Miss Kendall. He'd woken early the next morning feeling more rested than he had in ages. Almost human.

If she'd been able to help him sleep once, surely she could do it again.

He craned his neck above the sill and looked through the mullioned windows into the ballroom—a world so foreign and mysterious to him that it might as well have been two continents away. He was the second born, and while he'd attended a ball or two as a young buck, he'd eagerly traded in his formal wear for an officer's uniform. He'd given up the opera, theater, and men's clubs for rifles, fighting, and battlefields—and hadn't regretted it for a single moment.

But then, three months ago, the unthinkable had happened. Edmund, the older brother he'd worshipped, had died.

Reese had no choice but to return home. But part of him still bled in the trenches, still heard the moans of the fallen all around him. He could never go back to being the person he'd been before.

And he could certainly never replace Edmund, but, like it or not, Reese *was* the Earl of Warshire now. The title conveyed power, privilege, and a whole host of problems. The most pressing—and surprising, to Reese—was a distinct lack of cash. Fortunately, he'd always been good with numbers and felt sure he could do a better job managing the books than Edmund's old steward had. Reese wouldn't mind sacking a few crooked employees and tightening some belts. He'd turn the estate around and take care of it until the day it passed to the next in line—his cousin, if he outlived Reese, or his cousin's heir, if he didn't. Reese didn't much care who the title went to. Probably because it was never supposed to have been his.

He scowled at the scene inside Lady Rufflebum's glittering ballroom, where chandeliers glowed and the orchestra played. Elegant couples moved across the dance floor with the same precision as soldiers marching toward the front lines. On the perimeter of the room, matrons and older gentlemen gathered in clusters, forming encampments where they could safely observe the action without actually venturing into the fray.

Reese spied several young women with blond hair inside the house, but even from a distance he could tell that none of them was Miss Kendall. Though he'd only met her once, and they'd only conversed for an hour or so, everything about her had been indelibly imprinted on his mind. Her wildflower scent, her effortless grace, her lyrical voice. He saw her when he closed his eyes . . . and he suspected the valerian root was to blame.

He remained in his hiding spot, keeping company with the frogs and occasionally looking into the ballroom, hoping for a glimpse of Miss Kendall. The hours wore on, and just when he was about to abandon his post, he saw her.

Wrapped in an airy swath of emerald-green silk, she twirled across the parquet dance floor. Her hair was gathered in a knot at her crown, but a few honey-colored curls floated around her face and down her neck. She wasn't the most beautiful woman there. She didn't wear the most expensive jewels. She wasn't even the most accomplished dancer.

But she was the only one that he saw.

He blamed the damned tea for that, too.

She danced with a large, dark-haired man. Reese didn't know him, but he looked to be the sort who took everything for granted—his dashing looks, immense wealth, high-born status . . . *and* his current dance partner.

Reese rolled his shoulders and eased the tension out of his neck. Who cared if Miss Kendall danced with a rich, arrogant young buck? She could dance with the devil if she wished.

All Reese needed from her was the recipe for the brew she'd concocted. The one that had, by some miracle, given him a few hours of peace.

So he tried to be patient as she finished her waltz. Watched with interest as she joined two young women—sisters, if he had to guess—and embraced each of them warmly. He imagined it would be quite pleasant to be hugged by Miss Kendall, partly because she smelled nice, and partly because she cared about everything—people, plants, probably animals too.

She talked animatedly with her friends, and when she smiled, soft and true, the sight made his chest physically ache. He tried to rub the pain away, but it lingered like a phantom, taunting him. Telling him he'd never be enough.

Jesus. He tore himself away from the window, pressed his back to the brick wall, and closed his eyes. Clearly, he was in dire need of sleep. Any qualms he'd had about to-night's plan evaporated like a morning mist. He *needed* to speak with Miss Kendall.

He raked a hand through his hair and straightened his jacket before stepping onto the terrace and making his way toward the double doors leading to the ballroom. He re-mained outside but managed to flag down a gangly foot-man who circulated among the guests serving drinks.

The young man approached and bowed politely. "May I be of service, my lord?"

Reese thrust a hand into his pocket and withdrew the note he'd written before leaving the house. Handing it to the footman, he said, "Deliver this to Miss Kendall, please."

"Miss Kendall?" the lad said, shrugging.

"She's standing across from the orchestra." Reese nod-ded in her direction. "Wearing the brilliant green gown."

The footman followed Reese's gaze, and when he spotted her, his eyes widened in obvious appreciation.

"Your discretion is appreciated," Reese added, dropping a coin into the young man's palm. "But the sooner you can give her the note, the better."

With that, Reese withdrew into the shadows . . . and went to wait for Miss Kendall in the garden.

"Champagne, ladies?" A whip-thin footman flourished a tray, offering fizzing glasses to Fiona, Lily, and Sophie. Fiona declined, but Lily and Sophie eagerly helped themselves to crystal flutes. They had just raised their glasses in a silent toast when the footman surreptitiously handed Sophie a small, folded paper. "For you," he said under his breath before weaving his way through the crowd.

Something in the footman's demeanor caused Sophie to keep the paper concealed in her fist. If Fiona or Lily noticed the odd exchange, neither said anything. But then, perhaps they were distracted by the arrival of their handsome husbands, who hoped to steal them away for a dance. When the sisters hesitated, Sophie waved them onto the dance floor. "Go on," she said. "I'll take the opportunity to check on Mama."

While she waited for her friends to melt into the throng on the dance floor, the paper burned a hole in her palm. She, Sophie Kendall, was not the sort of young woman who routinely received mysterious missives. She'd never inspired a gentleman to write her romantic poetry. She'd never even passed a note to a classmate in the schoolroom.

She supposed the note could be from a member of the Debutante Underground, but that would amount to an infraction of rule number two, and she'd never had a member reach out to her outside of their established meeting time.

The most likely scenario Sophie could imagine was that the footman had delivered the note to her in error. Perhaps it had been intended for Lady Halton, who, like her, was wearing a green silk gown, but who, *unlike* her, currently had half a dozen men vying for her attention.

Sophie swallowed and turned the paper over in her hand. If it was meant for her, she fervently hoped it was *not* from Lord Singleton—who had already claimed a dance with her and had been keeping a watchful eye on her ever since.

As she casually walked toward a trio of potted topiaries at the back of the ballroom, she wondered if the person who'd delivered the note was watching her now. Whether he'd be gauging her reaction as she read his words.

She found a quiet spot near a spiral boxwood, carefully unfolded the paper, and read the bold, scrawling script.

Dear Miss Kendall,
I underestimated the power of your tea—and,
moreover, you.
      Please, meet me in the garden if and when you
are able.

Sophie's fingers tingled. Mr. Peabody had written her a note. Wanted to see her again. Tonight.

She scanned the paper once more before folding it and furtively slipping it into the top of her bodice, tucking it between her breasts in a manner that would have horrified her former headmistress, Miss Haywinkle.

Sophie paused to gather her wits. What on earth was Mr. Peabody doing at Lady Rufflebum's ball? And why hadn't she spotted him among the guests?

More to the point, why did the prospect of seeing the growly, sleep-deprived tailor again make her belly turn cartwheels?

Across the room from Sophie, Mama appeared to listen raptly as Mrs. Hartley gossiped and waved her fan demonstratively. Lord Singleton looked as though he were embroiled in some sort of political debate with several older gentlemen. Fiona and Lily still whirled on the dance floor.

Deciding no one would miss her if she took a short stroll in the garden, Sophie smoothed the front of her skirt and glided toward the French doors at the side of the room.

The moment she stepped over the threshold onto the terrace, she felt as though she'd ventured into another realm. The sound of the orchestra's violins faded into the chirps of crickets and croaks of toads. The scents of beeswax candles and pungent perfume faded into the lush smells of dew-kissed grass and blossoming peonies.

At the rear of the terrace, Sophie followed a winding stone path under an ivy-covered arbor and past a charming stone birdbath nestled in a cluster of hydrangea bushes. Lanterns placed at intervals along the path lit the way and added a soft glow to Lady Rufflebum's meticulously tended garden.

But Sophie instinctively knew that Mr. Peabody would not be waiting for her near the whimsical statuettes of fairies and sprites. He'd no doubt prefer to be away from the house and the lanterns and the other guests. At a bend in the path, she paused and squinted into the moonlit landscape beyond the garden.

"Miss Kendall." His voice, low and rich as chocolate, heated her blood.

She looked up to find him lounging beneath a large birch tree, his back pressed against the trunk. Dressed in a black jacket, trousers, and boots, he blended into the shadows; only the crisp white of his cravat stood out in the darkness.

He pushed himself off the tree and inclined his head politely. "Thank you for coming."

She took a few steps off the path, into the soft grass. Toward him. "Mr. Peabody," she said softly. "What are you doing here?"

He looked down at the ground. "My name isn't Peabody."

"I beg your pardon?"

"I'm not the tailor, but I happen to own the building." He met her gaze, his expression apologetic. "My name is Reese, and I'm the Earl of Warshire."

Sophie blinked. Not in a hundred summers would she have guessed that Mr. Peabody was an earl. He was too wild and unrefined. Too rough around the edges. "The Earl of Warshire," she repeated, combing through her mental files for any pertinent information. "Wait. I thought the earl had . . ." She stopped because she couldn't bring herself to say what she recalled about the former earl, who must have been Reese's older brother—that he'd died a few months ago after a tragic hunting accident. "Your brother?" she asked.

He nodded as though he didn't trust himself to speak.

"I'm sorry," she said simply. "You must feel the loss keenly."

"I do." His voice cracked a little, and he cleared his throat. "I should have told you I wasn't Mr. Peabody that night," he said. "I'm not sure why I didn't."

"Maybe because you thought I was trying to rob you blind?" she replied.

That garnered a half smile. "Maybe." He swallowed and looked at her earnestly. "In any event, I fell asleep before

I could thank you for the tea. You were right about me not sleeping much. And that's the other reason I asked you to meet me tonight."

She shook her head, confused. "I don't understand."

"Miss Kendall," he said, his voice sober. "I require your help. And I think we could strike a deal that would benefit us both."

Sophie moved a bit closer. Marveled at the way the moonlight cast his face in relief—the faint hollows of his cheeks, the straight line of his nose, and strong edge of his jaw. "What sort of help do you need?" she asked, her curiosity far outweighing any apprehension.

He hesitated, rubbing his chin before he replied. "I need you to spend the night with me."

Chapter 5

Miss Kendall's impossibly long eyelashes fluttered. "Forgive me," she said with a nervous chuckle. "It sounded as though you said you needed me to spend the night with you."

"I did, and I do." It was a bold request, but Reese saw no reason to prevaricate. Figured she'd appreciate his candor. "But before you misconstrue my meaning"—clearly, it was too late for that—"please allow me to explain. I'm not suggesting anything untoward. I simply need you to help me sleep. Like you did the other night."

"Oh," she said, her relief obvious—and unintentionally insulting. "There's no need for me to stay the night with you, Lord Warshire. I'll simply give you some more valerian root."

He shook his head firmly. "I've already tried it. I used the bag you left behind, and it didn't work."

She tilted her head. "But it's the same mix."

"I know. And it didn't make me fall asleep." On Saturday evening, he'd re-created the exact conditions on the night she'd been at the shop. Steeped the tea in precisely the same way. Reclined in the same old chair. Even tidied the room as she had, prior to drinking four cups of the damned potion. But he hadn't slept a wink.

The tea hadn't been effective on the three subsequent nights he'd tried it either. Apparently, the missing ingredient was Miss Kendall.

"Interesting," she mused. She tapped a finger to her lips, thoughtful. "Why don't I write out the exact steps and proportions I use and deliver the instructions to you in a letter?"

"You don't understand," he said as gently as he could, given the panic swirling in his gut. If she didn't say yes, he'd be reduced to begging. He was terrifyingly close to it already. "It wasn't the valerian root that helped me sleep for the first time in weeks. It was you."

A mixture of understanding, pity, and denial dawned on her face. "It's not me, Lord Warshire."

"Call me Reese," he said. "Please. Every time you use the title I'm reminded of Edmund, my brother." And how he should still be there. Only, he wasn't.

"Very well . . . Reese," she said tentatively. For some reason, the sound of his name on her lips made his heart gallop. "I'm truly sorry that you've been suffering from insomnia," she said, and the compassion in her voice gave him hope. "But if you think I had anything to do with your good night's rest, you are mistaken. I have neither healing abilities nor magical powers," she added with a shrug. "I simply brew a good pot of tea—and anyone can learn how to do that."

Shit. He'd been afraid she wouldn't believe him. But then, she didn't really need to *believe* she could help him. She simply needed to agree.

"All I ask is that you stay with me. A couple of nights a week."

She gasped. "Impossible."

"I'd let you use the building," he said, playing one of his last two cards. "Rent-free. As often as you wish."

She froze, her beautiful face impassive. But he could

tell from her eyes that she was sorely tempted. "You'd bribe me to spend the night with you?"

"It's not a bribe," he assured her. "More like a trade. You'd be doing me a service, and I'd be compensating you for your time. I wouldn't ask you if I wasn't . . ." He couldn't bring himself to say it—to reveal the depths of his desperation. "I wouldn't ask if I thought I had another option," he amended.

She paced in front of him, the emerald silk swishing around her feet like waves churning along the shore. He could almost see her weighing her desire to use the tailor's shop against her resolve to avoid trouble.

"No," she said at last. "As much as I'd like to help, I can't. Do you imagine for one second that my parents would permit me to spend the night alone with a bachelor? And if anyone learned of our little arrangement—innocent or not—my name would be trampled in the mud like primroses after a foxhunt."

"You were wandering the streets alone on the night we met," he countered. "If you managed to escape your house once, surely you could do it again."

"That's different," she said. "I wasn't doing anything wrong."

He arched a brow at that. She may not have been breaking any laws, but she clearly had a few secrets of her own. "I'm not asking you to do anything wrong either."

She held out her palms helplessly. "I'm sorry, Reese. I know you're convinced that I can help, but I can't. And I can't risk my whole future and my family's good name just to prove that to you." She shook her head regretfully. "I must go."

Despair hovered, threatening to smother him like a shroud. He couldn't—and wouldn't—force Miss Kendall to spend a night with him.

But he couldn't let her leave without playing his very last card, which wasn't a card at all. "Wait," he said. He reached behind the base of the birch tree and picked up the single rose he'd cut from his garden that morning. The yellow blossom, large as a saucer, had reminded him of her—bold and open, but soft, too. And the petals, brilliant gold with hints of orange at the edges, were as fresh as the sunrise. As warm as her smile.

He said none of those things, of course, as he gave her the flower, opting instead for, "This is for you."

Her eyes grew wide and her lips parted. "It's beautiful," she whispered, holding it up in the moonlight. "I've never seen a rose quite like this. Did you find it in Lady Rufflebum's garden?"

He shook his head. "It's from Warshire Manor."

"You have a garden?" she asked, as if he'd piqued her curiosity.

"I'm not certain you could call it a garden. More like a wasteland. A colorless collection of dead bushes and shriveled flowers."

"But this rose," she said, twirling the stem between her fingertips.

"It was the only blossom on the bush. Probably the one living thing in the whole damned place."

"Truly?" she asked, intrigued.

He took a step closer, determined to memorize the gentle slope of her nose and the bowed shape of her lips. He didn't blame her for refusing to help him. But if he wasn't ever going to see her again, he might as well leave her with the truth. "In a sea of decay and death, that rose was a stubborn spot of sunshine—and it reminded me of you."

He shoved his hands deep in his pockets and swallowed a mouthful of despair and loneliness. Tried not to think about the endless days and torturous nights that stretched out before him. He inclined his head and said, "Enjoy the rest of your evening," before turning on his heel and striding away.

He'd almost reached Lady Rufflebum's back gate when he heard Miss Kendall call out behind him. "Reese. Wait."

He froze, wondering if he'd wished her voice into his ears. But when he slowly spun around, she was standing there, her chest rising and falling with each breath.

"I still don't believe that I can help you sleep," she said, "but I'm willing to try."

A tiny seed of hope took root inside him. "Thank you," he said, his voice ragged to his own ears.

Her deep sigh said she was already regretting her decision. "Meet me at the shop on Friday. The same time as last week," she said smoothly. "We'll discuss the terms of our . . . arrangement then."

"Very well. I look forward to seeing you. On Friday." He was already counting the hours. "Good night, Miss Kendall."

She looked down at the yellow rose she held and smiled in spite of herself. "Good night." He remained standing there, watching as she gracefully turned and walked toward the house. When she glanced back at him, it felt like the sun had peeked through the clouds. "Oh, and Reese?" she said, as if she'd almost forgotten something. Something important.

His heart hammered. "Yes?"

"You may call me Sophie." She shot him a dazzling smile before she disappeared into the night like a nymph leaving the mortal world for her mystical realm.

Chapter 6

On Friday evening, at the conclusion of the Debutante Underground meeting, Sophie presented to Madam Laurent a pot of bright periwinkle asters nestled in a thick bunch of deep green leaves. Smiling at the dress-shop owner, she said, "On behalf of all our members, I'd like to thank you for allowing us to meet here for the last several weeks. You've been so generous."

The ladies sitting around the long table in the back room of the dress shop nodded and clapped appreciatively.

"But we've imposed on you for far too long," Sophie continued, "and I'm pleased to announce that starting next week, we'll be meeting in a vacant building just down the block. It's the old tailor's shop, and I've arranged for us to use it on Friday evenings. So, enjoy your week, and I look forward to welcoming you to our new location next time."

Everyone murmured excitedly as they filed out. Sophie quickly set the room to rights and called good night to Madam Laurent and Ivy before slipping out the door and heading down the alley toward the tailor's—and her rendezvous with Reese.

Each time she thought about seeing him again, her nerves stretched tight and her skin prickled. Partly because she had no idea what he expected of her. It wasn't that she feared him. If he'd wanted to harm her or take advantage of her, he could have done so the first night they'd met or shortly after, on the night of the ball. But he'd been a gentleman. A grumpy gentleman, to be sure, but always respectful of boundaries—and of her.

The truth was that much of her nervousness was born out of anticipation. She *wanted* to see him again, even though she knew she shouldn't feel that way.

That was why she'd been determined to resist his pleas, his bribes, and his silver tongue. She'd been unyielding as an oak, in fact, right up to the moment when he'd given her the rose. Then her resolve had blown away like dandelion seeds in the wind. In that moment, she'd caught the briefest glimpse of the man underneath all the despair and pain. He'd been honest and kind—almost poetic.

But she'd seen something else in him too—an appreciation for nature's power and beauty. Anyone who could see the world that way was not beyond saving.

She walked briskly to the green door, rapped twice, and placed a hand over her chest. Dash it all, if her heart didn't slow its beating, she was going to need valerian root herself.

Reese yanked open the door almost immediately— as if he'd been pacing the room, waiting for her. "You knocked," he said with a wry, disarming grin. "How refreshing." He waved her in, to the center of the room, toward the pair of leather chairs.

She faced him and prepared to launch into the speech she'd rehearsed earlier. The one where she explained in no uncertain terms that she would be dictating the rules of their deal and that she was prepared to walk out the door if he balked at a single one of her demands.

But the moment she saw him in the light of the lantern, the words died on her lips. His hair stood on end, and several days' worth of stubble covered his jaw. His eyelids were droopy, his cheeks sunken. "Reese," she said, setting her reticule on the piecrust table between the chairs. "You look awful."

"I should have made myself presentable." He touched his chin and winced. "My valet tried, but I can be stubborn."

"You don't say." Sophie crossed her arms. "Have you eaten yet today?"

He stopped to think about this, as if it were a tricky question. "I don't think so."

"Then that's the first order of business," she said in a matter-of-fact tone. "There's a tavern down the block. Go and eat dinner. We'll talk when you return."

"You're not coming with me?" he asked, and Sophie would have sworn she detected a hint of alarm in that deep, rich voice.

She shook her head firmly. "I can't be seen with you."

He met her gaze, his eyes wary and wounded. "I'm not hungry," he countered.

"It's not open for debate," she said. "You must eat before we discuss the particulars of our agreement."

He hesitated. "You'll wait here?"

She nodded solemnly. "I promise."

Grudgingly, he grabbed the jacket that was draped over the back of a chair and stuffed his arms into it. "I won't be long, but lock the door behind me, just to be safe."

She gave him a placating smile and waved him out the door.

When she was alone, she wandered around the room, eager to have a better look at the shop. Most of the merchandise had been removed from the shelves and counters, but a few pitiful items remained: a single glove, a mismatched pair of socks, a couple of cravats, and a cane.

Behind the counter, she found an assortment of cuff links, buttons, and feathers. But she was more pleased to find an apron and a bottle of dusting oil. Thinking she might as well start cleaning the room prior to next week's meeting, she slipped the long apron—which she guessed had belonged to Mr. Peabody—over her head and grabbed one of the cravats to use as a rag. She dusted the counter and shelves and even ran her cloth over the leather chairs.

She was so absorbed in the task that Reese startled her when he walked in, carrying a small sack in the crook of his arm. "What's that smell?" he asked, sniffing the air suspiciously. "And why does it look like a brigade of overzealous maids came through here?"

Sophie brushed off her palms, untied the apron, and lifted it over her head. "It's lemon oil," she said with a shrug. "The room was overdue for a cleaning."

"Thank you," he said with a frown. "I hope you know that's not why I asked you here."

"I know," she said—although she still wasn't entirely sure of the real reason. "How was your dinner?"

"I brought it back," he said, holding the sack aloft. "There's a sandwich in here for you as well, some cheese, and a couple of apples." He sat in one of the chairs and gestured at the other. When she didn't move, he said, "You're not going to make me eat alone, are you?"

Tentative, she took the sandwich he offered and sat across from him. It seemed strange to be eating dinner alone with a man—and even stranger that they had no napkins, utensils, or table. A little like a picnic, but without the pesky insects.

Feeling Reese's eyes on her, she nibbled at the sandwich. "Delicious," she said.

He unwrapped his and bit into it with obvious gusto. "Food was an excellent idea," he admitted. "I didn't realize how hungry I was."

They devoured most everything Reese had brought from the tavern, with the exception of the apples, which they set on the table between them.

The room had no clock on display, but Sophie suspected that the hour was close to midnight. Usually by this time on a Friday evening, she would have made her way from the meeting to Fiona and Gray's house, where she often stayed up late visiting with her friends before making herself at home in their lovely guest bedchamber. But earlier that day, she'd sent Fiona a note informing her that she wouldn't be able to spend the night and would arrive early Saturday morning, instead.

Sending the note had felt a bit like crossing into dangerous, uncharted territory. Miss Haywinkle had been fond of saying that the rules of proper behavior were in place to protect young ladies. Sophie had been skeptical, but as she sat across from the scruffy, brooding Earl of Warshire in the quiet, dimly lit room, she began to think that the headmistress may have had a point.

And that was precisely why Sophie intended to set up rules governing their interactions. She needed to establish clear boundaries. Lines that would not—*could* not—be crossed.

"As I mentioned in Lady Rufflebum's garden," she began, "I think it's important that we spell out the terms of this arrangement."

"I agree," Reese said earnestly. "But allow me to pour us some drinks first." Before she could object, he swept away the remnants of their dinner, disappeared into the back room, and returned with two glasses of brandy. He handed one to her, then clinked his glass against hers before raising it and taking a long swallow.

Sophie set hers down on the table without taking a sip. If there was ever a time she needed to keep her wits about her, tonight was it. "I am under no obligation to you," she began. "But to ensure there is no misunderstanding going forward, I wish to make a few things clear."

"Fair enough," he said smoothly as he settled back into his chair. "I know that my request is highly irregular, but I'm not proposing anything improper. It's not my intent to seduce you, Sophie."

Heat crept up her neck. Whether it was from talk of seducing or the velvet sound of her name on his tongue, she couldn't say. Either way, she was grateful that the lantern was on the counter and she and Reese were mostly in shadows.

"I wasn't suggesting that you have wicked intentions where I'm concerned," she said. "I realize that such a thing would be highly unlikely."

"Why is that?" he asked, incredulous.

Heavens. Now her cheeks were on fire. "Because I don't usually inspire those sorts of . . ." Dear God, this was humiliating, but she'd promised herself she'd be forthright in her discussions with Reese. That she wouldn't dance around difficult subjects. "I only meant that men generally don't . . . desire me in that way."

He blinked as though she'd managed to stun him. And then he chuckled—a deep, intoxicating laugh that she felt low in her belly. "Forgive me," he said, leaning forward and propping his elbows on his knees. "But as long as we're being truthful, I have a confession to make."

Sophie braced herself and resisted the urge to reach for her glass of brandy. "Go on."

"I was sincere when I said that it isn't my intent

to seduce you. But that doesn't mean I don't desire you, Sophie. In fact, it's difficult for me to imagine a woman more desirable." His gaze, undeniably hot, lingered on her face for several heartbeats.

Like a dormant bulb feeling the sun after a long, brutal winter, her body unfurled, blossoming with warmth. "The conversation seems to have veered off course," she said, doing her best impression of Miss Haywinkle. "The point is that I want to be clear about our agreement. You will permit me to use this room every Friday night between the hours of seven and eleven o'clock. Afterward, I shall endeavor to create an atmosphere that's conducive to sleep—but I make no guarantees."

He rubbed the back of his neck, wary. "What, exactly, is going to happen here between the hours of seven and eleven?"

Sophie purposely ignored the question. "That brings me to rule number one."

"We have rules?"

"You will make no inquiries about my use of the building and will stay far away during the aforementioned hours."

"Fine," he grumbled, arching a brow. "But this is a respectable tailor's shop. I hope you don't plan to turn it into an opium den."

"If I do, it's no concern of yours," she said briskly.

Reese took a swallow of brandy and shot her a knee-melting half smile. "I'm intrigued, Miss Kendall."

"Rule number two," she continued. "Absolutely no one may know about this arrangement," she said soberly.

Reese rubbed the stubble on his chin. "My staff?"

Sophie's neck prickled ominously. "Why would they need to know?"

"Because they're bound to see you at Warshire Manor," he said, as if it should have been painfully obvious.

"But I assumed we'd be meeting here in the shop," she said, even as she realized he had other ideas.

He shrugged. "In case you hadn't noticed," he said dryly, "there's no bed here."

She stood and paced in front of her chair. "You slept in the chair last Friday evening. Why can't you do it again?"

"Because I need you to stay with me, and you wouldn't be comfortable here."

She blinked. "Reese, I am *not* going to share a bed with you."

He arched a brow, amused. "I wasn't suggesting that."

"Good." She spun on her heel to hide her mortification. The earl had already said he wasn't trying to seduce her, and yet she'd rather recklessly injected the possibility into the conversation again. She'd assumed he had ulterior motives for wanting her to spend the night—but it seemed her worry was for naught. "However, I'm afraid that spending the night at Warshire Manor is out of the question."

"But you were prepared to spend the night here. How is staying at my house any different? It's only a short coach ride away—and far more comfortable. I've already had a guest bedchamber prepared for you."

Needing some distance, Sophie walked to the far wall and plucked a half-crushed derby off the shelf. She spun the hat in her hands, stalling for time. What Reese said was logical. How could she explain that going to his house felt far too personal? There she would run the risk of learning more about who he truly was. And then she might begin to care about him—as more than a grumpy, sleep-deprived earl.

Setting the hat back on the shelf, she faced him and

said, "You shouldn't have presumed I would be willing to go home with you. I'd prefer to stay here, in territory that's more neutral."

"I'm not an adversary, Sophie. I want you to be comfortable. If you wish to spend the night here, then that's what we'll do. I just thought that you'd like to have your own room and that . . ." His voice trailed off as he stared into his glass and shook his head. "Never mind. It's not important."

She took a few steps closer to him, curious. "What?" she asked. "What's not important?"

He pressed his lips together as if determined to remain silent, but she walked right up to his chair. Challenged him to look into her eyes.

He held her gaze for several seconds, casually set down his glass, and stood so that they were toe-to-toe. He was so close that she could see the gold flecks in his irises and the dark fringe of his lashes. "I was going to say that as long you were at Warshire Manor, I thought you might enjoy spending time in my garden."

"The garden where you found the yellow rose?" she asked, keenly intrigued. She could still see the flower's perfection in her mind's eye. Could still feel its velvet petals against her cheek.

"The same one," he confirmed. "But, as I mentioned, there's not much else to look at. The head gardener took ill last year and hasn't tended to it in several months. He's slowly recovering and is intent on returning to his duties as soon as he can. He's faithfully served my family for years, so I'm willing to wait, but in the meantime, the grounds look rather . . . bleak."

Sophie swallowed. If there was one thing she found nigh irresistible, it was a gardening project—and the greater the challenge, the better. But she had to weigh that against the risks. "I will consider going to Warshire Manor next week," she said. "Tonight we will stay here."

"Fair enough." Reese's eyes crinkled at the corners and a half smile formed on his lips. "Is it time for bed yet?"

Chapter 7

Sophie cast an assessing gaze at Reese's face. "You're not in the right frame of mind for sleep," she said.

That much was true. All his senses were on high alert around Sophie. His body thrummed with awareness of her—the sure, graceful way she moved, the unexpectedly sultry tone of her voice, and the defiant spark in her blue eyes.

Though he longed for sleep, he disliked the thought of wasting hours he could be spending in her company. "What would you like to do?" he asked. "We could play cards or go for a walk."

She looked around the room, thoughtful. "Let's move some furniture."

He glanced over his shoulder at the leather chairs. "What's wrong with the furniture?"

"Nothing. But I'll need more seating in here for next Friday, arranged in a circle."

Reese shrugged off his jacket and tossed it onto the counter. He didn't really give a damn what they did—just having her close gave him comfort. Distracted him from his big problems.

"There's a long bench in the back room. I can bring it out here," he offered.

"Perfect," she said. "There are a few stools behind the counter, too. Even ottomans will serve my purposes."

Reese desperately wanted to know what she planned to do there but couldn't risk asking without violating the rules she'd laid out only minutes before. So he rolled up his shirtsleeves and brought every seat he could find to the center of the shop's front room, moving each one according to her directions. The only chair she didn't want him to move was the one in the back room where he'd slept last week.

When they were finished, the hodgepodge of chairs, benches, stools, and even overturned crates formed a large, neat oval that could seat at least a couple dozen people.

"It's a fine start," Sophie mused, slowly turning in the center of the circle like a dancer on a dais. "Thank you for your help."

"My pleasure," he said, surprised that he meant it.

"I brought more tea," she said, gesturing toward her reticule. "Would you like me to prepare some?"

He thought about it for two seconds and decided he'd rather expire from lack of sleep than have her treat him like a feeble curmudgeon. "Thank you, but I think I'll stick with brandy for now."

She looked suddenly self-conscious. Almost nervous. "It's late, and I happen to know you're in need of rest. Perhaps we should go to the back room and see if we can make you comfortable."

Good God. He didn't want a nursemaid. In fairness to Sophie, he wasn't sure what he wanted. "Are you tired?" he asked. "You're welcome to curl up in the chair back there. I can stay out here, so you'll have some privacy."

She shook her head. "I'm not sleepy. Maybe if we play cards for a while our eyelids will grow heavy."

Reese took a deck of cards out of the side table's small

drawer and loosely shuffled them in his palms. "Shall I bring a larger table out here?"

Sophie grabbed a few cushions off the chairs and threw them onto the carpet in the center of the circle. "No need. We can play on the floor."

"Vingt-et-un?" he asked, sinking onto a cushion across from her.

"As long as you don't mind losing." There it was again. That sensual, slightly suggestive lilt to her voice. The one that made him feel like he'd just taken his first shot of whiskey.

He propped himself on one elbow and dealt the cards. "Care to make a wager, Miss Kendall?"

She met his gaze and pursed her lips, thoughtful. "I believe I would, my lord."

It seemed to him that the room grew warmer. More intimate. "What did you have in mind?"

"Money is too commonplace," she said, tapping her plump lower lip with an index finger. "Surely we can do better than that."

His blood heated a few more degrees. "I concur."

"I have nothing of value to wager," she drawled. "So we will need to be a bit more creative."

No problem there. He'd already imagined half a dozen wagers ranging from mildly improper to wildly wicked. "Name the stakes," he said. "Anything goes."

"Are you certain?" As she picked up the cards he'd dealt and glanced down at them, her face gave no indication of her hand.

"Positive."

"Very well." She set down her cards, slowly stood, and walked behind the counter. She bent down, and when she straightened, she was hiding something behind her back. Deliberately, she returned to their spot on the carpet and eased her way to her cushion, the skirt of her dress billowing around her like a frosted cake. "Tonight we will wager . . ."

She produced a crystal bowl from behind her back. A bowl filled with—

". . . buttons." She spilled them onto the carpet and then scooped them in her palms, letting them run through her fingers like pirate's gold.

"Buttons," he said flatly.

"The pink embroidered ones are the most valuable, obviously." She held one up for him to admire.

"Obviously," he repeated, impressed that she'd managed to surprise him.

"But the ones made of bone are also sought-after," she said matter-of-factly.

He shrugged, playing along. "Personally, I prefer the polished brass."

"Rather unimaginative," she teased as she began divvying up the pot. "Can't say I'm surprised. I hope you're prepared to lose your entire share."

"We'll see about that," he growled, but Sophie wasn't intimidated by his bluster. She merely picked up her cards, arched a brow at him, and made her wager.

An hour later, there were more buttons on her side than his, but he didn't mind in the slightest. He was too distracted by the strange, buoyant feeling in his chest. A sensation he vaguely recognized as enjoyment. It was a feeling he associated with his days at Eton and summers with his brother and the first time he'd kissed a girl.

A lifetime ago.

But as long as he played cards with Sophie, he wasn't thinking about his problems or his past or his inability to sleep. Instead he focused on his cards, and her blue eyes blinking at him above her hand, and the mesmerizing movement of buttons from one pile to another and back. His muscles relaxed. His breathing slowed. And some of the tension drained out of him.

As the night wore on, her eyelids drooped, and when he caught her trying to hide a yawn behind her cards, he took pity on her and tossed his almost-certainly-winning hand facedown onto the carpet. "You're exhausted," he said. "Why don't you go the back room and make yourself comfortable in the chair?"

She set down her cards, stretched out on her side, and tucked her elbow under her head. "I'd rather stay here and just close my eyes for a bit," she said, shooting him a sleepy, grateful smile.

"Of course." He grabbed one of the soft cushions and nudged it under her head.

She sighed as she nestled her cheek against it, and he suddenly felt intensely and irrationally jealous. Of her pillow.

"If I doze for more than a half hour, wake me," she mumbled, her eyelashes fluttering valiantly but ultimately losing their struggle.

"Sleep well, Sophie," he said, more to himself than her. When he sensed he could move without disturbing her, he quietly rose, retrieved his jacket from the chair, and gently laid it over her, covering her from her shoulder to hip. He turned the lantern low before returning to the floor, where he reclined and laid his head on a cushion across from her.

Somewhat shamelessly, he watched her. Wondered at the ease and perfection of her slumber. Someone who drifted off to sleep in the space of two sentences surely had a soul as pure as the driven snow, a conscience as clear as a cloudless sky—and Reese couldn't begin to fathom what that must be like.

He studied the subtle rise and fall of her chest, the slight parting of her lips. He observed the faint twitching of her eyelids and wondered if she dreamed of yellow roses or pink buttons or something else entirely.

As he watched her, he tucked his hand beneath the pillow and bent his knees, mirroring her pose. He inhaled and exhaled in time with her breathing. He closed his eyes and pictured her—greedily sifting buttons through her hands, helping him move furniture around the shop, smiling in the moonlight in Lady Rufflebum's garden.

He lingered with her in that peaceful twilight, calm and content, until eventually—miraculously—he fell asleep.

Sophie stirred, squeezing her eyes shut to protest the beam of sunshine slicing through the narrow opening between the drawn curtains. Her muscles felt a bit stiff, but she was warm and comfortable beneath a soft wool blanket that smelled like leather, brandy, and . . . Reese.

She moaned softly, rubbed her eyes, and peeked down at her torso to find that her blanket wasn't a blanket at all, but Reese's jacket. Heavens. She hadn't meant to sleep through the night. The whole point in her staying at the shop with him was to help *him* fall—

"Good morning." His voice, smooth and amused, caressed her skin like a field of buttercups, and he held out a steaming cup, offering it to her. "Tea," he said.

She pushed herself to sitting, reached for the cup, and took a fortifying sip. "Thank you." Blinking herself into full consciousness, she said, "I thought you didn't drink tea."

"I don't. But I know you do," he said with a shrug, looking much improved from the night before. His cheeks weren't quite so hollow, and his eyes weren't quite as lost.

"Did you . . . that is, were you able to sleep at all?" she asked.

"I did," he said, half incredulous, half relieved.

"That's good," Sophie said sincerely. "Although I think we've proven that you're quite capable of falling asleep without any assistance from me. I wasn't even awake last night. You did it all on your own, Reese."

"No," he said firmly. "I wouldn't have slept without you." He shot her a wary look. "You're not trying to renege on our deal, are you?"

She swallowed. "No. But I can't deny that I'm questioning the wisdom of it."

"Why?" he asked hoarsely. "You spent the night with me, and the world didn't come crashing down. The most scandalous thing that happened was a series of wagers involving buttons."

Sophie stared down at his jacket, still covering her lap. True, nothing untoward had happened—yet. But a strange heat had simmered between them. At times, she'd felt herself involuntarily leaning toward Reese, like a tulip stretching toward the sun. She couldn't admit such a thing to him, but she was fairly certain he felt it too, which was a very dangerous thing.

Because whatever attraction they might feel toward each other simply could not be acted upon.

She was all but betrothed to Lord Singleton and could not disappoint her family, who were depending on her, counting on her, to keep them out of the poorhouse.

"Are you worried someone will find out?" Reese probed. "Because I'll do everything in my power to protect you. To make sure not a single soul knows."

"Yes, it's partly that," Sophie admitted. But she was more afraid she might not be able to resist Reese. That she might begin to long for a future she couldn't possibly have.

"And you've established rules," he said, almost desperately. "I've sworn to abide by them. I wouldn't risk losing you—that is, your help—by violating the terms you set."

And that's when she realized what she must do, as a safeguard. As a last line of defense against her own, irrepressible desires: She had to tell Reese about Lord Singleton—and add one more rule, perhaps the most important of them all.

She set down her tea, handed Reese his jacket, and looked at him earnestly. "One of the reasons I must be especially careful is that I plan to become engaged in a few weeks."

"Engaged," he repeated dully.

"Yes," she continued, matter-of-fact. "To Lord Singleton. We've decided to wait till the end of the season to announce it."

"Singleton," he mused. "The tall, respectable-looking bloke you danced with at Lady Rufflebum's ball?"

"Yes."

"I see." He stared at the crystal bowl of buttons sitting on the floor between them, and the vigor she'd seen in his face only moments before vanished. "Sophie, if you want to extricate yourself from this deal—from *me*—I understand. I won't pretend to be happy about it, but I do understand."

"No," she assured him. "I agreed to help you, and I want to, if I can."

"You already have, just by being here."

She took a deep breath. "I'll promise to stay with you every Friday night until my engagement is announced, if you'll agree to one more rule. One that may seem rather . . . odd."

He gave her an encouraging nod. "Anything you want."

"Rule number three," she said softly. "We mustn't touch each other."

He shook his head as though confused. "I'd never touch you," he said gruffly. "Unless . . . unless you wanted me to."

"I know," she said evenly. "But the rule is absolute. No touching. Even if you want to. Even if I want to. And *especially* if we both want to."

He scrubbed his palms over his face. "I've got it," he said soberly. "No touching."

"Not even contact that could be considered innocent or incidental." She needed a clear, firm line. The Debutante's Revenge had explained how easy it was to succumb to desire. And it would be far easier to resist if she abstained altogether.

Reese gazed at her, his eyes unexpectedly hot. "You have my word."

"Excellent," she managed, as she stood and stretched the stiffness from her limbs. "We have a deal."

"I would offer to shake on it," he said, arching a brow, "but . . ."

"Your word is good enough for me, Reese. I'm trusting you." That much was true.

The person she *didn't* trust was herself. She was counting on rule number three to keep her feet on level ground and prevent her from tumbling headfirst over a perilous cliff.

And she hoped it would be enough.

Chapter 8

The members of the Debutante Underground approved wholeheartedly of the tailor's shop as a meeting place, nodding and exclaiming over the large, open room as they filed in and took their seats the following Friday. Compared to the cozy but cramped back room of Madam Laurent's dress shop, the tailor's felt like a palace. The women took advantage of the empty space at one end of the room, using it to stretch their legs and mingle.

Sophie was delighted that the group's numbers had consistently grown, and this week was no exception. That morning's edition of The Debutante's Revenge had created a stir, and all the women seemed eager to talk about it.

At eight o'clock, Sophie launched into her usual greeting and review of the rules before ceremoniously handing her copy of the *London Hearsay* to Ivy, one of the dress shop's seamstresses, to read the latest column:

> *Dear Debutantes,*
> *Young ladies are often taught to be passive and*
> *undemanding; to avoid creating a fuss. In a*
> *romantic relationship, however, it's important to*
> *make your desires known. Tell your partner what*
> *pleases you, or, if it is difficult to speak the words,*

show him. Do not be afraid to ask for the things
you want; encourage your partner to do the same.

A true gentleman will appreciate and respect a
woman who communicates her desires—and who
does not expect him to be a reader of minds.

The accompanying sketch depicted a couple in a field
of wildflowers. She sat among the blossoms, plucking the
petals off a daisy, while his head rested on her lap. They
looked perfectly content and at ease with each other—and
also very much in love.

As Ivy read the column, Sophie tried to picture Lord
Singleton's head in her lap. Tried to imagine speaking to
him about personal things—the sorts of things that weren't
discussed in polite company. The sorts of things that
mattered.

And she couldn't.

To be fair, she didn't know him very well. But he'd
never seemed very curious about her. Never sought to understand her. Not in the way Reese did.

As the discussion around the column began in earnest,
Sophie retreated to the side of the room near the counter
and recalled the night she'd spent with Reese on the floor
of that very room.

She knew she shouldn't be so eager to meet with him
again, but she'd thought of little else since waking that
morning. Last Saturday, before they'd said goodbye, she'd
agreed to meet him outside the tailor's shop at eleven
o'clock that night so he could take her to Warshire Manor.
He'd promised to dismiss the staff for the entire night so
she wouldn't have to worry about being seen—and becoming the subject of gossip.

Sophie's family and friends would have no inkling as
to her whereabouts. Mama assumed she was staying with

Fiona and Gray as usual, but Sophie had informed her friends that she wouldn't be sleeping over for the next few weeks, due to a project she was undertaking.

Fiona had arched a brow at that, but thankfully hadn't pressed Sophie to elaborate on what the *project* entailed. All she'd said was that any project Sophie undertook was destined to be a smashing success.

But all Sophie wanted was a bit of adventure. A taste of freedom. And if she could achieve that without bringing shame upon her family, she'd consider herself fortunate.

As the meeting drew to a close, Sophie stood by the door and bid each woman good night. One of the last to leave was a young, weary-looking woman with huge brown eyes in a too-pale face. Her dark hair was drawn into a no-nonsense knot at her nape, and her thin shoulders were wrapped in a faded yellow shawl.

"I don't think we've met. My name is Sophie," she said, warmly extending a hand.

"I'm Violet," the young woman replied. As she grasped Sophie's fingers, she swayed on her feet till Sophie swiftly steadied her by the elbow.

"Come, sit for a moment," Sophie insisted, guiding her to the nearest chair. "Forgive me for saying so, but you don't look well."

"I'm fine," Violet assured her. "Just a bit dizzy after sitting for so long, is all. You needn't worry about me."

"Nonsense." Sophie plopped a scone on a plate and thrust it at Violet. "Something tells me you haven't eaten dinner yet."

The young woman's cheeks pinkened, and she glanced at the floor.

"I wish I had something more substantial to offer than a scone," Sophie said, clucking her tongue. "But that and a cup of tea will have to do, for now."

She brought Violet some tea and sat beside her as she nibbled on the pastry. Sophie longed to know more about the woman, who looked to be about eighteen—too young to have dark circles beneath her eyes and tired lines around her mouth. But Sophie didn't want to pry. After all, most members were understandably skittish about sharing details of their personal lives. She did notice that the woman didn't wear a wedding band, and her chapped hands revealed she was accustomed to hard work.

"I'm glad you were able to join us tonight," Sophie said sincerely. "The size of the group can seem a little overwhelming at first, but I hope you felt at home."

Violet nodded vigorously. "Oh yes. Everyone was so welcoming and friendly, even though I'm just a . . . well, I *was* a maid."

"One of the things I adore about the Debutante Underground is that it brings everyone together." Sophie strolled around the tailor's shop as she spoke, stacking plates and cups on a tray. "Within these walls, it makes no difference whether you're a grand dame, a lady's maid, a shopkeeper, or a laundress. We all gather on Friday evenings for a singular purpose—to share our knowledge and experiences . . . and support each other."

"That's lovely." Violet sounded wistful and hopeful at the same time.

Sophie smiled as she gingerly watered Reese's potted plant, which, she had to admit, was looking marginally better. "It helps knowing that we're not alone."

Violet's cup clattered against her saucer, as though her hands trembled. "I'm afraid I must go," she said, standing abruptly.

"Of course," Sophie said, sympathetic. She retrieved her reticule from behind the counter, withdrew the few coins she'd brought, and pressed them into Violet's palm. "It's not much, but I'd like you to have it."

"I couldn't," Violet said, clearly appalled.

"Please, think of it as a small gift." The coins amounted to Sophie's share of last week's earnings from the newspaper column—the earnings that Fiona and Lily had insisted on splitting three ways from the start. "One day, if you wish, you can pass the kindness along to someone else."

"That's very generous. I don't know what to say, except . . . thank you."

"It's nothing," Sophie said with a dismissive wave.

Violet gave Sophie a wobbly smile, clutched her shawl tight around her shoulders, and turned toward the door.

"Take care walking home," Sophie called after her. "And I hope you'll be able to join us again next week."

"I hope so too," Violet said softly, before vanishing into the darkness of the alley.

Sophie's encounter with the frail young woman left her feeling uneasy as she finished washing the dishes and setting the shop to rights. But she had little time to dwell on the conversation because it was almost eleven o'clock—and Reese would arrive any minute.

When he rapped on the window of the back door, she grabbed her portmanteau, extinguished the lantern on the counter, and met him in the alley, her heart pounding as if she'd run a mile.

"Sophie," he said, sounding faintly relieved. "You're well, I hope?"

"Yes." She exhaled slowly, willing her pulse to slow. "And you?"

He shrugged. "Better now." He gestured toward her bag. "Would you like me to carry that? I have a hackney cab waiting for us one block over."

"Thank you." She handed him the portmanteau, taking care to avoid contact with his hand. Then she draped her shawl over her head like a hood, concealing herself just in case they encountered anyone during their short walk.

A few minutes later, they were in the cab, rumbling through the streets, on their way to Warshire Manor. Reese sat beside her, keeping a safe distance on the seat between them. Occasionally, he glanced over at her, almost as though assuring himself she was still there. But mostly, he stared out the window.

He looked much the same as he had the previous Friday evening—agitated, exhausted, and generally at his wits' end. Unfortunately, his weary state didn't detract from his attractiveness. The planes of his face were eminently masculine, from his straight nose to his pronounced cheekbones to his square jaw. The moonlight illuminated the light stubble on his chin and the golden streaks in his collar-length hair. His long, sinewy legs sprawled across the cab, and the muscles of his shoulders flexed beneath the stretched fabric of his jacket, making the interior of the coach seem rather intimate and warm.

"The drive won't take long," he said. "And, as you requested, I made certain that all the staff left for the weekend, and there's nary a maid nor a footman in sight. They're delighted to have some time off."

"I'm glad," she said. "Thank you."

"Of course, that means we'll need to fend for ourselves. We won't have a butler, housekeeper, coachman, or, most importantly, a cook."

"I feel certain we'll survive the night," she said with a smile.

The lights of town began to fade, and the landscape outside their windows changed from boxlike buildings and paved streets to lush fields and twisting roads. The farther they traveled from London, the more she relaxed.

For tonight, she wasn't Miss Kendall, the unfailingly proper, ever-dutiful daughter of a destitute baron who would soon be betrothed to a marquess.

She was simply Sophie.

And for once, the possibilities seemed limitless.

At last, the hackney cab rumbled up a long, winding path, leading to a striking structure that appeared one part medieval castle, one part soaring cathedral. Gothic windows, a massive arched door, and a pair of pointed turrets probably would have made the manor house look foreboding to most people, but Sophie found it strangely beautiful and unique.

When the coach rolled to a stop, Reese hopped out and turned to help her disembark before remembering himself and quickly shoving his hands in his pockets. He paid the driver and arranged for him to return at eleven o'clock the next day.

The driver readily agreed, and as he drove off, Sophie realized that for the next twelve hours she and the earl would be entirely alone—a prospect that both thrilled and frightened her.

Chapter 9

Reese led the way up the steps to Warshire Manor—the house he still thought of as Edmund's. Reese had lived there as a boy but had spent little time there as an adult—until three months ago.

That's when he'd received a cold and carefully phrased letter offering condolences and informing him that his older brother Edmund had "succumbed to injuries resulting from a tragic hunting accident."

The solicitor's missive had requested that Reese return home immediately to see to his brother's funeral arrangements, attend to several important estate matters, and take up his duties as the new Earl of Warshire.

But Reese hadn't been able to get past the first, soul-wrenching paragraph. The part that had said Edmund—the brother he'd worshipped—was dead.

In Reese's mind, this house would always belong to Edmund.

He was the one who had exorcised the demons their father had left behind.

He was the one who should have lived here until a ripe old age, secure in the knowledge that his children and grandchildren would carry on the family name and bloodline.

But Edmund was gone, and since the continuation of

the family line now depended on Reese . . . well, it didn't stand a chance.

He led Sophie up the brick front steps, resisting the urge, once again, to offer her his hand. "Watch your step," he said, wishing he'd thought to light some lanterns outside before leaving the house.

He pushed open the door and ushered her inside, pausing in the dimly lit entrance hall. Sophie's eyes grew wide at the sight of the room's cavernous ceiling, ornate buttresses, and elaborate stonework. "This is amazing," she breathed. "Otherworldly."

He couldn't say that he'd ever had such romantic notions about the house, but he liked that Sophie did. She could find the beauty in anything.

"Come," he said, picking up a lantern from the gilded side table flanking one side of the entrance. "I had a room prepared for you. I'll take you there so you can make yourself comfortable."

As he led her down the long, marble-tiled hall, she craned her neck to observe the ancient tapestries adorning the walls and the swirling geometric patterns gracing the second-story windows. "You grew up here?" she asked, with more than a little awe.

"I did," he said, thinking it best not to mention that he'd left it all behind at the first possible opportunity.

Halfway down the hall he waved an arm at the grand staircase, and she followed him up the steps to the first landing. "There's a sitting room and a library on this level," he said, noting the keen interest that sparked in her blue eyes. "Please, make yourself at home here. Wander anywhere you like."

"I'd love to see more," she said. "In fact, I wish it were daylight now, so I could roam the grounds and explore the garden."

"I don't see why we need to wait for dawn," he said with a shrug. "Let's place your portmanteau in your room, and I'll take you to the garden right away."

"Could we do that?" she asked, almost rapturous.

"We can do anything we like."

Reese led Sophie to a guest bedchamber that was three times the size of her room at home. Decorated in shades of gold and pale blue, it was fit for a queen. The four-poster bed that held court in the center was far grander than any she'd slept in before; even her bed at Fiona and Gray's couldn't compare.

"I hope you'll be comfortable here," he said earnestly.

"I'm sure I shall," she replied, a little breathless. "Where are your quarters?"

"Just down the corridor in my old room," he said. "I can't bring myself to move into the master suite."

Sophie nodded, filing away the information for future use. "You know," she said softly, "we don't have to go to the garden tonight. The whole reason I'm here is to try to help you sleep. If you're spending half the night escorting me around your estate, you'll miss out on precious hours of rest."

He leaned against the doorjamb, thoughtful. "Earlier today, I was so exhausted that I couldn't tie my own damned cravat. My head pounded, my fingers wouldn't work, and all I wanted was a few hours of sleep."

"And now?" she probed.

He dragged a hand across his jaw. "I just want to spend time with you, like a normal person."

She chuckled at that. "You *are* a normal person."

For several heartbeats he stared at her, his expression unreadable. At last he said, "Only when I'm with you."

A shiver, sensuous and sweet, stole over her skin—and

though she was halfway across the room from Reese, she felt as though he'd caressed her. With his words.

"How about this?" she said slowly. "We'll spend no more than an hour in the garden, then I'll brew some tea for you and see if I can coax you to sleep."

He nodded. "I'm beginning to think you could coax me to do just about anything," he said gruffly, making her body tingle again.

Flustered, she set her portmanteau on a bench and tossed her shawl on the bed. "You know, I think a brisk walk will do wonders for both of us. I'll follow your lead."

They wound their way through a maze of corridors and back staircases, eventually arriving at a pair of heavy wooden arched doors. "This is the entrance to the ballroom," he said, leaning a shoulder into one of the doors till it creaked on its iron hinges and slowly swung open.

Sophie ventured into the center of the room, huge, empty and dark, and slowly turned in the center, admiring every detail. The polished parquet floors were covered in intricately shaped shadows from the towering windows along one wall. Moonlight painted the room the color of a pale purple orchid—ethereal and exquisite.

"My brother used to host grand parties here," Reese said, as if trying to imagine the room filled with guests and music and revelry. "But I prefer it like this—quiet and bare."

"I like it this way too," Sophie admitted.

"This may surprise you," he said dryly, "but I'm not very fond of balls."

"You mean you're not fond of dancing?" she asked with mock surprise.

"As a rule, no." He walked up to her and held a hand above her head like they were waltzing. She spun a few times, careful not to brush against the planes of his chest

or the protective, almost possessive, arc of his arm. But
the brief make-believe dance left her feeling dizzier than
it should have. She chuckled as she pirouetted away from
him and caught her breath, pretending she found his gruff
charm only mildly amusing.

But the truth was that Sophie had loved that moonlit,
music-less dance with Reese. Wouldn't have traded it for
a hundred waltzes beneath glittering chandeliers.

Reese strode to a set of French doors at the rear of the
room and pushed them open as though he were her escort
into another kingdom. Sweeping an arm toward the terrace and the plants and trees beyond, he said, "Welcome to
Warshire Manor's garden."

Sophie stepped out onto the flagstone terrace and was
immediately enthralled. "Reese," she whispered. "It's unlike anything I've seen." It was just as he'd described—
dying, desolate, dark. But it was also *so* much more.

From her vantage point near the house, she could see
at least three distinct parts of the expansive garden. A foreboding stone pavilion stood in the center, like the hub of a
wheel. To the left was a thicket of gnarled black poplars,
prickly bushes, and creeping vines. The area to the right
was a sea of nothing but pale, ash-gray asphodel flowers, rippling softly in the warm evening breeze. Behind
the stone pavilion Sophie could barely make out another
section—perhaps the most enticing of them all. It was
difficult to discern in the darkness, but she glimpsed an
apple orchard and massive stone fountains that mimicked
waterfalls.

The stark contrasts within the garden enchanted her, but
its most unusual feature was perhaps the one directly in
front of her, lapping at her feet. The entire landscape was
surrounded by a moat.

"Watch your step," Reese warned as she approached

the murky river water, which swirled and eddied as though monsters lurked below the surface. "It's deeper than it looks."

She rubbed the gooseflesh on her arms. "You say that as if you've gone for a swim or two."

"Not so much a swim as a thorough dunking," he said good-naturedly. "Come on. There's a bridge over here."

She followed him to an elaborate footbridge made of dark wood planks embellished with iron and stone. On one side of the bridge stood a sculpture of a life-sized, sinister-looking creature that was half dog, half beast.

"This is the closest thing Edmund and I had to a pet," Reese quipped. "Sophie, meet Rex."

A chill skittered down her spine as she put it all together: the pavilion, the moat, the strange trees and plants . . . and the ferocious guard dog made of stone. "That's not Rex," she whispered.

Reese turned to look at her, his expression curious. "What do you mean?"

"That's Cerberus," she said slowly. "Hades' dog."

"But he only has one head," Reese countered.

Sophie reached up and ran a hand over the cool stone at the dog's neck. A couple of areas were not as polished as the others—almost as if the stone there had been chipped away and filed down. "I think he must have had three heads at one time."

"Cerberus," Reese muttered. "That would explain why our pet dog had such ferocious-looking teeth. But why place a statue of Cerberus here? It seems rather random."

"Not at all," Sophie said, more than a little awed. "It all fits perfectly. Unless I'm mistaken, this entire garden is modeled after the Underworld."

Chapter 10

Reese scratched his head, skeptical. "Granted, this might not be your typical English garden, full of obedient rose-bushes and tidy hedges, but . . . the *Underworld*?"

Sophie's blue eyes seemed to capture the light from every star that shone above, and she nodded as if delighted to discover that his garden was some sort of tribute to Hades, God of the Dead. "Isn't it fantastic?" she whispered, almost reverent.

"Wonderful," he said dryly. He gazed warily at the cloudy water lapping at the rocks beneath the footbridge. "Ready to cross the River Styx?"

She gave Cerberus's head an affectionate pat and strode to the center of the bridge before stopping abruptly. "I almost forgot. We're supposed to pay the ferryman." She inclined her head toward the water meaningfully.

"Of course we are," Reese grumbled, but he jammed a hand in his pocket, withdrew a coin, and flipped it into the water, where it landed with a plunk.

Sophie's gleeful expression made him want to toss a dozen more coins in the godforsaken moat.

All his worries that she'd find the house too imposing or dismal had been for naught. Indeed, she seemed to appreciate its oddities and eccentricities.

As he led her deeper into the garden, he could almost see her shrewd eyes assessing each area, wondering about the choices of flora, noting the spots that required attention. He could almost see her palms itching to prune and weed and tend.

"I need to brush up on my mythology," she mused. "I'm certain there are all sorts of clever clues hidden among the plants and sculptures."

"There are probably a few mythology books in the library," he said, making a mental note to look for them on one of the nights when he was prowling the house in search of something constructive to do.

"Did your father commission the garden?" she asked, running a hand over a balustrade of the stone pavilion.

"I don't know," he admitted, "but I can ask the old head gardener, Mr. Charing, next time I see him."

"I'd love to know who designed it."

Sophie was curious about everything, asking scores of questions about the grounds and the house. Unfortunately, Reese had few answers.

His brother, Edmund, was the one who had been groomed to take over the estate. The one who knew everything about their family's history and heritage. The one who'd been unfailingly honorable, noble, and true.

An unexpected wave of grief crashed into Reese, nearly taking him out at the knees.

As if she'd sensed the sudden change in his mood, Sophie turned to him, concern marring her forehead. "This has been lovely, but perhaps we should return to the house and brew some tea."

Heart pounding, Reese glanced up at the monstrous manor house and wondered why he'd never noticed that it resembled a tomb. A dark, desolate crypt that could swallow him whole. He shuddered, feeling as though a thousand maggots writhed across his skin. And though a sliver of his mind knew that none of that was real, he also knew he couldn't go inside.

"I'll walk you back," he choked out, yanking at his cravat. "But if you don't mind, I'd rather stay outside for a while."

"Why?" She reached toward his arm, then quickly drew her hand back, as though realizing he was covered in thorns.

Sweat broke out on his brow. "Sometimes, especially when I haven't slept in several days, it feels as if the walls of the house will collapse on me. I know it doesn't make any sense." Not to a sane, good-hearted person.

"Actually, it makes perfect sense to me," she said softly.

"It does?"

She nodded serenely. "Being close to nature always calms me."

"I've never seen you be anything *but* calm," Reese said, winding his way through the garden and leading her toward the house.

Her face clouded. "You know what they say about appearances."

An image came to his mind, unbidden: Sophie dancing with her beau in Lady Rufflebum's ballroom. She and Lord Singleton had looked perfectly matched. Perfectly happy. Perfectly in love.

But what if they weren't?

Reese mentally slapped himself. He had no business questioning Sophie's relationship. Jesus, he was pathetic for wishing for even one second that she might be miserable with Singleton.

"I have an idea," she said, drawing him back to the

present. They'd already arrived at the footbridge, just yards away from the terrace. "I'm going to go inside and grab a few things. Will you wait for me just outside the ballroom? I promise I won't be long."

"Certainly." He would have waited there all night if she'd asked him to. "Can you find your way around the house?"

She nodded confidently, took the lantern he'd set by the door, and gave him a reassuring smile before disappearing into the ballroom.

But watching the darkness devour her made his palms sweat and his hands shake. He needed something to distract himself while she was gone. Something to occupy his mind and keep the demons at bay.

He closed his eyes and pictured Sophie strolling through the garden like a goddess, spreading light and goodness everywhere she went. Twisted, tangled branches bowed before her. Pale, feathery flowers gathered at her feet.

And then he knew exactly what to do.

He had time before Sophie returned.

He just had to make a quick journey across the River Styx.

Sophie found her way back to her bedchamber, opened a chest at the foot of the four-poster, and pulled out two thick quilts. She traipsed down the stairs, glided through the ballroom, and rushed out onto the terrace, slightly breathless.

But Reese wasn't in the spot where she'd left him.

Her belly twisted and her heart lurched. She shouldn't have left him alone, not when he was so clearly exhausted and distressed. She dropped the quilts, cupped her hands around her mouth, and was about to call out his name when she spotted him, a few yards away.

He sat on a marble bench at the edge of the terrace, holding a bouquet of silvery, starlike flowers—asphodels.

"What are those for?" she asked.

"You'll see." He shot her an enigmatic smile and gestured toward the quilts heaped at her feet. "What are those for?" he echoed.

She scooped up the blankets and gave him a saucy smirk. "Follow me."

They left the lantern behind and relied solely on the glimmer of the moon and stars as they tramped across the lawn. For Reese's sake, Sophie wanted to put some distance between them and the house.

Maybe, if the conditions were right, she could coax him to sleep.

She wandered down a hill toward a copse of birch trees and stopped beneath the largest. She turned slowly, assessing the area. A balmy breeze rustled the leaves overhead, and a mattress of soft, fragrant grass tickled the tops of her feet. The house had all but disappeared from view, and nature surrounded them in a comforting cocoon.

"This is perfect," she said. "Will you help me spread out these quilts?"

He cast her a quizzical look but set down the flowers. Careful to avoid touching her, he took one side of a blanket, pinched the corners, and lifted it, letting it billow to the ground. They repeated the process for the second quilt, placing it a few inches from the first.

Sophie waved a hand at the blankets. "These shall be our beds tonight," she announced, kicking off her slippers and sitting in the center of one of the colorful patchwork quilts.

Reese's face was unreadable as he sat on the other blanket and faced her. "Have you ever slept outdoors before?"

She tapped a finger to her lips as she considered the question. "I have napped outside. Does that count?"

He picked up one of the asphodel flowers and tentatively plucked a few leaves off the stem. "I suppose so."

"Have you slept outside before? All night, that is?"

He nodded soberly. "I have. Many times."

"Do you enjoy it?" she probed.

Silence stretched out between them, and Reese suddenly seemed miles away.

She leaned closer, straining to see his face in the darkness. "Reese?" Maybe it had been foolish of her to bring him here. Perhaps she was only making matters worse.

He shook his head and frowned at the flower in his hand as though he'd forgotten he held it. "Forgive me," he said, his voice rusty and raw. "I was thinking about the last time I slept outside. It was during my time on the front lines in Portugal, and I was surrounded by fellow soldiers. We were cold and filthy, and our stomachs growled all night. But to answer your question—yes. In spite of all that, I did enjoy sleeping outside."

Sophie closed her eyes briefly, trying to imagine a fraction of the horrors he must have endured. Her mouth went dry. "I didn't know you were a soldier."

"Major in the 41st Foot," he said, dragging a hand down his face. "I bought my commission eight years ago and fought up until the day I received word about my brother. The next day, I left my regiment to come home."

She waited to see if he'd say more . . . but he didn't. Still, it was a start. In the few snippets he'd shared with her, he'd sounded both proud and melancholy. Dedicated and defeated.

"I'm sorry," she said earnestly. "About your brother . . . and about having to leave your company."

His gaze snapped to hers. "You're the first person who's said that you're sorry about me leaving the infantry," he said hoarsely. "Everyone assumes I'm grieving for my brother—and God knows I am. But no one seems to understand that I never wanted to come home. That I don't belong here."

Sophie's throat grew tight. "Reese. Things must feel strange right now. All of this"—she waved a hand in the direction of the house, hoping he understood she was talking about the title, the estate, and all it entailed—"is new to you. But you're not alone."

"I left all my friends behind," he said, his voice steeped in shame.

"You must have some family or friends here in London." She prayed he wasn't entirely alone.

"Just my valet, Gordon," he said flatly. "He's the only one I trust."

"It may take a while for me to prove it to you," Sophie said deliberately, "but you can trust me—and count me as a friend."

A flicker of relief and hope flashed in his eyes. "You can trust me too," he said, before turning his attention back to the flowers. One by one, he knotted and clumsily wove together the stems of at least a dozen of the delicate, lavender-gray blossoms.

"Are you going to tell me what you're making?" she teased.

"I should think it would be obvious." He held up a disjointed circle of squished petals, bent stalks, and wilted leaves. "It's a flower crown." With uncharacteristic, endearing shyness, he added, "For you."

"Oh," Sophie breathed. No one had ever made her a flower crown before, and she couldn't have loved it more if it were a diamond tiara. "It's lovely."

"It's my first attempt," he said with a chuckle. "And probably my last. But I'm glad if you like it."

"I adore it," she confirmed.

"Then it's time for your coronation." He moved closer to the edge of his quilt, assumed an appropriately serious expression, and propped an elbow on his bent knee. She scooted closer to the edge of her blanket, her legs bent to the side, and looked up at him, expectant. Only a few inches separated them, and her body thrummed with awareness of nature, the night, and *him*.

He cleared his throat and let his gaze sweep across the landscape—the lawn, the garden, the woods, and the dark violet horizon beyond. "Loyal subjects," he began in his deep, rich voice. "I hereby present to you Miss Sophie Kendall, your undoubted Queen."

She smiled at that, but his expression remained serious as he looked directly into her eyes. "Will you solemnly swear to preside over the grass, trees, and flowers?"

Because it seemed like the appropriate thing to do, Sophie raised her right hand. "I do so solemnly promise."

Reese lifted the flower crown from his lap and held it an inch above her head. "Then I pronounce you the queen of all you survey." Reverently, he let it drop onto her head. "God save the Queen," he said softly.

The tree boughs above them shook in the warm breeze, and a chorus of insects chirped enthusiastically. A delicious shiver stole over Sophie's skin, and she knew she'd forever remember the moment Reese proclaimed her queen of his garden . . . Queen of the Underworld.

"Thank you," she said, sitting back and stretching her legs across the quilt. "Are you ready for my first royal edict?"

He shot her a lopsided grin. "Probably not."

"Everyone in the kingdom must rest. Like this." She carefully set her crown on the quilt, reclined on her side, and tucked an arm under her head. Then she arched an expectant brow, waiting for him to lie down too.

"It's not easy being your royal subject," he grumbled, but he reclined on his quilt, facing her. Though their bodies were an arm's length apart, he seemed to radiate heat—like a stone that had been warmed by the sun all day.

If she really *was* a queen and free to do as she pleased, she might have wriggled close to him and soaked up that warmth. She might have even removed the pins from her hair and nuzzled her face to his chest. She might have done lots of things.

Instead, she rolled onto her back and stared at the leaves and the sky. "It feels like London is a world away," she whispered. "It's beautiful here."

"It is," he agreed. And though she didn't look at him, she could feel his heavy-lidded gaze on her. Could hear the gruffness of his voice.

"The stars shine brighter away from town. They look so close you'd think you could reach out and touch one." She turned to glance at him, flushed when she caught him staring at her, intent.

"Have you ever seen a shooting star?" he asked.

"No. Have you?"

"Yes." A cloud passed over his face. "But maybe it was only artillery fire."

"Did you make a wish?"

"I did," he said—so somberly, she knew without asking that it hadn't come true.

"Well, there's no artillery fire here," she said soothingly. "Just hundreds of twinkling stars. If we stare at them long enough, one is bound to streak across the sky. When it does, we'll both make a wish."

"I'll tell you what," he said softly. "You keep watch on the heavens. I'll keep watch over you."

Chapter 11

Reese felt grass sticking to one side of his face, the morning sun warming the other. His heart kicked into a gallop out of sheer habit, but then he recalled where he was. Lying on the lawn at Warshire Manor, with Sophie by his side.

He peeked at her through sleep-swollen lids, relieved to find her still resting next to him, covered with the quilt he'd placed over her last night. A few golden strands of her hair had slipped free from their pins, covering her eyes like a shimmering silk veil.

As though she'd sensed that he'd awoken, she brushed the hair off her face, stretched, and opened her eyes. "Did you sleep?" she asked.

"Aye." The last time he'd slept so soundly might have been when he and Edmund had gone swimming in the lake as boys. They'd jumped and splashed in the water till their fingers and toes shriveled and their lips turned blue. When they were finally too exhausted to float, much less swim, they dragged themselves out of the water, collapsed on the sandy ground, and napped for hours. "We should go swimming next week," he said.

Sophie shot him a curious look and rubbed her eyelids. "I wonder what time it is," she said worriedly. "I need to be at the house when the hackney cab arrives."

Reese reluctantly pushed himself to sitting. "I don't think it's very late yet, but we can make our way back and check the time. I'll round up something for us to eat, too."

She sat up, spied the quilt covering her legs, and frowned. "You gave me your blanket?"

He shrugged and scrubbed a few blades of grass from one cheek. "I'm used to sleeping on the ground. I didn't want you to be cold." He stood, and though he longed to help her to her feet, he settled for taking the quilts and shoving them under an arm.

"That was very thoughtful." She shot him a grateful smile as she slipped on her shoes and tucked a blond curl behind one ear. "But the whole point of my being here is to help *you* sleep."

"Right," he agreed, even if the reminder robbed a little of the glow from the morning. She was only there because they'd made a deal. She'd wanted the use of his building one night a week, and he required her help to fall asleep. She was the sort of soft-hearted person who probably routinely rescued stray mongrels and broken-winged birds. He'd essentially taken advantage of her good nature and begged for her help, knowing it would be nigh impossible for her to refuse.

That was the reason she was there, the reason she tolerated his company—for now. He couldn't let himself forget that.

She scooped her wilted flower crown off the ground, letting it dangle from her fingertips as they strolled back to the house in comfortable silence.

He took her through a back entrance and led her to the main corridor, where the grandfather clock confirmed they had half an hour before the hackney cab was scheduled to return.

"Why don't you take a few minutes to return to your

room and freshen up?" he suggested. "I'll see what I can find for us to eat and meet you in the dining room."

"Perfect," she said, placing a hand over her belly. "I'll return shortly."

He raided the larder and found a couple of hard-boiled eggs, a basket of pastries, and a variety of fruit that his cook had thoughtfully prepared before leaving for the weekend. Reese set everything on the dining-room table and grabbed plates and silverware from the sideboard while he waited for Sophie.

When she breezed into the dining room a few minutes later, she wore a pale pink gown embroidered with dark pink flowers that made the formerly dreary room feel like a garden party. She set her portmanteau by the door and allowed him to pull out her chair for her. "This looks delicious," she exclaimed, helping herself to a sweet roll. "I confess I'm famished."

While they ate, she asked a few questions about the house and the garden.

He asked her about her childhood and her favorite school subjects.

Neither of them dared tread too close to sensitive or revealing topics. With the end of their time together looming, Reese felt as though they'd already begun to say goodbye—at least till next Friday.

But then, shortly before it was time for her to leave, Sophie turned to him and said, "Could I ask you something rather bold?"

"Certainly," he said, hoping her question had nothing to do with his brother, his time on the front lines, or any other personal demons.

"Do you think your head gardener would mind if I provided a short list of chores for your groundskeeping staff to undertake?"

"I doubt it," Reese replied. "I believe he's been housebound for almost a year. I'm sure he doesn't expect the garden to remain untouched in his absence."

"I wouldn't want to overstep," Sophie said. "And the suggestions would be small improvements intended to restore the garden to its former glory. I have no wish to turn it into something else, because . . . well, there's something magical about it, just as it is. I'd hate for a well-meaning but overzealous member of your staff to try and change the essence of the garden."

"No, we'll ensure that it retains its Underworld quality, so Hades always feels right at home," he teased before adding, "I'd be grateful for your suggestions. What would you like to see done?"

"Why don't I write out a list?" she said, setting her napkin on the table. "With instructions you can give directly to your staff."

"Very well." He pulled out her chair and led her down the hall to his study, where he invited her to sit at his desk.

"You have a few unopened letters here," she said, pointing to three envelopes addressed to him, sitting near his quill.

"Yes." All of the letters were from the same woman. He'd never met her, and yet he knew a dozen little details about her—that her hair was the color of a sunset and her skin was as freckled as a quail's egg. That she made the best suet pudding and the worst kidney stew in all of England.

Her latest letter had arrived yesterday, but the others had been sitting there for at least a week before that. Taunting him, tormenting him. But he couldn't bring himself to open them.

So he unceremoniously swept them into a drawer and produced a clean sheet of paper for Sophie.

He prowled the study while she wrote. A few minutes later, she set down the pen and stood. "There," she said, leaving the paper on the desk. "This will make a fine start."

"Thank you." He moved away from the window, where he'd kept an eye on the pebbled drive in front of the house. "The hackney cab just arrived." He wanted to ask her where her family thought she was and whether she was going directly home now. He wanted to know if Lord Singleton treated her well and whether she looked at him the way she'd looked at Reese when he'd given her the flower crown.

But he knew damned well those things were *not* his business.

"Well then," she said with forced cheerfulness, "I suppose I shall see you next Friday evening. Same place, same time?"

"Yes," Reese said, already wishing away the days in between. "I will see you then."

He picked up her portmanteau, walked her outside, and stood back while Sophie spoke to the driver, presumably giving him an address. Then Reese paid the man and opened the cab door for her.

"Promise me that you'll take care of yourself," she asked, her forehead creased with concern. She took a satchel of herbs from her reticule and dropped it into his palm. "Ride your horse during the day and try to sleep at night. With the valerian-root tea or without it. In your bed or under the stars. Just . . ." She tilted her head as though searching for the thing that would help him most. "Just . . . think of me."

"I will," he said solemnly. At last, he'd made a promise that would be easy to keep.

"You're acting rather nervous today," Lily said, narrowing her striking green eyes at Sophie. "Like the time we hid a frog in Miss Haywinkle's bed, and you insisted on sneaking back into her room to take the poor creature out."

"I felt bad for Miss Haywinkle—and the frog," Sophie said with a laugh. "But you're right. I confess I am feeling anxious." She'd been frazzled ever since the hackney cab had dropped her off at Fiona's house an hour ago. Lily and Fiona were more like sisters than friends; Sophie wasn't accustomed to keeping secrets from them.

And Reese was a *very* big secret.

The trio of women had gathered that morning, as they did each Saturday, to discuss their plans for the next Debutante's Revenge column. They'd taken care of business quickly, which left them time to chat and catch up on the week's events. But for Sophie, the last twelve hours with Reese had eclipsed everything else in her world.

"Would your nervousness have something to do with your whereabouts last night?" Fiona asked, momentarily looking up from her easel. There was no hint of censure in her voice. Sophie knew instinctively that Fiona and Lily would never judge her harshly—even if most of the ton *would*. "Did something happen after the meeting?"

"Yes," Sophie admitted. She stood, walked to the window of Fiona's lovely studio, and swept aside a gauzy silk curtain so she could gaze at the trees outside, just beginning to bud. "I'm involved in a new project. It's only temporary," she said, feeling an unexpected pang. But she'd known her involvement with Reese couldn't continue once she was betrothed to Lord Singleton.

"I'm sure I'll tell both of you all about it one day soon," Sophie continued, "but I'm not quite ready to share." She was still sorting out her own feelings about Reese and didn't trust herself to talk about him without revealing more than she should. She knew Fiona and Lily would support her, no matter what. They'd encourage her to follow her heart.

But Sophie did not have that luxury.

It wasn't possible for her to pursue her own happiness—not when her family's future rested on her shoulders.

"You may confide in us if and when you wish," Fiona said sincerely. "We would never press you to reveal your secrets."

"Speak for yourself," Lily quipped, flashing a mischievous smile. "I want to know everything."

"Pay no attention to her," Fiona said, shooting her sister a slightly scolding look. "We know and trust you. Unlike a certain person in this room"—she rolled her eyes meaningfully in Lily's direction—"you'd never engage in behavior that was illegal or improper."

"Of course not," Sophie said, perhaps a bit too vehemently.

Lily laughed and rubbed her palms together with obvious glee. "Miss Sophie Kendall," she teased, "you *are* involved in something scandalous, and I, for one, cannot wait to discover what it is."

Chapter 12

At eleven o'clock the following Friday night, Reese knocked on the door of the old tailor's shop, feeling more like himself than he had in months.

Sophie's advice had helped. He'd forced himself to drink the bitter herb potion. He'd ridden his horse and spent time napping outdoors. But mostly, he'd thought about her.

He'd thought about her as he spent hours every day completing the list of gardening chores she'd provided. It had taken him two whole mornings of poking around in the moat with a fishing net to strain out all the algae and debris. He'd sanded and painted the footbridge; he'd weeded and trimmed the vegetation along the walkways and in front of Rex.

If he was uncertain whether he should remove a stalk or leave it, he always erred on the side of leaving it—because he knew that's what Sophie would want.

When an appalled groundskeeper discovered Reese working in the garden, he'd tried to take over, but Reese wouldn't allow it.

He wanted this project. Needed this work. Craved this connection to Sophie.

Every sore muscle and aching joint reminded him of

her, and somehow, that made it easier for him to sleep a few hours each night.

Now that Friday had arrived, he wanted time to slow to a crawl. The hackney cab waited one block over, ready to take Sophie and him back to Warshire Manor.

When at last she smiled and waved at him through the window of the tailor's shop, his chest squeezed. The next twelve hours were all theirs.

He'd known she'd be eager to see the garden again, so as soon as they alighted from the cab, he set her bag inside the front door, grabbed a lantern, and led the way through the house and out the back door.

The night was warm and overcast, making it difficult to see beyond the light of the lantern, but Sophie seemed to notice everything.

"The footbridge," she exclaimed. "Oh, Reese, the black finish is perfect—such a stark but beautiful contrast to the white stone of Cerberus. I love that he's in full view now, too, taking up his post as our loyal guard dog."

He tried not to grin at her use of the pronoun *our*, but felt his face crack anyway. "You can have a better look at everything in the morning. All the tasks on the original list are completed, so you'll need to let me know what you'd like to see accomplished next."

"Yes," she mused. "I'm sure there's more that could be done to restore this place, but I'll need to think on it . . . after I've spent some more time here."

He stroked his jaw to hide the smile that resurfaced at the thought of her spending more time at Warshire Manor. "Are you tired?" he asked.

"Not really." She slowly circled the large stone pavilion at the center of the garden till she met back up with Reese. "Are you?"

"No," he said. "I was thinking that if you don't mind walking a little farther, I could show you the lake."

"That sounds lovely," she said, wistful. "But I fear it's too dark for us to see anything properly."

"Why don't we give it a try?" he suggested. "If it's too dark, we'll head back to the house."

"I suppose it can't hurt," Sophie said, shrugging her slender shoulders. "And an evening walk might be just the thing to induce sleepiness."

"If you say so." He shot her a smile. Wished he could take her hand and hold it all the way to the lake.

It would have been completely natural for him to do so, and lately it was becoming more difficult to stop himself from reaching for her. Somehow, he knew that her skin would be soft and warm and that the pressure of her palm against his would be just right.

The more he'd come to know Sophie, the more he craved her touch. Thought about it day and night—while he worked in the garden and while he lay in his bed.

And he wanted to do a hell of a lot more than hold her hand.

Sometimes Sophie looked at him as if she wanted to touch him too. Maybe it was wishful thinking, but every so often, her gorgeous blue eyes seemed to glow with affection . . . and simmer with desire.

Even so, Reese resolved that he wouldn't be the one to cross the clear boundary she'd set. It was a matter of trust, and he suspected that the only reason she occasionally let down her guard with him was because she felt safe.

In some ways, their whole relationship depended on that trust, and he couldn't jeopardize it, no matter how much he might wish to hold her hand.

So he settled for picking up the lantern and holding it

between them as they ambled across the lawn, down the hill, and past the copse of trees where they'd spent the night last week. He led her through a wooded area, then paused just before they reached the clearing.

Sophie turned to him, expectant. "Is something wrong?"

"Not at all," he said, grinning as he held the lantern aloft. "Follow the path, right between those two trees— and then you'll see the lake."

Sophie looked down at the dirt path, taking care to step over sticks and small rocks. She thought it very sweet that Reese wanted to show her the lake, but she couldn't imagine there would be much to see, especially since there was no moonlight to speak of.

In fact, it was so dark she rather hoped that she didn't walk directly *into* the lake before she'd spotted it. But it did seem that they were almost to a clearing. The brush ahead wasn't so thick, and a breeze tickled the curls at her nape.

"There," Reese purred in her ear. "Look up, Sophie."

She did, and her breath caught in her throat.

At the bottom of a gently sloping hill, dozens of colorful lanterns bobbed from the boughs of a huge, ancient oak along the lakeshore. Like a swarm of glowworms celebrating the arrival of summer, the lights danced above, painting the water red, blue, yellow, and green.

Beyond the tree, a wooden pier extended several yards into the lake, and dozens of small lanterns placed at the edge glittered above the water like chandeliers at a mermaid ball. At the end of the pier, a collection of jewel-toned pillows and plush quilts beckoned.

The entire effect was dazzling.

"Reese," Sophie whispered. "How did you do this?"

"I wanted to surprise you," he said. "Do you like it?"

"Yes." Her voice cracked on that one little word. "I

love it." Her heart was so full of joy that her chest actually hurt. She hadn't known, till then, that joy could do that to a person. She rubbed the spot on her chest just above her heart, trying to ease the ache away.

"Go have a look," Reese urged. "It's all for you."

"It's for us," she said. "Let's go." With that, she picked up her skirts and ran down the hill toward the lake as fast as she dared, Reese on her heels. When she reached the oak, she was laughing and breathless and dizzy with delight. She leaned against the thick tree trunk, tipped her head back, and gazed up at the lanterns above. "You must see the view from here," she said to Reese. "It's like standing under a parasol made of rainbows."

He chuckled as he strode toward the oak and leaned against the opposite side of the trunk. He was so near that she could feel the frisson of heat between them. Her palms were pressed against the rough bark; his were too. All she had to do was slide her hands toward his—just an inch— and their fingers would be touching.

"You're right," he said, his voice a caress. "It's like a rainbow parasol."

They stayed like that for a few minutes, basking back-to-back in their private, colorful cocoon, listening to water lap against the shore. And though they never actually made contact, Sophie felt Reese all around her.

He was the rough, solid trunk pressing into her back. The long, fragrant grass tickling the tops of her feet. The warm evening air kissing her neck.

At last he said, "Would you like to walk out on the pier? There's a basket of food there if you're hungry."

She pushed herself away from the tree and twirled around till she faced him. The light of the lanterns created shadows beneath his cheeks, nose, and jaw, making him look distinctly masculine—and dangerously handsome.

"You thought of everything," she said, more than a little touched. "I'll never want to leave."

"Then don't." He stared back at her, his face impassive and intense. "You can stay as long as you want, Sophie."

The ache in her chest flared again, but she managed a smile. "Why don't we make the most of tonight?"

"Yes," he said, shoving himself off the tree. "We'll enjoy tonight."

She took her time as she walked along the shore, reaching down to let the tall grass run between her fingers. Reese followed a short distance behind, as though he wanted to give her time and space to explore the lake as she wished.

When she reached the pier, she paused, taking a moment to savor the view. The planks stretched out before her, illuminated by lanterns on both sides. She glided down the pier with the same solemnity, the same wonder, as a bride marching down the aisle on her wedding day.

She hadn't had much time to write in her journal of late, but she'd write about this. She needed to capture this feeling and preserve a little of the magic—to sustain her years from now, when her life would no doubt be tragically mundane.

Sophie walked to the very end of the pier, where she could almost imagine she floated in the middle of the lake. The quilts were spread there, side by side, with half a dozen pillows all around.

A nosegay of pink peonies tied with a white satin ribbon lay atop a sapphire silk cushion. She sank to her knees and lifted the bouquet to her face. "These are my favorites," she said, looking up at Reese. "I don't remember seeing a peony bush in the garden."

He grinned at her as he sat on the other quilt. "They're

not from the Underworld. They're from . . . someplace else. For you."

"Thank you," she breathed. She could already picture the blossoms pressed between the pages of her diary—along with the yellow rose and the flower crown she'd already tucked inside for safekeeping.

He gestured toward the basket. "Would you like something to eat? Maybe a glass of wine?"

"I'm not hungry, but please help yourself. And a glass of wine would be lovely."

He poured a rich, purple-red claret into a pair of goblets and handed one to her. "Shall we have a toast?" he asked.

"I think we must," she said, hoping he'd say something poignant and romantic . . . and also hoping he wouldn't.

He frowned as he thought for a moment, then said, "To guard dogs named Rex, rainbow parasols, and you." His eyes gazed deep into hers. "Your turn."

"Let's see," she mused before raising her glass. "To bouquets of peonies, starless nights, and you."

They clinked their glasses and sipped, thoughtful.

Reese stretched out his legs, leaned back on one palm, and looked out at the tranquil water. Sophie stared at his profile, trying to decipher the emotions that flickered over his face. "What are you thinking about right now?" she asked.

He swallowed and kept looking out at the lake. At first, she feared he wouldn't answer, but at last, he said, "I was remembering all the days Edmund and I spent here. Swimming, fishing, paddling around in a leaky rowboat."

"You must miss him," she said.

"He was the sort of person who charmed everyone he met. At ease anywhere from a pub to a ballroom to the floor of Parliament. Everybody loved him." Reese picked a pebble off the pier and flung it into the water. "He couldn't have been more different from me . . . but he was my best friend."

"I think that you are more like him than you realize," Sophie reasoned. "You've charmed me." That last part had slipped out before she could stop it, but she didn't regret saying the words. Reese deserved to know he was good and kind too, and if she could hold up a mirror to help him realize that truth, then she was happy to do it.

"I'm nothing like Edmund," Reese said flatly. "He was honorable and decent and good."

"So are you." She leaned forward and craned her neck, forcing him to look at her. "You are all those things."

"You don't know everything about me, Sophie," he said, adamant. "You don't know all that I've done. Trust me when I say that my brother's the one that should be here now."

"I'm so sorry that he's gone, Reese. I'm so sorry that there's a hole left in your heart. But I know this for certain—I'm very glad that you're here now. I wouldn't want to be here with anyone else."

"Except maybe Singleton?" He shook his head as though disgusted with himself. "I shouldn't have said that. I'm not sure why I did."

"It's all right," she said softly.

"You're still going to marry him?"

Her stomach clenched. "Yes. But I meant what I said just now. I wouldn't want to be here with anyone but you."

He said nothing to that, but quickly drained his glass of wine and abruptly stood up.

"Where are you going?" she asked.

"For a swim." He tugged off one boot, then the other.

"Right now?"

"I need to cool off." He'd already shrugged off his jacket and was tugging at his cravat.

Sophie endeavored not to stare as he grabbed the hem of his shirt and hauled it over his head. His torso was lean and muscular, with gorgeous planes and ridges and a smattering of scars over his chest and back. His skin, tanned and shimmering with perspiration, made her mouth water.

She parted her lips to speak but wasn't sure what to say. Why should she care if he went for a swim? The night was warm, and he had energy to spare.

A vigorous swim might be just the thing to help him sleep.

But the sight of him shirtless might be just the thing that made *her* lie awake in her bed for many, many nights to come.

Chapter 13

Stripped down to nothing but his trousers, Reese hurled himself headfirst into the water. It wasn't an artful, graceful dive, but an athletic, acrobatic one. He disappeared below the surface for several seconds, then popped up, spraying droplets everywhere.

"Will you be all right here for a few minutes?" he asked, treading water effortlessly.

Sophie crawled closer to the edge of the pier and looked down at him. "Of course."

He kicked onto his back and began floating away. "I'll return shortly," he promised, before rolling onto his stomach and swimming in earnest, churning water in his wake.

Sophie watched the easy, rhythmic strokes of his arms until he disappeared from view.

She waited on the quilt, sipping her wine and thinking how very warm the evening had grown—and how very inviting the water looked.

Perhaps she'd just dip her toes.

Spying a wooden ladder at one side of the pier, she kicked off her slippers, hiked up her skirts, and tentatively stepped onto the first rung, just above the surface of the lake. She held the ladder tightly as she bent a knee and swirled one foot in the water, sighing at the delicious coolness.

Ten years ago, while she was at away at school, Lily and Fiona had woken her in the middle of the night and tried to persuade her to sneak out of the dormitory and join them for a swim. Sophie had said no. She'd been too afraid—of the darkness, of things that lurked in the lake, and, most especially, of Miss Haywinkle's wrath.

Lily and Fiona had reluctantly gone swimming without her, and Sophie still regretted missing out. They'd taken a risk, gone on an adventure, and made a memory that would bring smiles to their faces for the rest of their lives.

And Sophie . . . well, her prudent behavior and superior judgment had gotten her nothing.

Except, perhaps, an impending engagement to a man she didn't love.

Something inside her snapped. This was a rare second chance, and she refused to spend the next five decades wondering why on earth she'd stayed high and dry on a pier when she could have been floating and splashing in the lake. With Reese.

Blast it all, she was going for a moonlight swim.

Abruptly, she scrambled back onto the pier, pulled all the pins from her hair, and loosened the laces at the side of her dress. She hastily rolled off her stockings and, before she could change her mind, hauled her gown over her head. Sucking in her breath, she wriggled out of her stays till she wore nothing but a thin cotton shift.

If she were *truly* courageous, like Lily, Sophie might have stripped naked before diving into the lake. On the other hand, swimming in her shift was far more daring than anything she'd contemplated doing that night. And it would still give her *plenty* to write about in her journal.

Her knees wobbled a little as she inched toward the edge

of the pier, curling her bare toes around the rough edge of a plank. She was a decent swimmer but had no intention of exploring the dark corners of the lake. She planned to stay within a stone's throw of the lanterns *and* the ladder.

Still, taking this plunge was about proving something to herself.

She couldn't see or hear Reese from where she stood, but she knew he was out there—and that she was safe with him.

All that was left to do was jump in—and she might as well do it properly, without settling for half measures. Determined, she took several giant steps backward and counted down in her head. *Three, two, one.*

She charged toward the end of the pier, leaped into the air, and hugged her knees to her chest. Her shift billowed and her hair floated around her for one interminable second—before the bracingly cold water swallowed her up.

Heart pounding, she scissor-kicked to the surface, slicked back her hair, and lifted her face to the night air, triumphant.

In the distance, Reese yelled, but Sophie's waterlogged ears couldn't make out the words.

"Reese?" she called back.

"Sophie!" This time, his panicked shout carried across the lake. "Hold on. I'm coming."

She spun around, bobbing and squinting at the darkness. "Don't worry, I'm fine!"

But he didn't seem to hear. He swam like a shark on the hunt, cutting through the water with breathtaking power and precision. Head down, he barreled toward her—as though his life depended on it. Or as if he thought hers did.

She swam to the ladder, sat on the top rung, and waved her arms, trying to draw his attention before he gave himself an apoplexy. "Reese!" she shouted.

He paused several yards away and looked up at her, gasping. "What the hell are you doing?"

"The same thing you're doing." She rubbed the tops of her arms and shrugged. "Swimming."

He frowned for a split second—then grinned. "You're swimming," he repeated.

"I *was*," she corrected. "Till you chased me out of the water."

"I thought you were drowning," he said, panting. "I was trying to save you."

It was a sweet sentiment, and Sophie smiled at him as she stepped off the ladder, slowly submerging herself in the water. But the truth was that no one could save her— at least not in the way she needed saving. There was no escaping the future that had been prescribed for her.

And that future was knocking on her door.

She dipped beneath the surface, then swam toward the colorful lantern lights hanging from the giant oak. Reese followed closely, as though he still feared she might be in danger of sinking to the bottom of the lake, never to surface again.

But after she'd demonstrated she was capable of floating, he seemed to relax a little.

"I can't believe that you, Sophie Kendall, jumped into the lake," he teased. His shoulders, impossibly broad and smooth, flexed with every subtle swish of his arms, and she wanted to run her palms over his skin.

"What's so shocking about it?" she said, punctuating the question with a playful splash. "Did you expect me to sit idly on the pier while you frolicked in the lake?"

"First off, I did not *frolic*. Second, I guess I did expect you to wait," he admitted. "But I'm glad you joined me. Swimming alone isn't nearly as fun."

They floated under the old oak tree, where the lanterns

above glowed like a treasure chest of rubies, emeralds, sapphires, and gold.

"It's not too deep here," Reese said, treading water beside her. "If you tire, you can head a few yards toward the shore and stand. Or . . ."

"What?" Sophie asked, trying to keep her chin above the surface.

"Or you could hold on to me."

"Reese," she said, speaking his name like a warning—mostly to herself.

"Only as a last resort," he qualified. "In case you were desperate."

"I don't think it will come to that," she said, a little breathless.

"Thank God," he said, his eyes crinkling at the corners. "There's a chance I'll escape this lake with my virtue intact."

"Very funny." She splashed him again, and this time, he retaliated by flicking a few drops in her direction.

Before long, their peaceful moonlight swim erupted into an all-out splash war.

He sank stealthily below the surface and circled around her, then popped up behind her and launched a surprise attack, spraying the back of her neck.

Sophie, on the other hand, exercised patience and tried to time her splashes for maximum effect. She waited until he came up for air, then squeezed her palms together to squirt a stream at his cheek.

He laughed—a deep, rumbling sound she felt low in her belly. "You'll pay for that," he said, a promise that was one part playful, one part wicked.

"You'll have to catch me first," she taunted, and her heart clattered in her chest as she started for the pier, kicking as though a sea monster nipped at her heels. Reese gave chase, but only half-heartedly. He could have overtaken her in the space of two seconds if he'd wished.

Sophie shouldn't have been disappointed that she reached the ladder before he caught her, but the victory felt slightly hollow. Almost as if she'd *wanted* him to catch her.

But now she was climbing the ladder, her chest heaving. Her hair dripped over her shoulders down her back. Her shift clung to her thighs and dipped low across her breasts.

The fact that all of this should have been entirely predictable didn't make it any less problematic. She stepped onto the pier and stood there, hugging her arms.

Reese clambered up behind her, and the sight of him emerging from the water with droplets running down his chest made her a little dizzy.

He scooped up his quilt and handed it to her. "Here. Wrap up in this."

"Thank you." She tossed it over her shoulders like a cloak, snuggling into the instant warmth. Exhausted, she sank onto one end of the blanket still spread on the pier and waved at spot beside her. "There's room for you to sit, too."

He eyed the vacant side of the quilt warily. "You're certain?"

She looked up at him, taking in his breathtaking bare chest and soaking wet trousers. No man should be that attractive, that irresistible. "Yes. I'm sure."

Reese lowered himself onto the quilt and sat cross-legged, as she did. Droplets clung to his shoulders, and his skin glistened in the soft glow of the lanterns. "Tell me something, Sophie," he whispered.

She tilted her head. "What?"

"How is it that someone as lovely, smart, and passionate as you hasn't already married?"

Heat crept up her face. "No one has captured my heart . . . before now," she added.

Reese sat very still. "Before Singleton, you mean."

Sophie shook her head, unable to lie to him. "Lord Singleton does not have my heart."

"Then . . . why?" he asked—and she knew precisely what he meant. Why would she willingly bind herself to a man she didn't love?

"It's complicated," she said, even though it wasn't. Not really. "My father has a tendency to drink too much, and, due to a series of poor business decisions on his part, my family's financial situation is . . . dire."

"I'm sorry." He gazed at her, his expression solemn and tender at the same time. "I know the toll that can take."

"You do?" She'd just assumed he was rich—and felt a twinge of guilt that she'd been blind to his struggles.

He shrugged. "Money worries are just one of demons that keep me up at night. When I inherited the title a few months ago, the books were in shambles and the estate was insolvent. But I'm going to turn it around," he said firmly.

"I'm sure you will." Sophie wished she had a penny for every time Papa had proclaimed he'd devised a plan to save them all.

Reese ran his fingers over the light stubble along his jaw. "So, you want to marry Singleton for his fortune."

"It's not a matter of *wanting* to. I must."

"I thought you had an older sister. Why is it solely up to you to make an advantageous match?"

"Mary was ill as a child, and her health is quite delicate. She's spent very little time in society." Sophie squared her shoulders and blew out a long breath. "I'm the only hope my family has left. I can't ignore my duty to help them . . . even if I might wish to."

"I see," he said, his voice so devoid of emotion that he

seemed a ghost of the man who'd been chasing her in the lake only moments before.

She needed him to know what he meant to her—even if she was still trying to figure it out herself. Deliberately, she shrugged off the quilt and let it fall onto the pier behind her. Her thin, transparent shift provided no cover from Reese's hot, hungry gaze.

"I want you to know I've never done anything like this before," she said. "I've never gone swimming in my underclothes in the middle of the night and I've certainly never spent the night with a man. I've been taking chances with you, Reese. A dangerous thing, to be sure."

He swallowed and looked at her, earnest. "I would never hurt you."

"Not intentionally," she said, knowing it was true. But she was already hurting. It was the agonizing pain of wanting something with all her soul and having that prize dangled in front of her, just beyond her fingertips. Knowing she would never, ever possess it.

"I wish I was free to follow my heart," she said. "I'm sorry that I'm not."

"You don't need to apologize," he said firmly. "I knew from the start that you were promised to another, and in spite of that, you were kind enough to help me."

"But?" she asked, sensing he wished to say more.

"But now I'm tortured in a different way, Sophie." His expression was naked with longing. "I want to touch you."

His confession made her whole body thrum with desire. How easy it would be to lean into him and press her lips to his. God, she wanted to—and yet, she didn't dare.

But perhaps there was some middle ground. She thoughtfully picked up the bouquet of peonies and slipped one free of the silk ribbon. Grasping it by the long stem, she brought its soft, feathery petals to her lips and briefly closed her eyes as she let its scent fill her head. Reese stared, tracking the movement of the flower as though it were a rare and precious jewel.

"We cannot touch," she said to him, her voice hoarse with regret. "But that doesn't mean I don't feel you—in the night breeze, in the soft quilt . . . in this flower."

Before she could change her mind, she reached out and touched the blossom to the side of his face. Ever so slowly, she swept it across his cheek and jaw, thrilling at the hitch of his breath and the heaviness of his eyelids. Emboldened, she brushed the petals across his lips and savored the moan that came from deep in his throat.

"You see?" she whispered. "We are connected in more ways than you know."

Chapter 14

Reese's blood was on fire.

Sophie sat across from him like a river nymph, or rather, a lake nymph. Her long blond hair hung in wet waves over her shoulders, and her skin seemed to glow from within. Her thin wet shift stuck to her like seaweed, leaving nothing to the imagination. And he'd imagined plenty.

But Sophie was right—their connection was more than physical.

Unfortunately, the closer they grew, the more he wanted her. In every way.

He gestured toward the pale pink flower resting on her shapely, half-exposed thigh. "May I?" he asked.

She moistened her lips with her tongue, then nodded. "Of course," she said, carefully handing him the flower by the stem.

He took it and gazed deep into her bottomless blue eyes for several seconds. "Sophie Kendall," he began. "You are as mysterious to me as a mermaid and as necessary as the sun. You are everything I'd hoped for and far more than I deserve."

"Reese," she said softly. "That's not true."

"It's absolutely true," he insisted. "I need you to understand it—and believe it. If I were an honorable man, I'd send you away and protect you from this . . ." He swallowed the knot in his throat. "This thing between us. But I'm a selfish bastard, and you . . . you are nigh impossible to resist."

Her lips parted and her eyes welled with tears.

He twisted the stem of the flower between his thumb and forefinger, cursing himself for what he was about to do. "I won't hurt you. I won't violate your rules. But you can be damned sure that I'm going to take anything you're willing to give me."

She gave him a wobbly smile. "That seems fair."

Dear God—if she only knew.

Deliberately, he used the flower to caress the arch of her foot, back and forth. Her toes curled in response, and she sighed but didn't pull away.

"How was that?" he murmured.

"Unexpectedly . . ." She blinked, searching for the word. ". . . Arousing."

"We've only just begun," he said, feeling hopeful— and, maybe, a little smug. Using the lightest touch of the flower petals, he traced a path from her ankle to her knee to her thigh.

She remained still as a statue, but he heard her sharp intake of breath. "Reese," she said, his name a plea on her lips.

"Will you lie down, Sophie?" he asked. "Lie down and try to relax."

She tucked a pillow under her head, stretched out on her side, and smiled. "Our roles have reversed. I'm supposed to tell you to lie down and relax."

"Then I'll lie down too," he said, propping himself on an elbow and facing her.

When she gazed at him sensuously, expectantly, he

chuckled. "You might be the death of me," he said. "And if you are, I can think of no better way to go."

"But I haven't done anything," she said, mildly affronted.

The rock-hard erection in his trousers was evidence to the contrary, and, if she happened to look in that direction, the proof would be difficult to miss.

"I meant it purely as a compliment," he assured her, trailing the flower lightly across her forehead. "Close your eyes, Soph."

Her eyelids fluttered shut and the corner of her mouth curled in a half smile. "Very well. But I'm only agreeable because I find myself exhausted after beating you so soundly in our race."

He chuckled again. "Stands to reason," he said, letting the petals drift over her eyes and cheeks and under her chin.

"That feels so . . . nice," she breathed, snuggling into her pillow.

"Imagine that it's me touching you," he whispered. "My fingertips running over your skin. My mouth tasting your lips." He brushed the peony over her bare shoulder and down the length of her arm, lingering on the back of her hand.

"You shouldn't say such wicked things," she teased, her thick lashes still flush against her cheeks.

"Saying wicked things isn't against the rules," he quipped. "Besides, there was nothing wicked in what I said."

"No?"

"No. I keep the wicked things in my head. It's a mad crush of improper thoughts in there." For example, at that very moment he was imagining ripping open the front of her shift and burying his head between her breasts before working his way down her belly, spreading her thighs apart and—

"Reese?" she said, her voice raspy.

He shifted to make more room for his erection. "Yes?"

"I'm pretending, like you said. I'm imagining that you're touching me, and while I know it's probably not as good as the real thing . . ."

"*Definitely* not as good," he confirmed.

"Yes. Well, I'm fairly certain that I wouldn't feel this way with anyone else."

Reese's jaw clenched at the thought of Sophie with anyone but him. "You're thinking too much," he said, chiding himself more than her. "Just feel."

He let the peony cruise over the swells of her breasts, freezing when her shoulders trembled. "Too much?" he asked.

"No." Her eyes fluttered open and she looked directly at him. "Are you familiar with The Debutante's Revenge?"

He shook his head. "Whatever it is, it sounds formidable."

"It is," she said proudly. "It's a newspaper advice column devoted to matters of the heart and subjects that are not discussed in genteel drawing rooms."

"And what advice would The Debutante's Revenge give right now?" he asked, brushing the flower across the delicate lines of her collarbone.

"Make your desires known," she said, as if she were quoting from the column. "Ask for what you want."

"What do you want, Sophie?"

"I want . . . I want you to move the flower a bit lower." She sat up and slipped the straps of her chemise off her shoulders, then peeled the damp fabric away from her breasts, down to her waist.

She was, without a doubt, the most beautiful woman he'd ever seen—graceful, kind, and courageous. He'd fought beside brave men, and Sophie was just as brave, in her own way. She knew something of sacrifice and honor; she'd lived it.

And now she sat a few scant inches away, baring herself to him. Her luminous, impossibly smooth skin begged to be touched. Her petite, perfectly rounded breasts made his mouth go dry.

"I would do anything to please you," he said earnestly. "Anything."

She shivered slightly and smiled. "I know," she said. "And I trust you."

"Good." He took a fresh peony from the bouquet as well as the silk ribbon that had bound it. He tied the ribbon in a knot just below the blossom and left the long ends free. Then, he used the flower and silk tie to do everything he wished he could do with his hands and mouth.

He caressed the curve of her neck and traced a slow, languorous path down her arm and across her flat belly. He teased the undersides of her breasts until a moan escaped her lips, then circled the tight, pale pink buds until she strained toward him.

"Better?" he whispered.

"Better," she confirmed, gazing at him beneath heavy-lidded eyes. "And worse."

"I know," he said, sympathizing. He was nearly mad with raw, hot need . . . but this moment was purely for Sophie.

He stared deep into her eyes as he deliberately grazed the taut peak of one breast, and she shuddered as though he'd flicked her nipple with his tongue. He continued to torment her with feathery, light strokes, gradually increasing the pressure of the satiny petals until she let out a soft cry. Then he turned his attention to her other breast, showering it with equal affection.

Sophie's chest flushed pink, her plump lips parted, and her pupils turned huge and dark. She was practically drunk with desire and trembling with need. It would have been an easy thing to convince her to abandon the rules she'd set.

But Reese couldn't do that. He already worried that she'd regret the things they'd done that night. And he wouldn't risk scaring her away. The knowledge that she would return the following week was the only thing that kept him halfway sane.

Of course, he knew their time together was finite. But he refused to think about that right now. What he needed to do was to bank the fire and douse the flames that leapt between them.

"Why don't you lie down again?" he suggested.

When she rested her head on the pillow, he reached for the quilt that had been around her shoulders and covered her torso with it.

"It's late," he said. "And you've had a long day. Rest your eyes and dream of rainbow parasols. I'll see you in the morning."

She shot him a grateful smile, snuggled beneath the blanket, and closed her eyes.

He watched as her body relaxed and her breathing grew even. And just as she was about to drift off, he touched the flower to her cheek in the lightest of kisses. "Good night, Soph."

Chapter 15

A cool drop plopped on Sophie's nose, but she was too cozy, too content, to bother brushing it away. The sun had only begun to rise, and they could afford a couple more hours of sleep.

But then another drop pelted her cheek, and another—and soon she was unable to ignore the onslaught. Reluctantly, she opened her eyes to find Reese already moving about the pier, shrugging into his shirt and gathering up her castoff clothes.

The clothes she was definitely *not* wearing.

She pressed a hand to her chest, confirmed she was approximately ninety percent naked, and felt her cheeks burn despite the chilly rain. Beneath the quilt, she wriggled her arms into the top of her shift, sat up, and made a valiant attempt to smooth the cloud of curls around her shoulders.

Reese looked over at her and grinned. "Good morning, Miss Kendall."

"There seems to be a leak in the ceiling of my bedchamber," she grumbled.

"Forgive me, madam. I shall take it up with the owner at the first opportunity. In the meantime, I think we must relocate you."

"But I'm fond of this room," she said with a mock pout.

Reese looked out at the lake, where raindrops plunked like thousands of tiny pebbles. "I think we can do better. I might even be able to secure a room with—brace yourself—a mattress."

She rubbed the small of her back. "That sounds rather ordinary, and yet . . . tempting."

He jammed on his boots and tucked her clothes under one arm. "I would suggest that we race each other back to the house, but I have no wish to be trounced again."

Sophie stood, stepped into her slippers, and wrapped the quilt over her head like a hooded cloak. "That's very wise of you," she said, picking up the peony with the silk ribbon. She deftly maneuvered around him and began heading up the pier toward the shore. "Because while my swimming is impressive"—she blinked at him with feigned innocence—"my running is even more so."

With that, she dropped the quilt and tore up the hill towards the woods as fast as her legs would carry her. Reese laughed and chased her, alternately leading the way and letting her surge ahead until they reached the house, soaking wet and gasping for breath.

He deposited the sopping quilts he'd been carrying on the kitchen floor, lit a fire, and draped her rain-soaked clothes over the backs of chairs that he slid close to the hearth. "It's still early," he said. "You could rest in your bedchamber for another hour or two if you'd like."

Sophie shook her head. Her heart pumped much too fast to even consider sleeping. "I'm not tired. Are you?"

"No. I slept well last night . . . thanks to you."

She opened her mouth to say she had nothing to do with his slumber but decided to bite her tongue. Reese believed she was helping him, and maybe, in a roundabout way, she was. She moved close to the fire and rubbed her arms.

"Would you like a hot bath?" he asked. "I could prepare one in your room."

She laughed. "As heavenly as that sounds, it's too much work. Have you forgotten that you gave your staff the weekend off?"

"I have not," he said, as though mildly offended. "I'm going to see to it myself." He lit the stove and placed several pots of water on top before turning his attention back to her. "Why don't you go upstairs and wrap up in a blanket? I'll bring the tub up shortly."

"You don't need to go to the trouble, Reese."

"I want to," he said, smiling. "You have been taking care of me. Now let me take care of you."

A lump lodged in her throat. She'd always longed for a relationship that would work that way. She'd always wished for a partner who'd do thoughtful little things like put cream in her tea and rub her hands when it was cold.

Never in a million years would she have dreamed that an ornery, if devastatingly handsome, earl would prepare a hot bath for her.

"I insist," he said, and when she shivered, he crossed his arms as though he didn't trust himself not to haul her against his chest.

"Thank you," she said simply as she twirled the stem of the wilted peony between her fingers. "I suppose I should go upstairs and dry off."

His face brightened. "While you're waiting, you could survey the garden. There's an excellent view of it from my bedchamber window, just down the corridor from yours."

"You don't mind me going into your bedchamber?" she asked.

His mouth curled into a wicked, knee-melting grin. "Do you really have to ask?"

Sophie swallowed. "I just meant . . . that is, you are a rather private person."

He slowly walked over to her and stood so close that she could see the sprinkling of hair covering his muscled forearms, which were crossed over his chest. "To be perfectly clear," he drawled, "you are welcome in my bedchamber anytime you like. And you may do whatever you like there. *Anything* you like."

Good heavens. Mere seconds ago, she'd been chilled. Now, she barely resisted the urge to fan herself. "That's very generous," she quipped. "But I think I'll content myself with admiring the garden."

"You could also make a list of further improvements you'd like me to undertake."

She narrowed her eyes at him, curious at his choice of words. "You?"

He shrugged off her question. "Feel free to use my desk and avail yourself of anything you need."

"Very well," she said, thoughtful. "I shall see you upstairs, then."

She quickly made her way to her room, stripped off her damp shift, and slipped on the soft, dry nightgown she'd packed in her bag. She carefully placed the peony and the ribbon in her portmanteau before heading down the hall to Reese's room.

Despite all his assurances that she was welcome there, she hesitated at the door. Crossing the threshold of a gentleman's bedchamber was a momentous occasion, but her trepidation was due to more than that. The more she knew about Reese, the more she cared about him. And the more she cared about him, the harder it would be to say goodbye when the time came.

Still, she couldn't resist the chance to learn more about him.

His bedchamber was neat and sparsely decorated. One wall boasted an austere landscape; the mantel was bare but for a small gold-faced clock and a candlestick in a pewter holder. A dark blue counterpane and two matching pillows covered the large bed, but there were no extravagant bed-curtains or decorative touches.

Everything was terribly orderly and utilitarian—much like what she'd imagine a military barracks looked like.

A mahogany desk tucked into one corner of the room was predictably tidy, with nothing on the top except for a small framed painting. Sophie moved closer to examine it, but she could already guess the portrait's subject—Edmund.

Indeed, the young man in the painting was a more refined, more civilized version of Reese. A handsome gentleman, perhaps in his midtwenties, stared back at her, his intelligent eyes full of a confidence that bordered on arrogance.

He was the brother Reese idolized and the one he feared he'd never live up to.

Carefully, she returned the painting to its spot, then looked around the room for any other personal items—books or trinkets or any other clues that might help her understand Reese. A razor rested on a towel beside his washstand, and a lantern perched on the nightstand next to his bed.

But then, a few items on the top of his bureau caught her eye—a brass key and a pair of gold braided epaulets. She could easily imagine the epaulets on the shoulders of a scarlet jacket, and she was sure Reese had cut a fine fig-ure in his officer's uniform, looking one part dashing and two parts fierce.

Though she'd never seen him behave violently, she had no doubt Reese would be formidable in a fight. Something told her that when it came to his principles, he'd rather die than forfeit. A chill ran down her spine, and she said a quick prayer of thanks that Reese's soldiering days were over.

She wondered about the brass key but left it and the epaulets on his bureau, then walked to a window, where she swept aside a gray velvet curtain panel and looked outside. The rain had slowed, and while the skies were still overcast, the sun had begun to peek through the clouds in a few spots.

The view of the garden was remarkable—from the third floor, she was able to see each of the main parts and features as well as the overall balance. Already it looked much improved from the week before. Vines no longer encroached on the walkways; weeds no longer lurked between the path's stones. Water in the moat flowed freely, and the footbridge boasted a glossy new coat of black paint.

The section of the garden devoted to the gnarled, twisted poplars looked appropriately intimidating, and on the other side of the rotunda, the field of asphodels appeared delightfully haunting. The most mysterious part of the garden glimmered just beyond the main pavilion, promising magic and beauty in equal measures.

The garden was well on its way, but Sophie had some ideas for coaxing it along.

Intent on jotting down her thoughts, she strode to Reese's desk, sank into his seat, and opened the top drawer in search of writing supplies. She found paper, pen, ink—

And something else: a small stack of letters. Unless Sophie was mistaken, they were the same letters she'd seen in Reese's study last weekend. But now they were in his room—still sealed with wax.

She hesitated for a heartbeat, then reached for them and

examined the three envelopes more closely. They were all from the same person; the handwriting outside was graceful and feminine, and the name in the upper left corner read *Mrs. S. Conroy.*

Clearly, Reese was reluctant to read the letters for some reason, but why?

She couldn't help but wonder if Mrs. Conroy was a past lover . . . or a current one. Sophie had no reason—and no right—to be jealous.

And yet, an unsettled, sickly feeling swirled in her belly.

She reminded herself that he was downstairs at that very moment, preparing her a bath. And that *she* was the one who would soon be engaged to another.

With a determined sigh, she proceeded to write her notes about the garden. When she'd finished, she put away the paper and pen—but she left the list she'd written and the unopened letters on Reese's desk.

When she returned to her bedchamber, she found that Reese had placed the bathtub in front of the hearth, where a cozy fire burned. A pair of thick towels and a bar of soap rested on a stool. He strode into the room, carrying a bucket of steaming water that he proceeded to pour into the tub.

"Perfect timing," he said. "I left a jug of cooler water near the tub in case you need to mix some in."

"Thank you, Reese," she said, more than a little touched by his thoughtfulness. "I can hardly wait."

"It was nothing," he said, shrugging. With his shirt-sleeves rolled to his elbows and a full day's growth of beard, he looked every inch the rogue. Just the sight of him made her belly flutter.

"It certainly *is* something," she countered. "At least to me."

"Well," he mumbled, uncharacteristically shy. "I'll leave you to enjoy. I'll be in the drawing room if you'd like to join me when you're done."

"You could stay," she blurted. "That is, we have so little time together, and if you wanted to stay so that we could . . . talk, I wouldn't mind in the least."

He froze at the door, one foot on the other side of the threshold. Heat flared in his eyes. "I don't think that would be a good idea," he said, stating the obvious.

"Maybe not." She leaned over the edge of the tub, trailed her fingertips through the deliciously hot water, and sighed in anticipation. "But I trust you."

"I know," he said soberly. "And I want to keep it that way." He pressed his lips into a thin line and uttered a curse before walking out of the room and closing the door behind him.

An hour later, Sophie wore a fresh dress, and all her damp clothes had been collected and packed neatly into her portmanteau. She and Reese stood on the front step of Warshire Manor as the hackney cab rumbled up the long drive.

"Have you noticed that saying goodbye grows more difficult each week?" she asked.

"Aye." He raked a hand through his sandy-brown hair, looking frustrated and impossibly handsome. "But I can bear it, as long as I know you'll return next week."

"Of course I will," she assured him. "Barring something unexpected."

His eyes turned wary. "Unexpected?"

She swallowed. "I don't anticipate that anything will prevent me from meeting you as usual, but you must understand how terribly risky it is for me. I just don't want to make promises that I might not be able to keep."

"I know." He scrubbed the back of his neck. "And I

understand. I would hate for any harm to come to you because of me. We'll be careful."

As the hackney cab rolled to a stop in the drive, her fingers tingled with mild panic. She worried that they hadn't made the most of their time. That the hourglass of their relationship was running out of sand much too quickly.

She longed to talk about what was happening between them, but it was far easier to discuss other things, like the garden. "I left a list of suggested garden improvements on your desk," she said.

He nodded, as though pleased. "Consider them done."

Summoning courage, she said, "I left something else on your desk too—the letters that were in your drawer. I don't mean to pry, but is there a reason you haven't opened them?"

Reese stiffened, and it was as though all the ease and affection that had flowed between them suddenly iced over. "Yes. There is a reason."

If the hackney hadn't been waiting, perhaps Sophie would have pressed him on it. But his fisted hands, distant stare, and clenched jaw said he wasn't eager to explain the unread letters.

"You don't have to share everything with me." Even though the words were true, and she meant them with all her heart, they made her a little sad. She couldn't tell him about the Debutante Underground. He wouldn't tell her about the letters. She'd grown close to Reese over the last few weeks, but maybe they'd come upon a blockade.

When he didn't reply, she sighed, picked up her portmanteau, and slowly descended the steps toward the hackney cab, keeping her chin raised so he wouldn't guess how much his silence hurt her.

She gave Fiona's address to the driver and started to climb inside.

"Sophie."

She turned to find Reese striding down the stairs. "Next week," he said, coming to a stop beside her. "Ask me about the letters and I'll . . ." He swallowed as though he were in physical pain. "I'll try to tell you."

She nodded and shot him a grateful smile. The wall that separated them was still there, but it seemed to Sophie that it shook and crumbled a little. "You have a deal, Lord Warshire. I shall see you next week."

Chapter 16

"How was last night's meeting?" Fiona asked.

"Hmm?" Sophie looked up from the potted fern she was watering, blushing as she realized that she, Fiona, and Lily were supposed to be discussing plans for the next Debutante's Revenge column.

Fiona arched an auburn brow and smiled knowingly. "Were there any topics of particular interest at your Debutante Underground meeting?"

Sophie frowned, trying to remember. Last night's gathering at the tailor's shop seemed ages ago, but a few snippets came back to her. "There was a lively decision about whether it's preferable for one's partner to make one big, grand gesture or several smaller, thoughtful gestures."

Lily sat on the edge of her desk, swinging her feet as she pondered the question. "Why must it be an either/or proposition? I think that a worthy gentleman should be capable of both."

"Agreed," Sophie said, and her mind filled with images of jewel-colored lanterns, flower crowns, and steaming baths. "But what if, for the sake of argument, you had to pick one or the other?"

Fiona looked up from her easel. "I'd choose small, thoughtful gestures. They're more meaningful."

"A big, grand gesture for me," Lily said. "The sort of thing that a woman will remember forever," she said dreamily, running her palms over the top of the gorgeous desk—a surprise gift from her handsome husband. "What about you, Soph? Which would you prefer?"

"The small things, I think," she replied. "More than anything, I'd like someone to hold my hand. To give it a reassuring squeeze at just the right times."

For a few seconds, the studio was silent. Then Fiona said, "I've the feeling you're thinking about someone in particular. Do you want to talk about him now?"

Sophie sank onto the sofa and leaned her head back against the cushions. It would be a relief to confess her feelings for Reese to her friends. "There's someone I care for, and I think he cares for me too. We've been spending time together . . . alone."

Fiona set down her paintbrush and came to sit beside Sophie. "Have you changed your mind about marrying Lord Singleton?"

Sophie shook her head slowly. "I can't. My family's financial situation grows more dire by the day. And the man I mentioned . . . he's not in a position to help—even if he were so inclined."

Fiona reached over and squeezed Sophie's knee. "I wish you'd let Gray and me assist you. He even suggested it again over dinner the other evening. I didn't mention it to you because I know your feelings, but if you've changed your mind . . ."

"No," Sophie said hoarsely. "My parents are too proud. I suppose I am too. Perhaps it's old-fashioned and unenlightened, but I can't bring myself to rely upon the generosity of friends—even the most wonderful of friends."

She sniffled, letting out a long sigh before she continued. "This problem won't go away with the wave of a wand. Even if I could, somehow, repay all my father's debts today, his profligate tendencies will land him back in trouble. For my family's sake, I must marry well, and soon. I could do much worse than Lord Singleton," she said firmly. Almost as though she was trying to convince herself.

Lily hopped off her desk and paced the room. "What about the man you care for?" she said. "If money weren't an issue, would he be a good match?"

"He would," Sophie admitted, even though she'd told herself not to dream of such things. "There's no denying we're drawn to each other. But I made it clear from the start of our relationship that I intend to marry another."

"People change their minds all the time," Fiona said, sympathetic. "I know you want to stand by your word, but if keeping your promise to Lord Singleton means you're miserable for the rest of your life, you shouldn't feel obliged to keep that promise."

"It's complicated. Reese—the man I'm fond of—only recently and reluctantly came into his title. I don't think he wants to marry anyone—at least not anytime soon."

"Even the most steadfast of bachelors has changed his mind about marriage after meeting the right woman," Fiona said sympathetically. "Have you considered that you might be that woman for Reese?"

Of course she had, despite her resolve to avoid imagining a future that could never be hers. "He's going through a difficult time and still mourning the loss of his brother. It doesn't seem right to broach the subject right now."

"Better now than after the reading of the banns for your marriage to Singleton," Lily pointed out. "What do you have to lose?"

Sophie fingered the silk sash of her dress as she pondered her friend's question. Maybe part of her recognized that Lord Singleton was the safer choice. He wasn't fiery or passionate. Their relationship would be pleasantly civil, and he'd demand very little from her. Which meant she'd never completely lose her heart to him, and there was no possibility of him hurting her.

But baring her soul to Reese was an altogether different proposition. There would be no wading in or half measures. If she confessed her love for him, and he couldn't or *wouldn't* love her back . . . well, she wasn't sure she could endure that sort of pain.

"I'll give it some thought," Sophie said. She still had a few weeks until her betrothal to Lord Singleton became official. Granted, it wasn't much time, but perhaps it would be enough for her and Reese to figure out what they meant to each other. Their relationship was like a beautiful, fragile orchid, and she wondered whether it would be able to survive outside the cozy hothouse they'd created for themselves at Warshire Manor.

"Thank you for confiding in Lily and me," Fiona said. "And even though there are at least a dozen more questions we'd love to ask, we shall refrain."

"We will?" Lily asked, obviously disappointed.

"Yes." Fiona pinned her younger sister with a stern stare—the sort that would have made Miss Haywinkle proud. "Sophie has a difficult decision to make, and she will make the correct choice, as she always does."

Sophie wasn't so certain, but she managed a weak smile. "I appreciate your faith in me. And I know I can count on you both, no matter what."

"No matter what," Fiona repeated, her blue eyes twinkling with affection.

"Perhaps this week's column will be about trusting

one's instincts—especially when it comes to assessing a gentleman's character," Lily mused.

"I'm sure the members of the Debutante Underground would find the topic intriguing," Sophie said. "Heaven knows I would."

Fiona pursed her lips thoughtfully. "I believe I have an idea for a sketch, too. I'll begin working on it this afternoon."

"Good," Sophie said, rising from the settee. "I'm rather tired, so if you don't mind, I think I'll head home a bit early. I could use a nap before dinner."

Lily propped a hand on her hip. "Miss Sophie Kendall," she teased, "I would hand over my best bonnet just to know what you've been doing for the past twelve hours."

Sophie winked at her friend. "You wouldn't believe it if I told you."

A half hour later, Sophie walked into her foyer, surprised to find the house unnaturally quiet. She hung her pelisse and hat before heading to the drawing room, where her mother and Mary perched on the edge of their chairs, dabbing the corners of their eyes with soggy handkerchiefs.

Dread slithered around Sophie's neck, squeezing her in a chokehold. "What's happened?" she asked, rushing into the room. "Is it Papa?"

"No, darling," Mama assured her. "He's fine. He's just upstairs . . . resting."

A sob escaped Mary's throat.

"What, then?" Sophie said. "Why are you both crying?"

Mama stood, smoothed her skirt, and raised her chin in a valiant effort to regain her composure. "I had to let most of the staff go this morning. The truth is, we haven't been able to pay them for several months. They've stayed out of loyalty, but when they heard that a wealthy merchant was setting up house in Mayfair, they asked for a reference . . . and I couldn't refuse."

"Mr. Wickett?" Sophie asked, thinking of their dear old butler—the one who'd been more like a grandpa to her than a member of the staff.

"He regretted that he didn't have a chance to say goodbye to you," Mama said soothingly. "He asked that I convey his sincerest apologies."

Sophie's throat closed painfully. "He doesn't owe me an apology," she whispered, sinking into a chair.

"That's not the worst of it," Mary whined. "Lottie's gone too. Who's going to help us dress and style our hair and make our beds?"

"We'll help each other." Sophie reached out and patted her sister's hand. To her mother, she said, "I didn't realize things had become quite so desperate. Why didn't you tell me?"

"I didn't want to worry you more than I already have," Mama said, looking thinner and older than she had just twenty-four hours ago. "Besides, what could you have done?"

"I would have thought of something," Sophie said, adamant. She would have gladly handed over the small sum she'd saved from her share of the column. Maybe she could have pawned a few items, just to keep them solvent until . . . until her marriage to Lord Singleton.

Mama forced a smile. "At least we still have Mrs. Appleby and Mrs. Pettigrew," she said, referring to their faithful cook and their longtime housekeeper. "And Mr. Crawford, of course," she added. "Your father simply can't do without his valet."

"No," Sophie said dryly. "Of course not."

"I know it's not an ideal situation," Mama said, "but it's only temporary."

Sophie felt her sister's and her mother's eyes trained on her. Knew just what they were thinking—that they'd re-hire the staff once Sophie married the rich marquess.

"I . . . I'm rather tired," she said, struggling to keep her voice even and her demeanor calm. "I think I shall go lie down for a while." She walked over to Mama and pressed a kiss to her soft cheek before picking up her portmanteau. She was just about to make her escape from the drawing room when Mrs. Pettigrew appeared in the doorway, look-ing unusually harried. "Forgive me, ma'am," she said, wiping her hands on her apron. "But Lord Singleton has just arrived."

Sophie's stomach dropped through her knees. "What's he doing here?" she asked Mama. "I didn't extend an in-vitation."

"That's rather ungracious of you," Mary said, sniffing. "I should think Lord Singleton would be welcome here any time."

Some of Sophie's dismay over the marquess's unex-pected visit twisted itself into resentment. "Then perhaps *you* should be the one to entertain him," she suggested.

"Girls!" Mama hissed. "That is quite enough."

Guilt sliced through Sophie, and she pressed her fin-gertips to her forehead, contrite. "Forgive me. I don't know what came over me. Of course I'll receive Lord Singleton." She set her bag behind the sofa, plucked a book from the shelf, and sat in a chair beside the win-dow. Opening to a random page, she mustered a smile for Mrs. Pettigrew. "Would you be so kind as to show the marquess in?"

"Of course, Miss Sophie," said the kindly, ruddy-faced housekeeper. "Shall I prepare tea?"

It had been on the tip of Sophie's tongue to say no, but Mama quickly replied, "Please, Mrs. Pettigrew. Lord

Singleton is an esteemed guest, and we must make him feel most welcome whenever he deigns to visit us."

Sophie swallowed the knot lodged at the back of her throat, because while her mother's words had been directed toward the housekeeper, Sophie knew that they were intended for her.

Mary quickly packed up her needlework, no doubt preparing to escape to her room, as she usually did. But then Mama lifted her chin and, looking uncharacteristically stern, said, "Mary, you will remain here for the duration of Lord Singleton's visit and endeavor to be both pleasant and engaging. Is that understood?"

Mary swallowed, set down her sewing basket, and patted her head self-consciously. "Thank heaven Lottie was able to see to my hair one last time," she said dramatically.

All three women—Mama, Mary, and Sophie—took their seats like actresses preparing for the curtain to go up on a scene. Mama sat at the desk as though she'd been tending to correspondence. Mary picked up the handkerchief she'd been embroidering. Sophie pretended to read.

A few moments later, Mrs. Pettigrew announced Lord Singleton, then scurried off to help Mrs. Appleby prepare tea.

To the marquess's credit, he acted as though he hadn't noticed the absence of the butler. Addressing Mama, he said, "Good afternoon, Lady Callahan."

"Lord Singleton," she said graciously. "How terribly kind of you to call. I believe you've met my oldest daughter, Mary."

"A pleasure to see you again," the marquess intoned, bowing over Mary's hand. He turned to Sophie and gazed at her with the bright blue eyes he was rather famous for. "Miss Kendall," he said smoothly. "I've brought something for you."

He reached into his jacket pocket and produced a small ivory carving. "I know how much you like roses," he said, placing it into her palm. The perfectly formed flower felt cold and hard and lifeless against her skin.

"Thank you. It's beautiful," she said diplomatically.

"How thoughtful of Lord Singleton." Mama clasped her hands beneath her chin.

"Yes," Sophie said. "Very kind." But she couldn't help comparing the ivory carving to the gifts Reese had given her. She missed her wilted crown of asphodels—and him.

She'd said goodbye to Reese only a few hours ago, but the marquess's visit had all but erased the warm, hopeful glow in her chest.

Her family's situation grew more desperate by the day.

Lord Singleton was throwing them a lifeline.

But he wasn't going to wait forever.

Chapter 17

On his third straight day of working in the garden that week, Reese wiped the sweat from his forehead, tossed his scrub brush into the bucket, and stepped back to survey the results. The entire surface of the pavilion gleamed bright white in the sunlight. He'd cleaned every inch of the steps, floor, pillars, and roof, just as Sophie had suggested.

During the hours he'd labored, he'd had plenty of time to think—mostly about her.

And he'd realized two things.

First, their relationship had reached a critical point— the precarious, pivotal moment when the scale could easily tip toward success or failure. He'd experienced the same moment in the midst of battle. Every minute felt like an hour, and every move could end in victory or defeat. In a fight that had lasted for days, the outcome hinged on one heartbeat in time.

Not that he and Sophie were enemies—far from it. But their relationship couldn't continue on as it was, couldn't stand still. They had a choice to make: charge ahead together or retreat to their separate lives.

The second thing that Reese realized was that if he

wanted to keep Sophie—and God knew he did—he needed to make a strategic move. Not pretty flowers or colorful lanterns or hot baths.

Sophie may have liked those things, but now she was demanding more. She wanted him to read the letters he'd been hiding away. She wanted him to face his ugly, shameful past. Which meant he was going to have to give her the one thing he'd hoped to keep buried forever—the truth.

It was risky as hell, and it was going to hurt like the devil.

But he'd been in this situation before—behind enemy lines, under attack, and down to his last bullet.

If there were any other option, he would have jumped at it, but he knew in his gut that this was the only way for him and Sophie to have a shot at a future together. He was going to have to bare his godforsaken soul and hope that she stuck around.

At least for another week or two.

"Rule number four," Sophie recited, finishing up her usual welcome to the members of the Debutante Underground. "We shall always speak the truth, the best we know it. Now then, I believe we're ready to begin. Would anyone like to read this week's column?"

Several women raised their hands to volunteer, but Sophie's gaze was drawn to Violet, the maid she'd met a couple of weeks ago. She sat on the edge of her chair, her face pinched and pale. Her thin shoulders trembled as though she was chilled, even though the room was toasty. "Violet, are you feeling well?" Sophie asked.

"Excuse me," the dark-haired woman mumbled, pushing her chair back from the table and rushing toward the door.

Sarah, the young widow seated next to her, popped out of her seat. "I'll make sure Violet's all right," she said to Sophie. "Please, proceed with the meeting."

Sophie nodded and selected another member of the group to read. But as soon as the discussion was underway, she slipped out the door of the shop to see how Violet was faring. Sophie found her and Sarah in the alley outside the shop. Violet leaned against the brick wall with her eyes closed, greedily inhaling the cool night air. Sarah stood beside her, giving her shoulder gentle, soothing pats.

Sophie shot Sarah a questioning look, and the pretty redheaded woman responded with a smile that was both sad and serene.

"Violet," Sophie said softly, "do you require a doctor?"

"No," she answered quickly. "This happens sometimes, but it always passes. I'm feeling better already."

Sophie cast a skeptical glance at the woman's pallor. "Are you certain?"

"I'm familiar with these symptoms," Sarah said, matter-of-fact. "I've two young ones myself."

Sophie blinked as Sarah's words sank in, and she chided herself for not guessing the truth sooner. "You're with child?" she asked, her voice tinged with both relief and concern.

The bright red flush on Violet's cheeks was answer enough.

"When do you expect the babe?" Sarah asked gently.

"I think I'm about six months along." A tear trickled down Violet's face. "I haven't told my family, although I'm sure they must suspect. I don't know what I'm going to do."

"It's going to be fine," Sarah said, but lines marred her normally smooth forehead. "Can the baby's father help?"

"No." A sob erupted from Violet's throat. "He fired me."

Flashing hot anger pumped through Sophie's veins. "Your former employer is the father?"

Violet nodded. "He was wonderfully kind at first. He treated me like he . . . cared. I knew he wouldn't marry someone like me, but I never imagined he'd turn so cold and harsh. When I told him I was pregnant, he called me a . . . a trollop. He said the babe wasn't his."

"What a vile, pathetic man," Sophie spat. She was already thinking of ways to hold him to account. Perhaps she could enlist help from Gray and Nash. Surely they could shame the cad into providing for Violet and her child.

"He behaved horribly," Violet agreed. "But I'm afraid I'm no better. I let him seduce me with pretty words and trinkets. How could I have been so daft?"

Sophie grasped Violet's slender shoulders and forced the young woman to meet her gaze. "Listen to me," she said. "You are *not* daft. He was your employer, and he took advantage of you. *He* is the one who should be ashamed of his behavior."

"Well, he's gone now," Violet said, sniffling. She took the handkerchief Sophie offered and fanned herself. "I'd rather not talk about him anyway."

"I understand," Sophie said, even though her blood still boiled. "What can we do to help?"

"I'm afraid there's nothing anybody can do. All I want is to be able to support myself and raise my baby without being a burden to my family. But no man will want me for his wife, and no employer will want me as a maid."

"You're in a difficult spot," Sarah agreed. "I know what it's like to raise a child by oneself. But you mustn't be too proud to accept help when you need it."

"I'll figure out something." Violet pushed herself off the wall and drew her shawl around her, hiding her belly.

Sophie desperately wanted to help the young woman,

but she didn't have the faintest idea how. "I'll give the matter some thought this week," she said. "At the very least, you need a safe, comfortable home for you and your baby. Let me see what I can come up with."

"You needn't worry about me," Violet said briskly—as if she were embarrassed by her uncharacteristic show of emotion. "I seem to cry at the slightest provocation these days, but I'm certain all will be well, eventually. In the meantime, I beg you both to keep my secret. I've no wish to bring shame upon my family—at least not until it's absolutely necessary."

Sophie was still thinking about Violet's predicament a couple of hours later, when Reese met her just outside the tailor's shop. But the sight of him pushed every thought, rational or otherwise, from her mind.

Moonlight glinted off his hair and dusted the broad shoulders of his fitted jacket. Silhouetted against the night sky, he stood there—a strong, silent Prince of Darkness—and her skin tingled with anticipation.

"Reese," she whispered.

"You're here," he answered, exhaling in relief.

"Yes." But there was a good chance that this weekend together would be their last. Since laying off the staff, her parents had been pressing her to announce her betrothal to Lord Singleton, and she didn't have a particularly good reason to delay—at least not one she could tell them. "I'm glad to see you."

"You have no idea how glad I am to see you." He raked a hand through his hair, which inevitably made her wonder what it might feel like to run her fingers through the thick, closely shorn strands. She curled her fingers into her palms so she wouldn't be tempted.

But her traitorous feet carried her toward him, stopping when she was an arm's length away. Never had she felt such a strong pull toward someone. She suspected that if she got too close to him, the force of their attraction would be too great to escape. They'd slam together like two magnets that had crossed a critical line of proximity—and they might never be able to separate themselves, might never willingly break the bond.

"Tonight feels different," she admitted. He was more sober than she'd ever seen him, and the vulnerability in his eyes took her breath away.

"It *is* different," he said, his voice deep and sure. "Every time we're together, you pull me a little farther out of the lonely shadows and into the warm sunlight."

"I'm happy to hear it," she said, her heart swelling. "No one should reside in the shadows."

"You say that now," he quipped. "But the sunlight is bound to reveal a lot of scars."

"I'm not intimidated in the least," she replied.

He arched a brow, skeptical. "Let's wait and see if you feel the same way in the morning."

A shiver slithered down her spine, but she tilted her head and looked deep into those beautiful, haunted eyes. "Nothing you show me, nothing you tell me is going to scare me away, Lord Warshire."

For the space of three heartbeats, he said nothing. Then, "I suppose we'll see. Let's go."

She sat beside him in the carriage, wholly preoccupied with maintaining a bit of space between them. It seemed she was constantly fighting forces that conspired to push them together. A rut in the road or a sudden turn could launch her across the seat and into Reese's lap. While the wicked part of her prayed for a violent jolt of the cab, the more sensible part of her held tightly to the door handle.

When they arrived at Warshire Manor a short time later,

Reese led her into the house and stopped in the dimly lit, marble-tiled foyer. As always, the sight of the stonework and buttresses filled her with awe.

"Would you like something to eat?" he asked. "There are sandwiches, fruit, and cakes in the kitchen."

She shook her head. "Thank you, but I ate an early dinner. Help yourself if you'd like something, though."

"No, I'm fine." He hesitated a moment, then frowned. "I'm sorry. I don't have any entertaining diversions or romantic surprises planned tonight."

"Reese," she said gently. "I adored our night in the garden and on the lake. But I also loved playing cards with you at the shop. You don't need to amuse me. I just like . . . being with you."

"I like being with you too," he said earnestly. "Maybe too much."

Her heart skipped a beat. "How have you been sleeping this week?" she asked briskly. Between his bronzed skin, gold-flecked hair, and strapping muscles, he certainly *looked* well enough. But the creases around his eyes suggested that the demons were never very far below the surface.

"You changed the subject," he said. "Usually, I'm the one who avoids difficult conversations. I must be rubbing off on you."

"You're right." But she wasn't certain how to tell him about the latest developments at home or the necessity of having to move up her engagement. Her relationship with Reese was like a tropical flower that was just about to bloom; the news that she had to marry sooner than expected would kill it as surely as a late spring frost. All she could do was pray that the flower was heartier than it appeared.

"We do need to talk. Would you mind if I went to my

bedchamber and changed first?" she asked. "You could join me there in a few minutes."

"I'll bring up a tray of refreshments," he said nodding. "In case talking makes us hungry."

She tossed a smile over her shoulder and made her way upstairs to her room.

Chapter 18

Once inside her bedchamber, Sophie unlaced her dress, wriggled out of it, and removed all her undergarments. Then she slipped a soft, airy nightgown over her head and splashed cool water from the washbasin on her face.

Slowly, the worries about her family, Violet, and Lord Singleton receded, lingering in the back corners of her mind. Tonight was about making the most of her time with Reese—and seeing if there was any chance that their feelings could blossom into something lasting and true.

Sophie sat at a small vanity and began removing the pins from her hair. When at last it hung loose down her back, she retrieved the hairbrush from her portmanteau and methodically untangled her curls until they slid through her fingers like silk.

When Reese knocked at the bedchamber door, she jumped up and let him in. He carried a tray full of fruit, bread, and cheeses, along with a bottle of wine and a pair of glasses, and when he saw her in her nightgown, his eyes flashed with heat and awareness. Her blood thrummed in response.

"You look . . ." He frowned, as though at a loss for words.

"Exceedingly comfortable?" she ventured. "In a state of utter dishabille?"

"No," he said firmly. "Beautiful. So beautiful, in fact, that I may have forgotten everything I wanted to say to you."

"Thank you," she said, accepting the glass of wine he'd poured for her. She sat in a soft, cozy armchair and tucked her feet beneath her. "I'm nervous too. But all we need to do is say what's in our hearts."

Reese sank into the chair beside her and set his wineglass on the low table in front of them. He'd shed his jacket, and his shirtsleeves were rolled to his elbows, revealing strong, sinewy forearms and large, tanned hands. Her mouth went dry, and she took a fortifying sip of wine before looking at him again.

When she did, he leaned forward, elbows propped on his knees, and gazed at her earnestly. "A little over a month ago, I was at the end of my rope, barely hanging on to my sanity. But on the night you walked into the tailor's shop, everything started to change."

"Isn't it strange," she mused. "If I hadn't needed to rent a space, I might never have met you." The mere thought left her feeling vaguely unsettled and hollow.

"At first, I assumed the valerian-root tea was responsible for the subtle changes, but I was deluding myself. It was all you. Once I realized that, I thought that seeing you once a week, adhering to your rules, and never crossing the boundaries we'd set . . . I thought it would be enough."

"I know that the rules are exasperating," she said. "They are for me too. But I'm afraid they can't be helped."

"There's something important I need to ask you," he said. "And I need for you to tell me the truth, even if you fear I won't like the answer."

"I've never lied to you," she said. But she did have a few secrets.

He pressed his palms together and swallowed as if he

were mentally bracing himself. His dark brown eyes shone with a mix of fear and hope. "My question is this: Do you love Lord Singleton?"

She blew out the breath she'd been holding and looked down at her lap. The safest course of action—for both of them, really—would be for her to say *yes*. If she did, Reese would retreat, and her future with Lord Singleton would be all but etched in stone.

Her heart pounded as she slowly shook her head. "I don't love him."

"Do you want to marry him?"

"No."

He dragged his hands down his cheeks. "Why didn't you tell me?"

"Would it have made a difference?" She'd tossed the question out lightly, but it felt as though her whole life teetered on the edge of his response.

"I don't know." He stood and paced the length of the bedchamber. "Maybe."

"Lord Singleton is fully aware of my family's financial predicament," she explained. "He still wants to marry me and has generously offered to help. Moreover, I believe he's a good and decent gentleman. Given the circumstances, it's very difficult for me to refuse his proposal."

"Even if you don't love him," he said, his voice distant and cold.

"I would do anything for my family," she said, a tad defensively. "And many people marry for reasons other than love."

"Many people do," he agreed. "But not you."

Anger bubbled up in her chest. "You have no right to judge me, Reese. I'm sure it's difficult to imagine yourself in my position. But if you were, I daresay you'd do the same thing."

He braced his arms on the back of his chair and dropped his chin to his chest. "You're right; forgive me. I just wish things were different."

"How so?" she whispered, perilously close to tears.

He pressed his lips together, thoughtful, then sat across from her once more. "I wish that I could touch and hold you. I wish there were no secrets between us. But most of all, I wish I could be the man you deserve."

"I don't even understand what that means," she said, frowning.

His eyes filled with regret. "It means I'm not—and I don't know if I'll ever be."

"I see." A wave of hurt and disappointment crashed over her, but she refused to let it pull her under. "Then it was definitely prudent of us to set some boundaries from the start."

"This conversation isn't going as I'd hoped," he admitted. "What I was trying to say is that I've begun to change. I'm still not whole, not worthy of someone like you. But if you can give me some time—"

"Reese," she interjected. Though she longed to hear more, she couldn't, in good conscience, let him go on. Not until she'd told him about her family's rapidly deteriorating situation—and how it might cut short their time together. "There's something you should know."

"What is it?" he asked, instantly wary.

"My parents had to let most of the staff go this week because . . . because we can't afford to pay them. I hadn't realized things were quite so desperate when I agreed to this arrangement, but now that I know, I'm afraid I don't have the luxury to delay my betrothal till the end of the season. I'm going to accept Lord Singleton's proposal this week—which means tonight must be our last together."

"Sophie." Reese said her name like a plea.

"You're going to be fine," she assured him, even though her own heart was breaking. "You already look much healthier than you did a few weeks ago. It's obvious that you're sleeping more soundly, even when I'm not here."

"But that's because I was anticipating your return. I looked forward to you coming back," he rasped.

"We both knew that our time together was limited," she said, trying to be stoic even though she wanted to bury her head in Reese's chest and beg him to never let her go. "We would have said goodbye in a couple of weeks anyway. In the long run, it will probably be easier this way."

"Nothing about saying goodbye to you will be easy," he said. "And just to be clear, this is not about me sleeping or not sleeping. This is about my feelings for you."

"What *are* your feelings for me?" she asked, knowing that the answer she most longed to hear would also be the one that crushed her.

"I think about you all the time. I always want to be with you. I live to see you smile." He dropped his head into his palms. "God, Soph. I don't know what I'm going to do without you."

She fisted her hands so she wouldn't reach out and caress the back of his neck or run her fingers through his hair. "Then I propose that we don't think about goodbyes right now. Let's enjoy the time we have left."

"Do you want to walk down to the lake?" he asked, and she could tell he was trying to compose himself for her sake. "Or maybe stroll through the garden?"

"No." She shook her head slowly. "I just want to stay here. With you."

Reese looked at Sophie, sitting in the chair beside him, apparently oblivious to the fact that the earth around him had started to crack and was about to swallow him up. His heart raced like he was about to dive off a cliff, and panic clawed at his chest.

All because this was their last night together.

He understood why she had to accept Singleton's proposal. She had no other options.

Maybe if Reese had met her a little sooner, or if she could have waited a little longer, he could have been the one to propose marriage. He'd have enough money in his coffers to swoop in and save her. But he had little of value to offer her. He was too broken. Too undeserving. Too weak.

He couldn't even bring himself to open a few goddamned letters. Couldn't even fulfill a solemn promise he'd made to a bosom friend.

Lately, Sophie had helped him to feel more human. Like perhaps he was capable of being the man she thought he was. But this latest news had sent him into a backslide. And without her, he'd never recover.

He gripped the arms of his chair, trying to ground himself. She was still there, in his guest bedchamber—at least for now. Dressed in a white nightgown, her hair a golden cloud around her shoulders, she was a vision to behold. But she was more than beautiful. She was kindness, patience, and courage personified.

And sometime in the past month, she'd become the sun that his dark, decaying world revolved around. The sun that had the power to heal him.

Now that their time was about to run out, he couldn't help but think he'd squandered it. She deserved to know how she'd helped him—and what she meant to him. He wasn't particularly good with words, but he knew one gesture he could make that might please her.

"Sophie, I want you to know that the tailor's shop is yours to use for whatever purpose you like, anytime you like, for as long as you like. In fact, I'm happy to draw up papers and sign the property over to you, to make it official."

She blinked at him, her blue eyes full of emotion and sadness. "That's incredibly generous of you, but I don't think I'll require the use of the shop much longer. Only a few more Friday evenings."

"I see," he said, pretending he wasn't devastated to learn that the one, tenuous connection he'd hoped to maintain with her would soon be severed as well. "I know I promised not to ask about your use of the building, but I have to admit I'm curious. Mostly because whatever it is—I can clearly see that it's important to you."

"It is." She pressed her lips together for a second, then continued slowly—as if choosing her words very carefully. "I've been hosting a weekly meeting there. I'm not at liberty to discuss the details, but it's something I'm passionate about."

"Are you as passionate about your meeting as you are about gardening?"

She smiled and tilted her head, thoughtful. "Almost."

"And yet, you're giving it up in a few weeks," he said, arching a brow in question. "Is that because you think Lord Singleton wouldn't approve?" Reese didn't know the marquess, but he already wanted to strangle him.

"Partly," Sophie said, pulling her knees to her chest. "It's complicated. And I don't think it would be right to keep secrets from my . . . future husband."

"But you don't feel like you can confide in him." Reese paused. "Just like you don't feel like you can confide in me."

"It's not like that. I *want* to tell you, and I trust you. I've no doubt you'd understand. But our members made a pact not to reveal the nature of our business, and I need to adhere to the rules—rules that I set forth." Her forehead wrinkled and her eyes pleaded for understanding.

"You're quite fond of rules," he teased. "I wonder why that is."

"I can tell you why," she said softly—and he knew she was thinking about the no-touching rule. "It's because rules keep people from doing things that seem like a good idea at the time but are actually quite counterproductive at best, dangerous at worst. Rules keep people from listening solely to their hearts when they should listen to reason and good sense. Sometimes rules are the only defense against scandal and impropriety—and utterly devastating heartache."

"That's true," Reese admitted. "But when you find a person who understands and supports you unreservedly, trust takes over. Then, maybe, the rules aren't necessary anymore."

Sophie blew out a long breath and stood. Her frothy white nightgown swished around her lithe legs like foam on ocean waves. "I trust you, Reese. I wouldn't be here with you if I didn't. But trust is a two-way proposition. You have secrets too."

"What do you want to know?" he asked simply, hoping she couldn't tell that inside, he was shaking like a rabbit.

She walked toward the bed, turned, and leaned her back against one of the tall posters. "I want to know everything about you. What are the things that make you happy? What are the things that keep you awake at night?"

"There's a long list of things that keep me up at night." A hundred haunting images flashed through his mind, and the hairs on the back of his neck stood on end. "Are you sure you want to know what they are?"

She nodded soberly. "Why don't you take off your boots

and join me on the bed? I'll turn down the lamp; I always find it easier to talk about difficult things in the dark."

She had a point. Maybe with the lamp turned low, she wouldn't see the sweat on his brow or the panic in his eyes. He tugged off his boots, cravat, and waistcoat, then joined her on top of the soft feather mattress. She slipped under the covers, and he stayed on top—just so there wouldn't be any accidental contact.

Once they'd both settled their heads on their pillows, he inhaled deeply.

And prepared to unleash the demons.

Chapter 19

Reese's heart pounded, echoing in his chest like artillery fire. Most days, he spent a considerable amount of energy trying to avoid thinking about his time on the front lines—and specifically his last week there.

But now Sophie was lying beside him, asking him to remember those days. To walk through those minefields and relive the horror so that she could understand. For her, he was willing to subject himself to the pain and misery. She deserved to know how damaged he was, how broken. Even if exposing the wounds left him bloody and raw.

Though the bedchamber was fairly dark, Sophie's eyes glowed encouragingly. He focused on her like a sailor spying a lighthouse through a storm.

"It feels like another lifetime," he began, "but it was only a few months ago. I was on the front lines in Portugal, when a messenger arrived at our encampment—with an urgent message for me." The memory, vivid and raw, made him shudder involuntarily.

"Before I read the letter, I think I knew what it would say. The dread in my bones was so cold, so heavy, I had to force myself to break the seal on the letter. When I did, the nightmare was unleashed. Edmund was dead."

"Oh, Reese," Sophie said, her throat thick with empathy. "I'm so sorry. That must have been awful—especially when you were so far from home."

"I couldn't help but think that I should have been here with him. That maybe I would have been able to prevent it."

"No," she said firmly. "You cannot blame yourself, Reese. Not even a little bit. What happened to your brother was a tragic accident—and accidents, by their very nature, are unpredictable."

"He was the one person I'd always been able to rely on," he said. "My mother took ill when I was a child, and after she died, my father turned angry and cruel. Edmund was the one who always looked out for me. He devoted much of his life to raising me and taking care of the estate."

"No wonder you were so close," she said softly.

Reese let out a shaky breath. "Do you want to know the ironic thing? Edmund begged me not to purchase a commission in the army. He said that it was too dangerous. That he couldn't bear the thought that I might not come home."

"I'd feel the same way if I thought my sister was placing herself in danger," she said. "We always worry about the ones we love."

"That's just it." He gave a hollow laugh. "I didn't worry about him when I left. He was supposed to be safe here. I never dreamed any harm would come to him."

"It must have been a terrible shock," she said soberly.

Every muscle in Reese's body coiled tight, and his arms twitched with pent-up emotion. "It should have been me," he whispered. "Instead of him. He should be alive now. God, fate, the universe—whatever you want to call it—made a mistake."

Sophie reached out a hand like she wanted to touch his

cheek, then pulled back, her eyes shining with regret. "Edmund shouldn't have been taken from this world in the prime of his life—but that doesn't mean *you* should have been. Sometimes awful, tragic, pointless things just . . . happen. It's why we need to be thankful for every day we have on this earth." She paused and swiped at her eyes. "I'm thankful that you're here, too—and that I've had the chance to know you."

Reese breathed in through his nose, then slowly exhaled through his mouth, trying to let the anguish drain out of him. "There's a lot you don't know about me, Sophie."

"Maybe not. But I know you're a good, kind person."

He snorted at that. "If I was, I'd sleep a hell of a lot better at night."

"You're not going to scare me away," she said serenely. "I'm here—and I'm not going anywhere. You say that I don't know you, but I want to. Desperately. So why don't you start by telling me what it is, exactly, that haunts you."

His fingertips tingled and his head began to buzz. He opened his mouth to say something, but the words caught in his throat.

As though she could sense his distress, she scooted a little closer to him. The scents of rain and earth and sunshine filled his head, calming him slightly. "I assume it's related to your time in the infantry."

He nodded, grateful that she seemed to understand.

"Tell me," she said gently. "Drag the monsters out of your head and name them; perhaps then, you'll rob them of their power."

"I made a promise to my men. To my friends," he choked out. "I told them that I'd always fight beside them, that I'd never desert them. They knew I couldn't promise that we'd all make it home alive, but I swore I'd stand by them, no matter what."

"But then Edmund died," Sophie said, her voice tinged with sadness.

"Yes." Reese turned on his back and stared at the ceiling, blinking back tears. "I didn't want to leave them, but I . . . I had to see to my brother's final arrangements. I had to say goodbye to Edmund."

"I'm sure your men understood."

"They couldn't have been more supportive." He'd been half in shock at that point, and yet he remembered saying goodbye to Conroy and the others. They'd given him bracing slaps on his shoulders and promised to make him proud. Brave and charismatic with a wickedly dry wit, Conroy was a captain, and the obvious choice to take over in Reese's absence. In an uncharacteristically sober moment, he'd given Reese's hand a firm shake and told him he'd make a fine earl.

That handshake and those words had hit him like an ice bath. It was the moment he'd realized he'd never return to the front lines. Never fight alongside his friends again.

"The very next day, it happened," he rasped out.

"What happened?" Sophie asked.

"A surprise attack on my troop." Reese's stomach clenched with a potent mix of anger and pain. "They fought valiantly, but Conroy and two others were mortally wounded. They died on the battlefield," he said, his voice somewhere between bitter and hollow. "Brutal, tragic deaths. And I wasn't with them."

He scrubbed his face with his hands and blinked up at the ceiling, too ashamed to look Sophie in the eyes. "You asked what haunts me," he said raggedly. "It's the memory of their faces as I left them. They tried to act tough, keeping their chins up and puffing their chests out. But we were close as brothers and I could see the fear, cold and stark, in their eyes. They were scared out of their bloody minds, Sophie. But I still rode away that night. Still left them there to fight alone."

"It wasn't your fault, Reese," she said firmly—like she believed it. Like it was the end of the story.

At last, he turned to look at her, hoping to drive home the truth. "I broke my solemn promise. I came home; Conroy and the others didn't."

"I'm so sorry about your friends." The raspiness in her voice made his eyes sting. "I understand why the memory tortures you. You loved them, and you felt responsible for them."

"Exactly."

"But I stand by what I said earlier. It wasn't your fault," she said fervently. "And if you want to find a measure of peace, you must believe that."

He nodded, pretending to be agreeable. But the truth was that he didn't deserve to find peace. The sleeplessness, the nightmares—those were his penance. A constant reminder of his failings as a human being.

"In any event," he said, "now you know what haunts me."

"Thank you for confiding in me," she said sincerely. "Despite what you might think, nothing that you told me changes the way I feel about you."

"No?" he asked, skeptical.

"Actually, it does change my feelings," she admitted, and his stomach clenched again as he braced himself for what came next. "Now that I know some of what you've been through, I admire you, care for you, even more than I did before."

Reese released the breath he'd been holding and managed a weak smile. "You also asked about what makes me happy."

She smiled back and looked at him, expectant. "I did."

"That's an infinitely easier question with a much shorter

answer. There's only one thing that makes me happy, and that's being with you."

Sophie longed to reach out to Reese. She wanted to wrap her arms around him and make his pain go away. She wanted to will him to believe that all she said was true. But mostly, she wanted him to know that she loved him.

He'd just bared his soul to her, and words . . . well, they simply didn't feel adequate to express the emotion in her chest.

His large, tanned hand rested on the coverlet between them. It would be so easy, so natural, to lace her fingers through his. The problem was that Sophie already knew that holding his hand wouldn't be enough. She'd want to wriggle against the hard planes of his chest and press her lips to the skin above his collar. She'd insist on slipping her palms inside his shirt and running them over his shoulders and down his back.

And still, she'd crave more of him.

Worse, she knew that if she ever had a taste of physical intimacy with Reese, it would be infinitely harder to say goodbye to him. So, even though her whole body ached with the need to hold him, she couldn't.

Nor could she reveal the depths of her feelings—not when she was about to accept a proposal from another man. Since it would have amounted to torture for both of them, she settled for giving him a muted version of the truth.

She gazed at him lying next to her, more vulnerable and handsome than ever. "Earlier tonight, outside the tailor's shop, you told me you wished things were different."

"I remember," he said.

Tears welled in her eyes, and she was grateful for the

relative darkness. "I wish things were different, too," she said.

"How?"

"I wish we were both free to follow our hearts."

He gazed into her eyes but didn't say anything—at least not out loud. But the expression on his face revealed more than he probably knew: relief, frustration, and affection.

Sophie didn't delude herself into thinking that Reese loved her like she loved him, but they had a connection that was deep, intense, and true. Perhaps it was silly of her, but she imagined that maybe years from now, sometime after she was married to Lord Singleton and after Reese had battled his demons, they'd still think of each other.

Maybe they'd remember how they felt on this night and take comfort from the knowledge that they'd been friends . . . and more. No matter what happened, they'd always share this connection.

"Your eyelids are drooping," Reese said, his voice affectionately gruff. "Why don't you rest?"

Sophie sighed, snuggling her cheek against her pillow. "You'll stay here with me?"

"Yes," he said. "At least until you fall asleep. And after that, I'll be in my bedchamber, just down the hall."

She frowned but was too tired to protest. Reese was with her now . . . and that was enough.

Chapter 20

Sophie woke suddenly to a bedchamber that was almost completely dark. Reese no longer lay on the mattress beside her, and for some reason, the hairs on the back of her arms stood on end. Instantly alert, she threw off the covers, sat up, and lit a candle on the nightstand.

The house was eerily silent, and her heart raced as she tiptoed into the corridor and headed for Reese's room.

Earlier that night, when he'd shared a glimpse of the harrowing experiences he and his men had faced, it was clear to her he'd lanced wounds that had only just begun to scab over. She'd seen the raw pain in his face as he'd opened up to her, and she hoped he wasn't suffering the same way now, hours later.

The door to his bedchamber was slightly ajar, and she moved quietly as she peered into the room. He was sprawled across the large bed, the sheets tangled around his legs as though he wrestled a ghost. As she moved closer, she could see he was still asleep, but perspiration covered his face and chest, and the expression on his face was tortured.

He rolled over, thrashing on the mattress, and his low, anguished moan broke her heart.

"Reese," she said softly, not wanting to startle him. "It's me, Sophie."

But he continued to groan and struggle against an invisible enemy, deaf to her words.

"Reese," she said more loudly.

He fisted his hands in the sheets and let out a hoarse cry. "*No*," he murmured, oblivious to anything, apparently, but the nightmare playing out in his head.

Oh God. She had to do something. Couldn't let him suffer another minute.

She scrambled onto the bed beside him and firmly placed her hands on the sides of his face.

"Look at me, Reese," she said. "It's me, Sophie. I'm right here with you, and you're safe in your room."

He woke with a jolt, grasped her wrists, and blinked at her with wide, wild eyes. His chest heaved and his muscles twitched involuntarily.

"You're all right," she said, smoothing the pads of her thumbs over his cheekbones. "You were having a nightmare."

He seemed to be frozen, stuck somewhere between the horror in his head and the hope in his heart. His eyes flicked to his fingers encircling her wrists like he couldn't believe what he was seeing.

"What are you doing?" he asked, panting.

She swallowed and let her palms drift slowly across the rough stubble on his jaw. "Touching you."

He released her wrists and closed his eyes. "Sophie," he said, half warning, half begging.

"You were hurting," she said. "I had to do something, anything, to stop the pain."

"Even break your own rule?" he said with a weary smile.

"Even that." She slid her fingertips into his hair and let

the soft, thick strands tickle her palms. Her whole body tingled with a strange, magnetic pulsing, and she wondered if he felt it too. "I was worried about you. Would you like me to fetch you some water? Or a cool cloth for your head?"

"No," he said quickly. As though he didn't dare risk breaking the spell. "I just want you to stay with me. Like this."

"If I must," she teased, tracing the shells of his ears with her fingertips.

A cloud passed over his face, and he looked away.

She went still. "What is it?"

"I've dreamed of this," he said, his voice barely a whisper. "You touching me. I wanted it more than anything."

She tilted her head, puzzled. "Then what's wrong?"

"I don't want you to pity me. I mean, *I* know that I'm damaged. Beyond redemption. But I never wanted you to see me that way."

Her eyes burned as slowly, deliberately, she stretched out next to him and rested her cheek on his bare, hard chest. She placed her hand over his heart and said, "When I look at you, I see someone who's brave and loyal and caring. You're still grieving for the brother and friends you lost, but you're *not* broken. This darkness and despair you're feeling . . . it's not forever."

"How do you know?" he asked, as though her answer mattered very much.

She lifted her head and looked deep into his eyes. "I know because Edmund and your men would have wanted you to live your life without taking a single day for granted. And deep inside, I think you know that living a full, meaningful life is the best way to honor their memories."

For a few seconds, he said nothing. "Sometimes you can

know something with your head, but it takes your heart a while to catch up."

"That's true," she said. "But you must believe me when I say that my touching you tonight had nothing to do with pity. I'll admit I was worried about you, but I've imagined this moment"—she skimmed her palm over his chest and felt him shiver in response—"for a very long time."

"I have too," he said, low and deep. "It feels even better than I thought it would."

Sophie's belly flipped at his admission. Still, she couldn't help but notice that apart from initially holding her wrists, he'd made no move to touch her. His hands lay flat on the bed, almost as though they'd been strapped down. "What now?" she asked.

"That's entirely up to you," he said. "But if you're in need of ideas, I have plenty."

"Please," she said, her voice surprisingly raspy. "Tell me what you think we should do."

He leveled a heavy-lidded gaze at her and let out a low growl. "I think we should kiss, long, slow, deep, and hot. I think we should press our bodies together till I can feel your heart beat against mine. I think I should worship every inch of you with my hands and mouth till you cry out with pleasure." He shot her a lazy, wicked smile. "That's the abridged version of what I think we should do."

Her heart fluttered like it might fly away. "Abridged or not, your ideas have merit."

He suddenly rolled onto his side, propped himself on one elbow, and looked at her with an intensity that curled her toes. "I want this, Sophie, but only if you want it too. If all we have is tonight, then I'll take tonight. I just need you to say the word."

She thought briefly about her family and Lord Singleton. She thought about her friends and the Debutante

Underground. She even thought a little about Miss Haywinkle and all the cautionary tales the headmistress had shared.

And then, she decided she was tired of thinking about all those people, all those things. She was tired of thinking, period. Because she knew what she felt for Reese, and she knew what she wanted for herself.

She wanted him.

"Yes," she said, brushing a lock of hair off his forehead. "Yes to breaking our rules. Yes to seizing a night that is just for us."

The words were barely out of her mouth before he reached for her hand and laced his fingers through hers. The pressure of his hand made her feel like she was wrapped in a warm blanket and, at the same time, like she was about to dive headfirst off a cliff. Her whole body tingled, and she knew her world would never be quite the same.

Holding Reese's hand felt as momentous, as irreversible, as crossing the River Styx. Each of their souls was forever changed, and no matter what happened after that, they'd always belong to each other.

He raised her hand and reverently pressed his lips to the back of it, sending a chill through her arm. "I knew it," he murmured, his dark eyes glowing with desire. "Your skin tastes like honeysuckle."

She wriggled closer to him and tipped her forehead to his. "You mentioned something about deep, hot kisses."

Instantly, he slanted his lips across hers and groaned into her mouth. His tongue traced the seam of her lips and teased them apart. He pressed her onto her back and eased one leg between hers as he plundered her mouth and fisted his hands in her hair.

She was tumbling, falling, soaring.

Touching Reese was everything she'd hoped and feared it would be. But if she'd known it would feel so devastatingly exhilarating—so incredibly *right*—she never would have been able to resist him these past few weeks.

This kiss, primal and fierce, was far outside the realm of anything she'd felt before, but she refused to let inexperience hinder her. Using passion as her guide, she kissed him back, kissed him with everything in her heart.

She tangled her tongue with his and arched her body against his chest. She let her hands explore the smooth, muscled planes of his back and clung to his strong, broad shoulders when the heat thrumming in her veins threatened to overwhelm her.

"Tell me I'm not dreaming, Soph," he murmured against her neck. "Tell me I'm really holding and kissing you."

She speared her fingers through his hair and sighed as he slid a hand down her spine and cupped her bottom, pulling her closer. "This is no dream," she whispered close to his ear. "It's better."

Her words seemed to unleash something inside him, and he kissed her harder, held her tighter—as if afraid she'd slip through his fingers at any moment. She soothed him, running her hands over impossibly hard biceps and wrapping a leg around his.

Breathless, he lifted his head and gazed down at her, his eyes full of affection and wonder. "I don't deserve you," he said. "But God help me, I can't resist you."

"Do you want to know what I think?" she said, loving the slightly drunk expression on his handsome face.

He nipped at her ear. "Always."

"I think we both deserve—and need—this. I feel like a seedling that's lain dormant all winter. You were the sun I needed to make me fully alive."

"*You* are the sun, Sophie. You're everything that's good and true in my life." He stared at her like he was tattooing her picture on his heart. Then, he slowly slid a hand up her side, over her nightgown, grazing the side of her breast. She held her breath, waiting as his palm drifted over her shoulder and down her back. Inch by inch, he skimmed his large, warm hand up her rib cage, tenderly caressing the underside of her breast and circling the nipple till it pebbled beneath the silk of her nightgown.

With a smug smile, he lowered his head and drew the tip into his mouth. A little cry escaped her throat as he suckled her through the thin fabric. When he paused to blow on her taut nipple, she arched her back, demanding his mouth once more.

He'd touched her breasts before with the peony, but this . . . this was a million times more intense. Exponentially better. The pleasure he wrought swept through her body like a summer storm—powerful, wet, and wild.

But even the thin barrier of her nightgown proved ridiculously vexing. Wanting nothing between them, she tugged on the drawstring at her neckline. Reese murmured his approval, but when the knot stuck, he growled and proceeded to tear the gown down the front, all the way through the hem.

Deliberately, with something akin to awe, he parted the ripped fabric and let his eyes rake over her body, lingering on her breasts, hips, and legs. Deliciously cool air kissed her skin as she sat and shrugged her arms out of the nightgown's remnants.

"You're so beautiful, Sophie," he said, his voice balancing on the edge of ecstasy and anguish.

She felt her skin flush as she basked in the glow of his hungry, appreciative gaze.

But there was plenty for her to appreciate too. His hair hung low across his forehead, giving him a wicked, dangerous air. His tanned chest glistened in the flickering light of the candle, and his muscular arms rivaled any blacksmith's. The bedsheets were slung low across his narrow hips, and the ridges of his abdomen made her mouth go dry.

Shamelessly, she stared at him, admiring everything from his stubbled jaw to his muscled chest, to the fuzz beneath his navel.

And that was when she noticed the very obvious, very large bulge beneath the sheets that covered his lower half. Thanks to The Debutante's Revenge, she knew something of a man's anatomy . . . but this wasn't some hypothetical man she was reading about in the pages of the *London Hearsay.*

This was Reese. And she thrilled in the knowledge—the irrefutable evidence—that he desired her as much as she desired him.

"You're beautiful too," she breathed. "And I want to see all of you."

Chapter 21

Reese sat up without taking his eyes off Sophie. The house could have been on fire, the walls crumbling around him, and he still wouldn't have looked away. Hell, he didn't even want to blink for fear she'd disappear from view.

Her luminous skin glowed in the dim candlelight, and her hair hung in thick golden waves around her shoulders. She was everything he'd known she'd be—passionate, daring, trusting. Now, as she sat beside him, she was eyeing his body with naked appreciation—and asking to see more of him.

"I'm not wearing anything under this sheet," he warned.

"I'm not deterred in the slightest," she said with a sultry smile. She probably wasn't aware that she licked her kiss-swollen lips, but the sight made him even harder than he already was.

"You can see as much of me as you want, Soph. Nothing is off-limits." He waved a hand at the sheet covering his lower half in an unspoken invitation, then let his arms drop to his sides.

The corners of her mouth curled into another smile as she moved closer and boldly smoothed her hands over his chest. A bit more tentative, she pressed her lips to his shoulder, nipping it lightly. But then her mouth, perfectly wet and warm, drifted lower. She tasted his skin and murmured her approval. Her hands roamed down his sides and low across his abdomen, making his cock twitch in anticipation.

At last, she reached for the sheet and slowly pulled it off him, tossing it to the end of the bed without a second glance. All her attention was focused on his hard length, and she stared with a mix of wonder and curiosity. "May I touch you?" she asked.

"Nothing is off-limits," he repeated—but he did worry that one touch from her would make him lose control. So he fisted the sheets and braced himself. For the most exquisite form of torture imaginable.

She placed a hand on his thigh at first, then slid it up his shaft and over the head. He shuddered with pleasure and restraint.

Her forehead creased. "Have I hurt you?"

Shooting her a wry smile, he said, "You could never hurt me."

She leaned into him, nuzzling his neck and sliding her palm over his abdomen. "Show me how to touch you," she said. "Show me what pleases you."

"That's easy, Soph. Everything you do pleases me."

"You know what I mean," she said, impatient.

He *did* know and was more than happy to show her.

Before long, she was kissing the crook of his neck and eagerly taking him in her hand, stroking with just the right rhythm, just the right amount of pressure to drive him wild. His ears began to buzz and fireworks flashed behind his eyelids. His breathing turned ragged and his muscles tensed. "Sophie," he gasped, reaching for her hand. "Wait."

She stilled and snuggled against his side while he

caught his breath and attempted to regain control. He had to think clearly, damn it.

If he and Sophie only had one night together, he needed to make it special. So that she'd know, somehow, what she meant to him. So that years from now, she wouldn't have any regrets about what they'd done. And maybe, when she thought about him, she'd smile.

"Do you remember the night we met?" he murmured against her hair.

"When you accused me of breaking and entering the tailor's shop?" she teased.

"I think I knew the moment that you walked through that door that you'd turn my world upside down."

She arched a knowing brow at him. "Your world was already upside-down."

"That's true." He grinned as he laid her back on the mattress, then braced himself above her, his arms on either side of her shoulders. "But you shook it up even more. Since I met you, my head's been spinning . . . in the best possible way."

She reached up and cupped his cheek in her palm, brushing his lips with the pad of her thumb. "You have a similar effect on me, Reese. I'm going to miss you more than you know."

A lump lodged in his throat. "I'm here now, and so are you. If you ever miss me, I want you to think of this." With deliberate tenderness, he lowered his head and took her mouth, pouring everything he felt for her—emotions he couldn't even name—into his kiss.

When they were both a little breathless, he paused and looked deep into her eyes. "Or, if you like, you could think of this." He moved lower and kissed a trail down her neck and over her breasts, teasing the hardened tips with his tongue.

"No danger of me forgetting," she rasped, arching her back toward him. "I never knew I could feel this way—so dizzy and alive and free. It's like swimming naked in the lake . . . but better."

Chuckling, he slid even lower. Her skin tasted like nectar, pure and sweet. He kissed and licked his way down her belly, over her hip, and around her thigh, stopping short when she drew in a sharp breath.

"Reese?" She looked down at him, her heavy-lidded eyes clouded with confusion.

"I want to taste you," he said, rubbing his cheek against the impossibly soft skin of her inner thigh. "In the worst way. But only if you want me to."

"Oh." Sophie felt her cheeks flush with a mixture of embarrassment and desire—but mostly desire. "I trust you," she said firmly. "And if anything makes me uncomfortable, I'll let you know."

"Good." Reese's voice vibrated through her like a purr. "Because I think you're going to like this."

Good heavens. His touch was sure and gentle, his mouth warm and wet. He seemed to know how to apply just the right amount of pressure in precisely the right spot. Though it took her a minute or two to relax, she soon surrendered to the exquisite sensations he ignited inside her.

He nudged her legs farther apart and grabbed her hips, holding her like he'd never let her go. His mouth and tongue teased her mercilessly, and a lovely, insistent pulsing began to echo in her core. The feeling was so intense that she might have pulled away, but then Reese reached for her hand and laced his fingers through hers. "Stay with me," he murmured, renewing his efforts with an enthusiasm that humbled and enthralled her.

Every wicked flick of his tongue and brush of his lips

carried her higher, lifted her closer to the sun. Her belly tightened, her breath caught, and, suddenly, she was floating. Drifting through the air like a dandelion seed, blissfully light and free.

He held her all the while, ensuring she drew out every ounce of pleasure to be had. And when her body was deliciously sated and limp, he lay beside her and pulled her close, trailing his fingertips over her back in light, soothing strokes.

"You were right," she said with a smile. "I *did* like that."

He shot her a wicked grin. "So did I."

She nuzzled his neck, kissing his warm, salty skin. Never had she felt so close to someone, so safe, so . . . loved.

With a contented sigh, she reached between their bodies and curled her fingers around his smooth, hard length. A low groan escaped his lips, and she swallowed it, kissing him with all the fervor in her soul.

She found the rhythm he liked and stroked him till his eyes closed and sweat beaded on his brow. Knowing he was hovering on the edge, she gave a long, slow caress from the base of his shaft all the way to the top.

"Soph," he said raggedly. "I can't . . ."

"Yes, you can," she whispered, increasing the pace and pressure. She continued stroking as she lowered her head to his chest and ran her tongue over a flat nipple.

Stifling a curse, he placed his hand over hers and tensed as he climaxed, pulsing, hot, and wet in her palm. For several seconds, they lay together without moving. Her cheek rested on his chest, and his heart beat wildly. "You are amazing," he said, looking at her with awe and affection.

"I think it's more accurate to say that *we're* amazing," she said. "Together."

He pressed a kiss to her forehead. "Wait here. I'll fetch a wet towel."

When he returned to the bed, they laughed as they took turns washing and drying each other. And when they grew chilly, they snuggled beneath the sheets, her back to his chest.

While she lay there, Sophie wished for the impossible—to be able to fall asleep like that every night, with Reese's strong arms around her and his breath blowing softly in her hair. If circumstances had been different, it might have happened. She might have felt beautiful and sated and loved forever.

But her fate had been determined before she ever set eyes on Reese, long before she'd fallen in love with him. Tomorrow, she'd have to say goodbye, but at least she'd had one perfect night—and she'd always be grateful for that.

Chapter 22

Sophie awoke the next morning tangled in sheets that still smelled like Reese—only, he wasn't there. She sat up and found him on the other side of the room, sitting at his desk, his expression sober. "Good morning," he said.

She rubbed her eyes and blinked at him. He wore trousers but was still gloriously naked from the waist up. "Good morning," she said, stretching. "What are you doing over there?"

He held up a small stack of envelopes, then tapped them on the surface of the desk.

"Trying to summon the nerve to open these."

"I see," she said, suppressing the shiver that stole over her skin. She pulled the sheet from the bed, wrapped it around her torso, and padded across the room. Leaning her bottom on the edge of the desk, she said, "You don't have to tell me about them if you don't want to. But if you do want to talk, I'm listening."

He dragged a hand down his face. "They're from Conroy's widow. The first one arrived a couple of months ago, and . . . I still can't bring myself to read it."

"Why not?" she asked, even though she had some idea.

His face turned a shade paler. "What if she asks questions I can't"—he swallowed—"or don't want to answer? What if every word she writes is full of pain?"

Sophie's heart ached for him. "You're grieving for Conroy, just as she is. It might bring you a measure of comfort to talk to someone who knew him well and misses him as you do."

Reese shook his head. "That's just it. I was his friend and can hardly bear the loss. His wife must feel that tenfold—and I'm partly responsible."

"No," she reminded him. "You're not." But she understood his reluctance to read the letters, which would undoubtedly hold up a mirror to his own suffering. "Would it help if I read one of them first?"

He shook his head again, slowly. "I need to do this myself. That much I know."

She moved behind him, leaned her chest against his back, and circled her arms around his neck, savoring the physical intimacy that was still so new and heady. "You should read them before I go. That way you won't be alone."

"No. I'll read them after you leave," he said, a bit curt. "I've burdened you enough. I just wanted you to know that I'm not going to run from this anymore."

"You're not burdening me, Reese." She wanted to be someone he could count on. Someone he could share everything with. But now, just when they were on the brink of understanding each other, their time had run out. "I want to know what you're going through and help if I can. Even if we can't be together anymore."

"I won't subject you to more of my problems," he said flatly. "You are moving on to a new chapter in your life, and that's . . . as it should be. But I will say this: If you're ever in trouble, you know where to find me."

Sophie's eyes stung with unshed tears and she glanced at the clock on the mantel, desperate to make the hands stop moving. In less than an hour, she'd be in the hackney cab on her way to Fiona's house. And if she ever saw Reese again, it would likely be from a distance or in a crowd of people. She'd never have him to herself again. Not like this.

"Come back to bed," she whispered in his ear.

He reached up and cradled her head in his palm. "The morning's almost over, and I was going to bring you breakfast."

"I don't want to eat," she said, running a hand over the smooth planes of his chest. "I want to make love with you."

He hauled her onto his lap and searched her face, his eyes dark with desire and regret. "How can we, when we're about to say goodbye?"

"I can think of no better way to spend the minutes we have left," she said.

For several seconds he sat there frozen, his expression unreadable. Then he stood, hoisting her in her arms, and strode toward the bed. As he laid her on the mattress, his arm muscles flexed, and his hair hung low over his brow. He looked gorgeous and dangerous, like an angel of darkness.

"Aré you sure about this?" he asked.

She tugged at the sheet, slowly unwrapping herself. "I've never been surer."

Reese ignored the warning signals in his head—the ones that said he should safeguard Sophie's heart, and his.

He pulled her close and ran his hands over her body, savoring every sweet indentation and curve. When she threaded her fingers through his hair, he ground his hips against hers. She wrapped her legs around his and slid against his cock, driving him wild. Everything about her was perfect, from the satisfied sounds in her throat to the intoxicating taste of her skin to the unchecked passion in her eyes.

She caressed his neck and opened her mouth to him, tangling her tongue with his in a kiss that was demanding, reckless, and exactly what he needed.

Their bodies collided with a hungry, frenzied fervor, and he knew he'd die if he didn't have her. She pulled at the waistband of his trousers, and he slid them off in record time. He buried his face in the crook of her neck, licking and sucking while he caressed every inch of her body—the ripe mounds of her breasts, the soft indent of her waist, and the lush curve of her bottom. When he brought his palm up her thigh and felt the slick heat between her legs, she writhed beneath him.

"I want you, Reese," she said, her beautiful blue eyes imploring.

He positioned himself at her entrance and held her face in his hands. "Tell me if you're hurting," he said. "Even a little."

When she nodded and smiled, he eased himself inside her, an inch at a time. She felt impossibly tight and hot and perfect. When she began to move beneath him, he groaned. "You're everything I've ever wanted, Soph. Everything."

She looked up at him with such affection and trust that he thought his chest might explode. "I like this. You inside me, on top of me, around me. No matter how much I have of you, I always want more." As if to prove her point, she clenched her inner muscles around him, and he nearly lost control.

"Hold on," he said, thrusting harder. "But don't hold back."

She clung to his shoulders as he found a rhythm and angle she liked. Her eyes fluttered shut, her head fell back, and her lips parted, as they crashed into each other, perfectly, fiercely attuned.

Heat and pleasure shimmered through his veins like a drug, and his body begged for release—but he needed her to come first. So he moved a little faster, thrust a little harder, and reached between them to touch her. With a few strokes, she was whimpering, right on the edge.

"Yes, Sophie," he said raggedly. "Come for me."

She locked her gaze with his and cried out, her body pulsing all around him with wet heat. Somehow, he managed to wait out her climax, but sweat beaded on his forehead, and his muscles ached from the effort.

When she reached up and kissed him with utter abandon, he let himself spiral higher and higher. Everything inside him wanted Sophie—her essence, her goodness, her soul—and for that one moment, she was his.

Just as release barreled toward him, he pulled out, moaning and spending himself on the sheets.

For a full minute, they lay there, catching their breath and staring at each other with wonder.

And for the life of him, Reese couldn't say whether they'd just made the best decision of their lives—or the worst.

Chapter 23

A few hours later, Reese sat at the desk in his bedchamber. Alone.

He'd promised Sophie that he'd read the letters from Conroy's wife, and he intended to.

In an odd way, the task seemed less daunting now. Loving Sophie and letting her go had been the hardest thing he'd ever done or would do. If he'd survived that trial, he could survive anything.

He'd wanted to scream as she walked to the hackney cab. He'd wanted to drop to his knees and beg her not to go. The thought of her marrying someone else made him physically ill—as though his whole body rejected the knowledge that he wouldn't be the one who woke up next to her and who gave her flowers. The one who made her smile.

But he couldn't ask her *not* to marry Singleton. Her family meant everything to her, and he admired her for wanting to help them. The truth was that he couldn't offer her a better future than Singleton.

Marriage to the marquess would give her status, security, and stability. She'd have someone to escort her to balls and the theater and the opera. She'd be embraced by the highest echelons of society and move in the finest circles. She'd never have to worry about her family's finances.

Most importantly, she'd never wake in the middle of the night to find the man beside her thrashing in sweat-soaked sheets and crying out like a madman.

Swallowing the bitterness in his throat, Reese broke the seal on the letter he held and unfolded it. His hand shook as he began to read.

Dear Lord Warshire,

I write to you with a heart that is surely broken beyond repair. William was the center of the world for me and for our two young daughters. Even when he was away, he made sure we wanted for nothing. In his frequent letters he never failed to tell us how deeply we were loved.

In those letters he also told me a little of his daily life and often mentioned you. It's clear he held you in the highest regard, and I felt compelled to tell you how much William respected and admired you.

I understand you recently lost your own brother and offer my deepest condolences. If your grief is anything like my own, it feels like huge waves are crashing over you, threatening to drag you under. But I take some solace in knowing William was doing what he loved, for the people he loved, alongside men he loved like brothers.

If you are ever in London and have an hour or two to spare, I would greatly appreciate the chance to meet you in person and hear your memories of my dear William. Please call on us at any time.

Sincerely,
Mrs. Sarah Conroy

Reese set down the letter, dropped his head in his hands, and—for the first time in his adult life—sobbed.

All week long, Sophie felt like she'd been wandering through a fog, numb and sad. But now that Friday had arrived, she missed Reese more than ever.

As she slipped through the door of the tailor's shop to prepare for that night's meeting of the Debutante Underground, she saw memories of Reese everywhere. The buttons they'd wagered in their game of vingt-et-un. The pillows they'd laid their heads on as they slept on the floor. Even the ivy plant she'd begun nurturing back to life on the night she'd met Reese made her miss him. Perched on the counter where she'd left it to ensure it received some afternoon sun, its heart-shaped leaves drooped a bit—as if it shared in her sorrow.

Sophie gave the potted plant a little attention, then began heating water for tea and setting out little plates for scones and cakes. The Friday night meetings of the Debutante Underground had become such an integral part of her life, and she wasn't sure how she was going to bring herself to tell the members—much less Fiona and Lily—that her time chairing the meetings was quickly coming to an end.

But once she and Lord Singleton were married, she wouldn't be able to sneak out of the house and disappear for hours on end. She couldn't lie or keep secrets from him, and she certainly couldn't tell him the truth—for their relationship was nothing like Fiona and Gray's or Lily and Nash's, which were based on mutual respect and love. But her friends' marriages were the exception.

Like most gentlemen, Lord Singleton would expect his wife to be unfailingly proper and obedient. And Sophie supposed she owed him that much.

Reese wouldn't be waiting for her after tonight's meeting. Instead of going to Warshire Manor, she'd be spending the evening at Fiona and Gray's house. During her visit, Sophie planned to tell her friends everything she'd been keeping bottled up—and perhaps have herself a good, hard cry. But first, she had to muddle through tonight's meeting.

By the time members eagerly began filing into the shop, a dozen candles lent the room a cheery glow, the aroma of freshly brewed tea filled the air, and plump silk cushions brightened the shabby furniture. Sophie pasted on a smile as she greeted everyone, and at eight o'clock she took her place at the podium. After giving her official welcome and usual review of the rules, she invited Violet to read this week's edition of The Debutante's Revenge.

The young woman wore a long shawl that concealed her expanding belly. Her face was still a bit thin, but her cheeks had a healthy pink glow. She accepted the copy of the *London Hearsay* that Sophie offered with a shy smile, cleared her throat, and began reading.

> *Dear Debutantes,*
> *Do not despair if circumstances require you to be*
> *apart from a gentleman you admire. Prolonged*
> *separations can be difficult but are not a death knell*
> *for a relationship—unless you allow it to be so.*
>
> *Use the time away from your partner to*
> *ascertain your true feelings. Write him letters if*
> *you wish, but do not spend your days pining for*
> *him. If the connection you have with your beau*
> *is genuine, nothing will sever it. Neither time nor*
> *distance will keep you apart—and your hearts will*
> *find a way to be together.*

As the women immediately launched into a lively discussion about the column, Sophie retreated to a corner where she didn't have to pretend to agree with the column's advice. Usually, she believed every word, but this week . . . the sentiment simply didn't ring true. If a genuine connection was enough to reunite lovers, she would be spending the night with Reese. She'd be spending the rest of her life with him.

But some obstacles—like duty to one's family and the scars of war—couldn't be overcome. Not even with true love.

At the conclusion of the meeting, Sophie sought out Violet and handed her a basket filled with fruits and cheeses. "A little something for you," she said surreptitiously. "How are you feeling?"

"Large and unusually clumsy," Violet said mirthfully. "But I cannot complain. I told my mother about the babe, and she took the news better than I expected: one day of hysterics, followed by two days of not speaking to me, followed by a great deal of worrying." The dark-haired woman gave a matter-of-fact shrug of her shoulders. "It was the best result I could hope for."

"I'm glad you told her." Sophie stacked a couple of plates and teacups on her tray, eager to finish tidying the shop so she could head to Fiona's house. "You must be relieved to have someone you can talk with about your situation."

"Yes, but I'd rather hoped to see Sarah tonight. She shares more information than my mother does. Whenever I ask Mama a question about pregnancy or childbirth, she just looks at the ceiling, wrings her hands, and tells me I mustn't dwell on such things."

Sophie had noticed Sarah's absence too. "It's not like

her to miss a meeting," she said. "I hope neither she nor the girls have taken ill."

"She's been so kind to me," Violet said. "Even though it's obvious she misses her husband terribly and has her hands full with the young ones."

Sophie set down her tray and tilted her head. "Do you know what happened to her husband?"

"He was in the army," Violet said. "He died fighting on the Continent."

"How awful." A strange awareness, a sort of tingling, shivered down Sophie's spine. Surely, Sarah's husband couldn't be . . .

Using last names was a clear violation of the rules, but Sophie had to know. Quietly, she said, "Forgive me for asking, but would you happen to know Sarah's surname?"

Violet nodded. "She gave me her address a couple of weeks ago and told me I shouldn't hesitate to call on her if I needed anything. I believe her last name's Conroy."

Chapter 24

Later that evening, Sophie sat on the settee in Fiona's studio, wringing her hands as she and Fiona waited for Lily to arrive—so she could tell them what she'd decided.

"You're worrying me," Fiona said, pacing in front of her easel. "You're not ill, are you?"

"No," Sophie quickly assured her.

"Good." Fiona halted, then snapped her concerned gaze to Sophie's. "Please, tell me you're not moving far away."

"I'm not. At least, I don't think I am." She painted on a smile. "Nothing so dire," she said, even though the thought of giving up something so precious filled her with a keen sense of loss.

"I can't stand the suspense," Fiona said with a frown.

"I'm sorry. Lily should be here any minute." Fiona and Lily needed to hear the news at the same time, and Sophie didn't want to wait till their usual meeting time in the morning.

Now that she'd made her decision, every moment she kept it to herself felt like a betrayal of her friends. Sophie wasn't used to keeping secrets from them—especially not about The Debutante's Revenge, which was the project of their hearts and seemed to be at the very center of their friendship.

Almost on cue, Lily breezed into the room, her dark curls floating around her face. "I came straightaway," she said breathlessly. "Are you all right, Soph?"

"Of course," Sophie said. "I didn't mean to alarm you. But I do have something important to say."

Lily sank onto the settee beside her, reached for her hand, and gave it a squeeze. "Does this have something to do with the gentleman you've been spending time with? If he's hurt you in any way, I'll find out who he is and—"

"No," Sophie interjected. "This is about Lord Singleton. I'm meeting with him tomorrow, and I'm going to tell him I'm ready to move forward with our . . ." The word stuck in her throat like a dry scone, but she choked it out. ". . . Betrothal."

"Oh," Fiona said, searching Sophie's face. "That's, erm . . . wonderful?"

Sophie exhaled. There was no use in pretending to be happy. Her friends would see through her if she claimed to be thrilled about the prospect of marrying the marquess, but she owed him her respect, nonetheless.

"It's not the love match I'd hoped for," Sophie confessed. "Not like the relationships you both are so fortunate to have. But Lord Singleton has generously offered to assist my family and I'm sure he'll be a kind husband. I'm hopeful that, over time, our feelings for each other will grow into something warm and . . . affectionate."

Lily's nose wrinkled as though she'd smelled a rotting mushroom. "You do not love him."

"Not yet," Sophie said, doing her best to inject a bit of enthusiasm into her voice. She simply couldn't imagine herself ever feeling something like passion for the marquess. "Perhaps in time."

"And what of the gentleman you've been seeing?" Fiona asked. "How do you feel about him?"

I love him, Sophie wanted to say. But revealing the truth to her friends would only make matters worse. "My feelings for him are irrelevant. I need to do what is best for my family—and so I shall."

"Must you rush into this?" Lily asked, her beautiful green eyes tinged with sadness. "Why not wait a few more months? Perhaps your family's circumstances will improve."

Sophie shook her head firmly. "I'm afraid time has run out. Mama has already had to let most of the staff go. Worse, yesterday I found out that Lord Singleton paid off several of my father's debts with the understanding that we'd soon wed."

"Oh, Sophie." Fiona rushed to her other side so that she was sandwiched between the friends she loved like sisters. Pulling her into a hug, Fiona said, "You should have told us. Lily and I would have helped."

"I couldn't ask you to do that," Sophie said, cursing the sob that threatened. "Besides, it would only have delayed the inevitable. I made a promise to Lord Singleton, and I must keep it." She gave a hollow little laugh. "Listen to me, complaining about marrying a decent, handsome man and having to assume the duties of a marchioness. I must be mad to feel even a twinge of sadness. Pray, do not waste your pity on me."

"You don't need to pretend with us," Lily said, squeezing her hand tighter. "I wish there was another way."

So did Sophie. But there wasn't. Even if she could find a solution to her family's financial woes and bring herself to break things off with Lord Singleton—which would be unforgivable, considering the kindness and patience he'd shown—it wasn't as though Reese had offered marriage. He was too preoccupied with fighting his demons, too busy enumerating his shortcomings, to envision a future that included love or happiness or . . . her.

"There's no other way," Sophie choked out. "But I intend to make the best of my situation and be a supportive, dutiful wife."

Lily squished her face again, but Fiona shot her a scolding look. To Sophie, she said, "Whatever you do, we will support you. Our trio sticks together, no matter what."

Sophie swallowed the enormous knot in her throat. "There's something else," she said. "It's about The Debutante's Revenge and the Debutante Underground. As much as I've loved being a part of both projects, I'm afraid it's time for me to step back from them. I can't tell Lord Singleton about my role, and it wouldn't be fair for me to continue sneaking around once we're married."

Both Lily and Fiona sat beside her, frozen and speechless.

Sophie felt her eyes sting. "I don't want to give them up, but if I wish my relationship with Lord Singleton to succeed—and I do—I cannot begin by lying and keeping secrets from him."

"But it's always been the three of us," Lily said in a hoarse whisper. "Since our days at Miss Haywinkle's."

"You're like our sister." Fiona swiped at her eyes. "You're the rock that grounds us. We can't continue the column or the secret society without you."

"Nonsense," Sophie said, even though her heart was breaking. "You'll still create your beautiful, breathtaking drawings." Turning to Lily, she said, "You'll still write your witty, insightful articles. The column won't suffer from my absence in the least."

"That's not true!" Lily exclaimed. "We rely on you in more ways than you know. On the days when I'm staring at a blank sheet of paper and feel like I have absolutely nothing to say, you're the one who gives me ideas."

"And when I'm certain that nothing in my sketchbook will suit a particular column, you somehow flip to the page with a perfectly matched drawing," Fiona said.

"And let's not forget the impact of the Debutante Underground," Lily chimed in. "You've created something truly wonderful—a space where women from all walks of life can freely discuss romantic relationships and matters of love without fear of being ridiculed, or worse."

Sophie mustered a smile. "I've loved every minute that I've worked with both of you. It's been an honor to be a part of The Debutante's Revenge."

Fiona's expressive blue eyes welled. "You're talking as though you're already done with it—and us."

Sophie grasped Fiona's shoulders and met her gaze. "I'll always be your friend. And I can continue working with you on the column and conducting my meetings for two more weeks. At next Friday's meeting, I'll announce that I'm stepping down as the chairperson and hope that one of our members will volunteer to continue in my stead." She tried her best to sound matter-of-fact and optimistic, but she felt the same sense of foreboding as Fiona. Their friendship just wouldn't be the same once she'd disassociated herself from the projects.

Sophie had no doubt that Fiona and Lily would continue to be warm and supportive and loyal toward her, but it saddened her to think that she'd no longer be involved in the day-to-day workings of the column or participate in their passionate, entertaining conversations.

Instead, she'd open up her copy of the *London Hearsay* at breakfast on Friday mornings and read the new edition just like every other young woman in the ton. And the thought depressed her terribly.

It seemed her impending marriage to Lord Single-ton was already driving a wedge between her and her friends—and she wasn't even officially engaged.

But that, like everything else, would soon change. In fact, she'd written to the marquess earlier that day and invited him to call on her tomorrow.

She'd procrastinated all week in the hopes that Reese would reach out to her in some way through a visit, a letter, or even a flower delivery. But he had not, which was probably for the best. It had made it easier to write the note to Lord Singleton.

Now that she had, it felt like there was no turning back.

When Lord Singleton called on Sophie the next day, Papa requested a meeting with him in the study. Sophie hoped that her father wasn't asking for another payment or loan—but rather suspected he was.

When the marquess finally joined Sophie, Mary, and their mother in the drawing room, he greeted Mama first, then turned to Sophie.

"Lord Singleton," Sophie said as she curtsied and offered him her gloved hand. "What a pleasure." His dark hair looked like it had been freshly cut, and not even the hint of a beard marred his perfectly sculpted jaw. His cravat, white as a calla lily, was tied in an elaborate knot that must have raised his chin by two inches. Indeed, he could have posed as a model on a gentleman's fashion plate. He didn't scowl, and there were no shadows beneath his eyes; he was the picture of vitality and health.

But the sight of him didn't make her heart beat faster in the slightest.

Lord Singleton pressed a brief and very proper kiss to the back of Sophie's hand, then gallantly bowed over Mary's hand as well. "I'm delighted to see you again, Miss

Kendall," he purred, causing Mary to blush to the roots of her flaxen hair.

Sophie squashed a sigh. If her sister left the comforts of her bedchamber now and again to attend a social gathering, perhaps a simple greeting from a gentleman wouldn't have had the power to fluster her so. An admittedly uncharitable thought, but it crept into Sophie's head, nevertheless.

She shook off the sentiment, for there was no reason for her to take her decidedly ill humor out on Mary. It wasn't her fault that she'd been protected and sheltered all her life. The marquess would soon be her brother-in-law, and Sophie resolved to put her sister at ease.

At Sophie's invitation, Lord Singleton settled himself on the settee between her and Mary. Before long, he was regaling everyone with a tale wherein he found himself quite lost in the countryside during the Duke of Harkenwood's house party. The story, which was charmingly self-deprecating and funny, involved a broken boot heel, a drunken villager, and an eight-hour ordeal in a forest.

"I thought that if I climbed high enough up the tree," the marquess was saying, "I'd be able to get my bearings and find my way out of the woods. Instead, I fell."

Lord Singleton paused as all three women gasped appropriately.

"Fortunately," he continued, "my sleeve snagged on a branch and prevented me from landing too hard."

Mama fanned herself, and Mary stared at the marquess with a mixture of horror and relief—as though she could scarcely believe he'd escaped the greedy clutches of death.

"Unfortunately," he said dramatically, "my jacket ripped from shoulder to shoulder. By the time I returned to Harkenwood's house, I was barely recognizable and utterly unfit to be seen. I attempted to sneak past the guests and up to my bedchamber to change but was intercepted by the duke's near-sighted grandmama. She latched onto my arm and insisted I escort her into the dining room without delay."

"Oh no," Mama breathed.

Lord Singleton nodded and grinned wryly. "When we walked in, the entire dinner party was aghast. Upon seeing me, the dowager duchess dropped her fork and Lord Brockton toppled his wineglass. Then Harkenwood started laughing . . . and carried on for at least an hour."

Sophie shot him a sympathetic smile. "I imagine he won't let you forget the incident anytime soon."

"No," the marquess said. "And I can't say I blame him."

Mary and Mama giggled, their faces glowing with admiration. But while they were thoroughly entertained, Sophie was valiantly struggling to stifle a yawn. She found his story too practiced and polished for her liking. He delivered it so smoothly, one had to wonder if he'd rehearsed it in front of a mirror a dozen or more times.

But she knew she wasn't being fair. There was absolutely nothing wrong with Lord Singleton. Nothing, except . . . he wasn't Reese.

"Sophie, dear," Mama drawled. "The sun is shining and it's an especially lovely day. Perhaps you'd like to show Lord Singleton the garden?"

The marquess's eyebrows shot halfway up his forehead. "I should very much like to see it."

"Of course," Sophie said, leaping at the suggestion. Perhaps if she moved, she'd be less likely to nod off. Besides, she could no longer put off the inevitable. The garden was as good a location as any to tell him she was finally ready.

And willing to become his fiancée.

Chapter 25

The garden area behind her parents' townhouse was tiny, so Sophie had populated the space with miniature hedges, small flowerbeds, and a narrow stone path leading to a single bench tucked beneath a vine-covered trellis. It was an ideal spot to read a book or sip a cup of tea. And it would have been a perfectly lovely spot to accept a marriage proposal—if only that offer had come from the man she loved.

"I confess I was surprised to receive your letter," Lord Singleton began. He sat beside her on the bench, sweat glistening on his forehead. "You said there was something you wished to discuss?"

She'd already decided to approach the conversation in as forthright a manner as possible. "Yes, my lord."

"I think we should dispense with formalities," he said kindly. "Please, call me Charles."

"Very well . . . Charles. I'm ready to announce our engagement." The words were easier to say than she'd anticipated. Perhaps because there was no feeling behind them—it was almost as though she were hollow inside.

"That's . . . that's wonderful," he said with gusto, clearly hoping to convince her. Granted, she probably should have summoned a little more enthusiasm, but she didn't want to be false with him.

"Forgive me for speaking plainly," she said earnestly. "I admire and respect you, but the truth is that it may take a while for my romantic feelings to develop. I hope you understand."

"I do." He swallowed, then smiled a bit too brightly. "Rome wasn't built in a day."

She laid a hand on his forearm and gave it an encouraging squeeze. "You should know I intend to be a dutiful wife. I'll do my best to make you happy."

"You'll make a fine marchioness. And I hope to make you happy as well."

Sophie nodded but couldn't imagine she'd ever be truly happy again. Not without Reese. But perhaps she'd have peace of mind—the kind that came from knowing her family's future was secured. She'd be comfortable and content, which, she reminded herself, was not a terrible trade-off for happiness.

"Now that it's decided, I think we should move ahead as quickly as possible," she said firmly.

"Agreed." Lord Singleton—Charles, that is—slapped his hands on his knees. "But an engagement is a momentous event and must be celebrated in the proper way."

Sophie shrugged. "I could ask Mama if we have a bottle of champagne," she said, knowing full well that their wine cellar was almost dry.

"No," he said excitedly. "We can do better than that. I shall host a ball—two weeks from now—and we shall announce our betrothal there."

Sophie suddenly felt as though someone were mercilessly yanking on the laces of her corset, tightening them inch by inch. "Excellent," she managed. "You must let me know what I can do to help."

Charles waved away the offer. "My staff will see to the preparations. All you must do is find a gorgeous gown, so that when you glide into my ballroom, the other guests will be stunned by your beauty."

"Is that all?" Sophie said with a hollow laugh. She felt oddly detached from her body—as though she were simply an actress performing a part onstage.

"I have every confidence in you, my dear." Charles stood, pressed a perfunctory kiss to the back of her hand, and arched a dark brow as he met her gaze. "I shall see you in a fortnight."

Reese stood on the Conroys' doorstep, a potent mix of guilt, fear, and grief churning in his gut. But he needed to fulfill his promise to the man he'd fought alongside. To his friend.

He'd brought a bouquet from his and Sophie's garden, where he spent a couple of hours each day sweating in the sun, working in the dirt, and exorcising his demons. The flowers, hollyhocks—he'd looked them up—had come from the best part of the garden, hidden in the back, behind the rotunda. Reese had surmised that the lush, tranquil area was meant to represent Elysium—the part of the Underworld reserved for the worthiest of souls.

In other words, not him.

But it was the area of the garden with the most potential, so he'd spent the last several days there, doing his best to restore it to its original state. He'd found at least a dozen different kinds of flowers hidden among the weeds and overgrowth, but he suspected Sophie would have loved the hollyhocks' tall stalks and bell-shaped blooms in every shade of pink.

He'd brought the bouquet for Sarah Conroy, but as his clammy palm clutched the stems, he realized he'd brought it for himself too. As long as he held the hollyhocks, he had a little piece of Sophie with him, and knowing that gave him the courage to knock on the door.

A few seconds later, a woman with auburn hair and a riot of freckles sprinkled across her nose answered the door. "May I help you?" she asked warily.

Reese nodded. "I'm Henry Reese, Earl of Warshire."

He'd barely managed to get the words out of his mouth before Sarah threw her arms around him, crushing the bouquet and knocking the wind out of him.

"You came," she said, choking back tears. "I knew you would." She unceremoniously pulled him into the modest apartment and invited him to sit.

Reese held out the slightly crumpled flowers. "These are for you," he said, clearing his throat. "I visited your husband's grave before I came here. I left some flowers there as well."

Sarah's eyes welled, but she laughed softly. "He never brought me flowers," she said without a hint of bitterness. "But he showed me he loved me in countless other ways. Thank you for these," she said, taking the hollyhocks. "I'm going to fetch a vase. May I bring you some tea or a glass of port?"

"No, thank you," he said. "I don't want to trouble you."

"It's no trouble at all," Sarah protested, even though he could see she had a pot of something cooking on the stove and a basket of laundry sitting by the back door.

"I should have told you I was coming, but I was in the neighborhood . . ." he said, letting the lie trail off his lips.

"I'm just glad you're here." She placed the flowers in a pitcher of water and set them on the table before gracefully removing her apron and hanging it on a hook by the door. Tucking a long red curl behind her ear, she said, "Your timing happens to be perfect. The girls are down for their naps"—she inclined her head toward a room in the back—"so we have a moment to talk."

He sank into an armchair, and she took a seat on the sofa opposite him, smoothing the skirt of her lavender gown. "William wouldn't have wanted me to wear black for months on end," she said self-consciously.

"No," he said firmly. "He wouldn't have."

She shot him a grateful smile. "He thought the world of you, my lord."

"Please, call me Reese," he urged.

"William said that on the coldest, loneliest of nights, you always found a way to make him and the rest of the men laugh. He said that even when it seemed the enemy was breathing down your necks, you were never afraid."

"That's not true," he said. "William was the bravest of us all. The men looked up to him, and when I had to leave—after my brother's death—he was the one who stepped in to take my place." Reese looked deep into Sarah's eyes. "And I'm so sorry that I left him. That I left all of them. I'm so sorry that he didn't come home to you."

Sarah shook her head slowly. "You have nothing to apologize for, my lord."

"Actually, I do," Reese said. "I apologize for taking so long to reply to your letters. For taking so long to visit. And especially for waiting so long to deliver this message from William."

"He gave you a note for me?" she asked, her expression devastatingly hopeful.

"Not exactly. He said that if anything were to happen to him, I must tell you three things."

"Three things?" she repeated.

Reese nodded. "Sometimes at night, while we sat around the fire, he'd make me repeat them back, just to be sure I memorized them."

Sarah covered her mouth with her hands to stifle a sob, and Reese hurriedly dug his handkerchief out of his pocket and handed it to her.

He gave her a few moments to compose herself, and when she nodded at him, he began. "First, he said he loved you and the girls more than anything—even more than your suet pudding, but that it was a very close call."

"Goodness." She dabbed her eyes with the handkerchief and shot him a watery smile. "That sounds just like William."

Reese cleared his throat and continued. "Second, he said not to mourn him for too long. Three months at the most. He wanted you to be happy, and eventually, to love again."

Fresh tears fell down Sarah's cheeks, and she drew in a shaky breath. "How like my husband, to think he could dictate such things. I may refuse to smile again, just to spite him," she teased, but there was a softness in her eyes that made Reese's chest ache. "And the third thing?" she asked.

He forced himself to look directly at Sarah, to absorb some of her pain. "Third," Reese said soberly, "he said he wasn't sure where he was going, but he hoped they had skies as clear and as blue as your eyes. He said he'd know he was in heaven if they had sunsets the color of your hair."

For several seconds, Sarah sat there, gripping the arms of the chair as though she was trying to hold herself together. But then her chin trembled, and her whole body seemed to collapse. Sobs racked her shoulders, and she smothered her cries with his handkerchief. Reese couldn't recall ever feeling so useless.

He went to sit beside her and patted her back in a stilted attempt to comfort her. But she didn't seem to notice his awkwardness; instead, she rested her head on his shoulder and cried until she hiccupped. When her tears ran out, she sniffled and looked up at him, her nose red as a tomato.

"Thank you," she said. "For coming here. For giving me one more wonderful piece of my William. And thank you for letting me soak the sleeve of your jacket."

Before Reese could reply, two small urchins padded into the room. The taller one had a head of ringlets a few shades brighter than her mother's; the other had straight dark hair, like her father's.

"These are my daughters, Rose and Julia," Sarah said, quickly gathering herself and somehow pulling both of them onto her lap. "Girls, this gentleman was a friend of Papa's."

They both beamed at him, and his heart squeezed. "I'm happy to meet you," he said. Turning to Sarah, he added, "I should go, but I wanted to tell you that for as long as you live here your rent will be taken care of. You'll also have a monthly allowance—plenty to pay for food, clothes, and other necessities." He'd find the money to support Conroy's family—even if it meant selling the silver at Warshire Manor in the short term.

"My lord," she breathed, clearly stunned. "That's extremely generous but not necessary. We have William's pension, and I earn a little with my sewing."

"It will make me feel better to know you and the girls are taken care of," he said, adamant. He didn't expect it to help him sleep at night, but at least he wouldn't have to worry that Conroy's daughters were going to bed with empty bellies.

Sarah frowned but then looked down at Rose and Julia and nodded. "Thank you."

He stood and bowed in Sarah's direction. "I'll see myself out."

She moved the girls from her lap to the sofa and hurried to her feet. "I do hope you'll visit us again," she said, her blue eyes pleading. "You are most welcome any time."

"I'm not certain when I'll be able to come again. But do send word if there's anything you need." All Reese could think about was walking out the front door of the apartment, loosening his cravat, and breathing huge gulps of fresh air. "Good day, Mrs. Conroy."

She curtsied politely and smiled as though she sensed his discomfort—and understood. "Thank you for everything."

Reese turned and headed for the exit. But when he was one step away from the door, something—or rather, someone—clamped her arms and legs around one of his boots. He looked down and found Julia had fastened herself to him.

"Julia!" Sarah said, her tone lightly scolding.

"It's all right," Reese muttered while Sarah attempted to remove her daughter from his leg, but it seemed her thin little limbs had turned to tentacles.

"Piggyback!" Julia demanded.

"I'm sorry," Sarah said. "William used to give her piggyback rides." She managed to peel Julia off him and propped her on a hip.

Reese pretended not to see the little girl's arms stretching toward him as he inclined his head and rushed out the door.

It was only after he clambered into his coach and yanked off his cravat that he realized he had nowhere to rush to.

Worse, he had no *one* to rush to. He missed Sophie—and the way she'd made Warshire Manor feel like home.

Chapter 26

At the conclusion of Friday night's meeting, Sophie moved to the front of the tailor's shop and addressed the members, who were seated in their usual large circle. "Before we adjourn," she said, "I have an announcement to make."

The women quieted and looked at her expectantly.

Sophie swallowed as she scanned the faces she'd come to know so well: debutantes and spinsters, married women and widows, heiresses and maids. Somehow, they'd all become important to her. Sometime since the inception of the Debutante Underground, all of the members' challenges, fears, and triumphs had become her own.

Just last week, when a self-proclaimed wallflower mentioned that she'd summoned the courage to strike up a conversation with the gentleman she'd pined after for almost a year, the whole room had erupted in cheers. Sophie's chest had felt like it would burst—in the best possible way.

But everything would soon be changing for her, and it was time to pass the reins to someone else.

She tried to keep her tone light and upbeat as she spoke. "I'm afraid that next Friday will be the last time I'm able to chair our meeting. It's been such a privilege for me to play a part in bringing this amazing group of women together, but after next week, personal circumstances will make it impossible for me to continue."

A chorus of dismayed gasps and moans rolled through the group. "But we need you, Sophie," Violet said. "You're the one who made me feel welcome at my first meeting."

"And you're the one we all trust," another woman said. "It won't be the same without you."

"Nonsense," Sophie said. "All I do is recite the rules at the beginning of the meeting. It is *you* who bravely share your worries and your wisdom with each other. *That* is the heart of the Debutante Underground, and it will go on regardless of who chairs the meeting."

Several members clucked their tongues, others murmured doubtfully, but Sophie pressed on. "Fortunately, we have permission to continue using this space indefinitely." Her voice cracked a little, and she knew it was because she was thinking of Reese. It seemed she was *always* thinking of him. "If any of you would be interested in taking over my role, please let me know at next week's meeting. I'll be happy to make some notes for you and answer any questions you may have."

The women blinked back at her, silent, and the mood turned unnaturally somber.

"Well then," Sophie said, "that concludes tonight's meeting. I look forward to seeing you all next week."

The women said their goodbyes in hushed tones and filed out of the shop, one by one. Sophie spotted Sarah speaking with Violet at the back of the room and went to join them. Sophie loved that the Debutante Underground had brought the pair together—especially since they seemed to need each other. They looked up as she approached, and both smiled wanly.

"I confess your announcement surprised me," Sarah

said. "I can't imagine anyone leading our meetings besides you."

"Nor can I," Violet chimed in, absently rubbing her swollen belly. "All is well with you, I hope?"

"Yes," Sophie said firmly. She might have elaborated if she wasn't so choked up. Instead, she turned to Sarah. "We were worried when you didn't show last week."

"Oh, my sister was busy and couldn't stay with Rose and Julia," Sarah explained.

"That's too bad," Sophie said. "But I'm relieved that the girls weren't ill."

"Physically, they're healthy as can be," Sarah said, her eyes softening at the thought of them. "But Rose wakes throughout the night. She's been asking for her papa." She swallowed. "Sometimes I forget that the girls miss William just as much as I do."

Wrapping an arm around the widow, Sophie said, "He must have been a wonderful father."

Sarah sniffled. "The best. It breaks my heart to think that they might not remember him when they grow up, so I try to remind them of the good times—how he'd swing them high into the air, tell them funny bedtime stories, and even brush their hair. But the more we talk about him, the more my chest aches."

"I'm so sorry," Sophie said, feeling guilty for being wrapped up in her own sadness while Sarah suffered the grief of losing her husband and best friend.

"The week wasn't all bad, however," Sarah said. "William's friend from the army—his commanding officer, actually—came by to visit."

Sophie's belly flopped like a fish stranded on the shore, but she managed to ask, "He did?"

Sarah nodded. "He spent a bit of time with me, met

the girls, and delivered a message from my husband. Just talking with Lord Warshire made me feel closer to William . . . and gave me a sense of comfort."

Sophie gulped. She wanted to ask whether Reese had a wild, lost look in his eyes. She wanted to know if he seemed as empty and sad as she'd felt since the day they'd said goodbye. Instead, she said, "I'm glad Lord Warshire visited you."

She was proud of him, too. If he'd been reluctant to open the letters from Sarah, he must have been doubly apprehensive about meeting her in person. But he'd promised to do the right thing where Sarah was concerned, and he had—in spite of the demons that plagued him.

Sarah swiped at her eyes. "He was a bit reserved but very kind. He even—" Sarah turned and blinked at Violet, who'd begun to vigorously fan herself. "My dear," she said, putting a supportive arm behind the pregnant woman's back, "are you overly warm?"

"No," Violet said, but all the color had drained from her face, making her eyes look even larger and browner than usual. "It's just the name . . . Lord Warshire. I wasn't expecting to hear it."

Sophie tilted her head at the young woman, concerned by the tremor in her voice. Something had clearly upset her. "Do you know the earl?" she asked gently.

Violet swallowed, and for a moment looked as though she might be sick. "I knew the former earl," she said flatly. "He's . . . he's the father of my baby."

Sophie shook her head, wanting to be certain she'd heard correctly. Unless she was mistaken, Violet was talking about Reese's older brother. "Lord Warshire was your employer?" she asked. "The one who took advantage of you?"

"Yes." Violet's jaw twitched. "And when he discovered

I was with child, he . . . he refused to believe it, much less acknowledge he was the father."

"What a cruel, insufferable scoundrel," Sarah exclaimed, rubbing Violet's back soothingly. "I'd heard he died in a hunting accident. Perhaps that was fate's way of exacting justice."

"Please, don't say that," Violet said. "As angry as I was—and still am—I never wished for him to die. I only wanted him to take some responsibility for the life we created together." She sighed and cradled her belly in her arms. "That's impossible now."

The women sat in silence for several seconds. Then, Sophie said, "I don't know if fate played a part in the previous earl's death, but I do think that a greater force wove the threads of our lives together. We're all struggling in our own ways . . . but maybe we can help each other."

"You both have already helped me more than you know," Violet said.

Sophie swallowed and looked at her earnestly. "I need to ask you something. Would you mind if I told someone else—someone I trust—about the babe?"

"Why?" Violet said, frowning.

"It's rather complicated," Sophie said. "But I'm hoping that the truth will help all of us heal . . . at least a little."

"I trust you." Violet shrugged and smiled weakly as she patted her protruding stomach again. "And, in any event, the truth is becoming more and more difficult to deny."

"Thank you," Sophie said. She wasn't entirely sure how Reese would react to learning about his brother's baby, but she knew the man he was, deep inside. He'd do the right thing in the end.

Already, her traitorous heart bounced at the thought of seeing him again. It had only been two weeks since they'd said goodbye, but it felt like two months.

And although it would be torturous to see him and not be able to touch or kiss him, she needed to tell him about his brother in person. Reese deserved to hear the news from someone who cared about him. From someone who loved him.

Visiting him at Warshire Manor was risky—especially since his staff were likely to be there. But an idea was already taking shape in Sophie's mind.

And, if all went as planned, she'd meet with Reese tonight.

Chapter 27

The rushing waterfall behind Reese spilled into a shallow pool surrounded by colorful flowers that bowed over their rippled reflections. Usually, the splashing soothed him, but tonight his emotions churned like the water beneath the seven-foot drop.

Sophie's note, delivered by his footman, had simply said, "Meet me at midnight by the waterfall."

She referred to the most remote section of the garden, tucked away behind the field of grey asphodels and the grove of black poplars like a hidden treasure. He'd left the house half an hour before midnight, placing a few lanterns along the path to light the way for Sophie. He brought a few more lamps to the patch of grass near the waterfall, and they illuminated the whole area with a soft, hazy glow.

Nearby, a large swing hung from the branch of an ancient bur oak—the kind that could have been home to fairies and pixies. Reese threw a quilt onto the wooden swing seat and paced in front of it, scrubbing the back of his neck as he contemplated what might have prompted her to write the note.

Since the day she'd ridden away from Warshire Manor, he'd had a huge, gaping hole in his chest. In a vain attempt to fill it, he'd spent countless hours reviewing ledgers, eliminating extravagant expenses, and finding ways to make the estate profitable. He spent almost every afternoon sweating in the garden, clearing out dead trees and overgrown shrubs. He reasoned that if he kept busy, he wouldn't have time to dwell on the hollow, aching feeling inside him. But he'd been wrong about that—along with a host of other things.

Now he couldn't help but wonder if Sophie was giving him a second chance. And there was no way in hell he was going to waste it.

He sensed her presence even before she appeared in the garden. The crickets' song grew louder, the flowers danced in the breeze, and the clouds in front of the moon parted in deference to her. Reese turned and watched as she approached, her golden hair shimmering in the pale light. Dressed in an elegantly simple gown of silver satin, she emerged from the foliage like a goddess.

"Reese," she said softly.

"Sophie." He longed to haul her close, to crush her against his chest, to slant his mouth across hers. "I've missed you."

Her eyes welled with affection—and maybe regret. "I've missed you too," she said. But she didn't run to him or throw her arms around his neck.

"You have no idea how happy I am to see you," he confessed. "There's something I need to say."

She tilted her head, curious. "Yes. That is, I've something to tell you as well. I thought it best to discuss it in person."

The skin at the back of his neck prickled ominously as he gestured toward the swing. "Would you like to sit?"

She nodded, and he carefully spread the quilt over the swing's seat before she settled herself on one end. He sat on the other and basked in her nearness. Soaked it up. Let it soothe his wretched soul.

"How have you been?" he asked.

She hesitated before answering. "Fairly well, I suppose. You?"

"Miserable, as usual," he said with a grin. "I'm nothing if not consistent."

She smiled, filling a little of the emptiness in his chest. "You are remarkably consistent," she said. Sobering slightly, she added, "There are two reasons I wanted to see you tonight."

"I'm glad to see you, no matter the reason."

Her cheeks pinkened. "The first is to tell you how proud I am of you—for reading the letters from your friend's widow and for visiting her."

He dragged a hand down the side of his face, perplexed. "How did you know?"

"It turns out that Sarah and I are acquainted—but I only recently realized she was married to Conroy." Sophie stared into the night, the wisps around her face moving slightly as the swing swayed. "Sarah didn't share the details of your conversation, but I do know that your visit meant a great deal to her."

Reese shook his head. "I couldn't find the words . . . to tell her how great a man Conroy was. To tell her what he meant to me. I'm afraid all I managed to do was upset her."

"No," Sophie said quickly. "You comforted her more than you know. Besides, what you said wasn't as important as what you *did*. You went to her and shared in her grief, and I know that couldn't have been easy for you."

Reese shrugged, embarrassed to admit just how much he'd been sweating, how hard his heart had pounded as he'd stood on the widow's doorstep. "It was nothing compared to what Sarah's suffered. What she's still going through. I should have visited her weeks ago."

"You went. That's the important thing," Sophie said, her tone brooking no argument. He'd forgotten how powerful and persuasive she could be. How fiercely she defended something she believed in. And for some inexplicable reason, she believed in *him*.

"Talking with Sarah also made me realize how lucky she and Conroy were. In this big, messy, unpredictable world, they were able to find each other. And they held tight to the very end. They had far too few years together, but maybe they had more than most of us ever will."

Sophie gave him a watery smile. "I suppose that's true. We all expect to live to a ripe old age, but there's really no telling how long we have."

"That's why I need to tell you how I feel."

She swallowed and gazed at him. "Go on."

He cleared his throat, acutely aware that his happiness—his whole future—depended on him expressing what was in his heart. God, he hoped he didn't bungle it. "I need to explain how I feel when I'm with you."

Her eyes crinkled at the corners. "I'm listening."

"Being with you . . . well, it's a bit of paradise. Just like this garden." He waved a hand at the lush beauty around them. "It's the rush of a waterfall and the sturdiness of an oak. It's wonder and breathlessness and a sense of peace. It's the comfort of being rooted in the earth but also the thrill of gliding above it." He raked a hand through his hair and muffled a curse. "Damn it all, I'm not making sense."

He glanced up and saw her blue eyes shining with understanding and, maybe, something else. She reached across the swing bench and took his hand, lacing her fingers with his. The simple contact of her palm against his made his heart pound like he was racing on horseback at breakneck speed.

"You're making perfect sense to me," she said, her voice tinged with sadness.

He gazed into her eyes, determined to show her everything inside him—his flaws and fears, his scars and his love. "I know you have your future planned out, and I respect that. But I also need to explain what you've meant to me. What you'll *always* mean to me. I love you, Sophie. You stole a piece of my heart on the day you first walked into the tailor's shop, and you've owned it ever since."

"Oh, Reese," she breathed.

"I should have told you before. I wanted to, but I was afraid of dragging you down and dimming your happiness. Now I know you're too strong for that."

She shook her head. "I don't feel very strong right now. But I do know that your love could never bring me down. It couldn't bring me anything but joy."

"Then marry me." He lifted her hand and pressed a long, tender kiss to the back. "Let me spend the rest of my life taking care of you. Let me wake up beside you every morning and lie down beside you every night. Just . . . let me love you."

Sophie felt as though she were drifting through a lovely dream. She and Reese were rocking on a swing in the middle of an exquisite, exotic garden, and he was holding her hand.

Telling her he loved her.

Asking her to marry him.

It was a fantasy turned real. A dream come to life. Perfect in every way but one.

Because the man she loved had given her the proposal she'd longed for—and she couldn't accept it.

"Reese," she said softly, even as her own heart was breaking. "If I could wish for one thing in this entire world, I would wish that I was free to say *yes*."

He blinked slowly, then looked at her, his eyes imploring. "You *are* free. Say yes to me. Say yes to *us*."

"I cannot," she said, her voice cracking with regret. "I've already accepted Lord Singleton's proposal. Our engagement ball is next weekend."

"But . . . but you don't love him," Reese said. "You could break it off. People might gossip for a while, but they'd move on to a new scandal before long."

She shook her head sadly. "If the only obstacle to marrying you was a little gossip, I'd wed you tomorrow."

"I know about your family's financial woes," he countered. "I don't have a vast fortune to offer you, but everything I have is yours. I've already begun making payments to creditors and balancing the books. The problem is, it's a big ship to steer . . . and it's going to take a little time."

"My time has run out. My father is greatly indebted to the marquess. Charles has paid off all of Papa's creditors, including several substantial gambling debts."

Reese shook his head firmly. "I don't see what that has to do with you."

"I think you do. Charles made those payments as part of the marriage settlement that he and Papa negotiated. But the payments are also a favor to *me*, because they mean I don't have to jump out of my skin every time there's a knock on the door, fearing that someone's come to haul my father away to debtors' prison. They mean Mama and Mary will be provided for and their future is secure."

"I want to be the one to take care of you and your family."

"But you can't," she said softly. "Not yet."

Reese looked at her like she'd driven a dagger through his chest. "Not yet," he repeated hollowly.

As much as she hated to see the hurt on his face, she wouldn't apologize for surviving—or for choosing the path that would save her family. Raising her chin a notch, she said, "I've been truthful from the beginning. My relationship with Charles is nothing like the one I have with you, but I must make the best of it."

"I know," Reese said, apologetic. He hopped off the swing and paced in front of her. "But you shouldn't have to settle. You deserve to be happy, Soph. If you were mine, I'd make you smile every goddamned day. No one could possibly love you more than I do."

She could hear the urgency in his voice; she could see the earnestness on his face. His declaration filled her heart with bliss—and still, it couldn't change anything.

"That is the most lovely thing anyone has ever said to me," she whispered. "And I appreciate the sentiment more than you know."

He dropped to his knees and reached for her hands, clasping them between his. "It's not a sentiment, Soph. It's the *truth*. You've changed me in ways I never expected. You've made me see there's more to life than nightmares and guilt and pain. You showed me that behind the shadows there are also light and hope and love."

A tear trickled down her cheek and plopped onto their joined hands. "Of course there are. No matter what happens, there are always light and hope and love." She needed him to believe that now, more than ever.

He rested his forehead on her thigh, sending shimmers of desire through her body. "There's something so right about the two of us, together," he murmured. "You can't tell me you don't feel it."

"Of course I do." She slid off the swing and knelt

beside him on the soft, thick grass, cupping his face in her palms. "I love you, Reese. But I cannot break off my engagement."

"So you're saying we can't be together," he said, incredulous. As though he still couldn't bring himself to accept it.

"You'll always be in my heart," she said, letting her fingertips trail along his jaw and down his neck. "I'll never see a rose without remembering the night we met in Lady Rufflebum's garden. I'll never see an asphodel without thinking of the flower crown you made me. And I'll never see a peony without recalling the night we swam in the lake. Every night with you was a gift—and I'll cherish those memories forever."

Reese speared his fingers through her hair and cupped her head in his hands. "You can walk out of my life. You can even marry another. But it doesn't change the fact that we belong to each other. Our souls are so entwined that I don't know where mine ends and yours begins. A month ago I would have sworn I was incapable of love . . . but somehow, because of you, it just happened."

Sophie nodded because she didn't trust herself to speak. But she knew she'd never regret loving Reese, and he was right—they would always belong to each other.

Time slowed as they knelt on the fragrant grass, face-to-face and chest-to-chest. The lanterns around them illuminated the exquisite beauty of the garden. The splashing waterfall, the rippling pool, and the exotic flowers combined in the perfect balance of movement and tranquility.

Reese's warm fingers caressed her scalp, sending delicious shivers through her limbs. He tipped his forehead to hers, and their breath mingled in the space between them. She could feel the potent heat from his body and the desire that always simmered low in her belly when he was near.

"I want you, Soph," he said with a growl. "Say you want me too."

"I do." There was no use denying it. "But all I can give you . . . is tonight."

Chapter 28

Reese had known the odds weren't in his favor. He'd pro-
fessed his love for Sophie and made his heartfelt proposal. He'd laid everything on the line . . . and it still hadn't
been enough.

Maybe if he'd come to his senses sooner. Perhaps if he'd
bared his soul to her a fortnight ago, her answer would
have been different. But maybe not.

The truth was, she'd been clear about her intentions
from the beginning. And even though his and Sophie's
connection was undeniable, he had to respect her decision
to put her family first.

But he refused to dwell on any of that now—not while
Sophie was in his arms.

She was giving him the gift of one night. And if that
was all she could give him, by God, he'd take it.

He crushed his mouth to hers and hauled her body
against his. He'd tried his best to tell her how he felt with
words. Now he'd show her.

And he couldn't help but hold out hope, however foolish and naïve, that Sophie would realize how good they
were together—and change her mind.

One taste of her lips was all it took to send him reeling.

He ran his hands over her body, savoring the fullness of her breasts and the flare of her hips beneath his palms.

She clutched the lapels of his jacket in her fists as she kissed him back with equal fervor. Breathless, she shoved his jacket off his shoulders and pulled at the buttons of his waistcoat. He tugged at the laces of her gown, and they wrestled with each other's clothes until they were both naked, surrounded by a heap of silk and wool, slippers and boots.

When she would have pulled him down onto the soft, cool grass, he stopped her. "I have an idea," he said, helping her to her feet.

Her hair hung around her shoulders, half up and half down, in beautiful disarray. Her lips were swollen from his kisses, and her blue eyes were dark with desire. "Do you?" she asked, shooting him a smile so soft and sensuous that it melted him from the inside out.

He slid his palms down her arms, caressing her from shoulders to elbows. "Are you nervous?"

She pursed her lips and smirked. "Just intrigued, my lord."

"Good." In one smooth motion, he gently grasped her waist, lifted her, and placed her on the swing behind them. When she arched a questioning brow at him, he leaned forward, kissed her neck, and whispered gruffly in her ear. "Part your legs for me."

Sophie drew in a raspy breath but did as Reese asked, settling herself against the soft quilt he'd draped over the swing. Slowly, he sank to the ground in front of her and kissed the sensitive spots on the insides of her knees.

She gripped the back of the bench as he nuzzled her thighs, loving the way his light beard grazed her skin. Each time he moved against her body, the swing retreated slightly—until his hands, strong on her hips, brought her back to him. The subtle push and pull, the hypnotic swaying, aroused her till she was pulsing with need.

"Reese," she breathed, threading her fingers through his thick hair. "I feel like I'm floating. Like this is just a dream."

"It's real," he murmured, the deep timbre of his voice sending sweet tremors through her core. When he looked up at her, his expression was heartbreakingly sober. "You're mine, Soph. No matter who you marry or where you go, you'll remember this night. And you'll know I loved you enough for a lifetime."

One hand still firmly on her hip, he lowered his head again. She gave herself up to the night breeze drifting over her skin, the beauty of the garden, and the wondrous pressure of his mouth at the very center of her pleasure.

With the teasing strokes of his fingers and the wicked flicks of his tongue, he wove a spell, entrancing her. Desire coiled deep inside; her breath came in gasps. The rush of the waterfall began to crescendo in her head, the sound impossible to separate from the pounding of the blood in her veins.

And then she was hurtling toward release. She cried out as powerful currents swept her over the edge and sent her tumbling through the air, unfettered and free. For those interminable seconds, there was nothing to hold her back—no duties, no responsibilities—only the love she felt for Reese and all the joy and heartache that was wrapped up in it.

When the last tremors of pleasure subsided, her body went limp and soft. Reese sat on the bench beside her and pulled her against him, soothing her with warm, sure strokes down her spine.

Utterly sated, Sophie leaned her cheek against the hard

muscles of his chest and let her hands roam—down the side of his neck, across his broad shoulders, and over his perfectly defined biceps. She skimmed her palms over the ridges of his abdomen and down his muscled thighs, then wrapped her fingers around his hard, thick length, loving the way he moaned when she began to stroke him.

"Soph, I need you," he said, his breath coming in ragged gasps. "In every possible way. To brighten my days and calm my nights. But right now, I need to be inside you."

She slid her tongue into his mouth and kissed him with her whole heart. "I need you too," she whispered. "To hold me tight and free my soul. But right now, I just want you inside me."

"That," he said with a rakish grin, "can definitely be arranged." He reached for her thigh and gently pulled her leg across his lap till she straddled him and his eyes were level with her breasts. "I knew this would be a good idea," he said, just before he captured a one taut, rosy tip in his mouth, suckling her and making her whole body shimmer with warmth.

His hands cruised over her waist and her bottom, alternately caressing and squeezing. He gazed at her face as he positioned himself at her entrance, teasing her with gentle nudges, hot pressure . . . and the promise of what was to come. Impatient, she lowered herself slowly, taking him deep inside.

He groaned and buried his head in the crook of her neck, kissing and sucking the spot just below her ear. She tried rocking her hips a little, and Reese moaned as though he liked it. She did too. He kept his feet anchored on the ground so that the swing didn't sway wildly; rather, it moved just enough—like they were making love on a boat on the calmest of lakes.

Reese showed her how she could lift herself and find

the angle that made her dizzy with longing. She held tight
to the bench back behind him and moved faster and faster,
setting up a rhythm that had them both reaching and soaring and—

"Oh Reese," she cried, stars exploding all around her.

He wrapped his arms around her as she climaxed,
held her as she spiraled downward like a maple seedpod.
Filled with wonder, she blinked at him. His body was still
tightly coiled, his jaw clenched with restraint.

"Reese," she began tentatively. "Were you not pleased?"
She'd thought he'd felt what she had, but perhaps she'd mis-
read the signs. This intimacy was all so new and lovely
to her.

He closed his eyes and chuckled softly—as though
she'd asked the most foolish question imaginable. "Everything about you—and this—pleases me. More than you'll
ever know. I don't want it to end too soon."

She wriggled a bit, surprised to feel an echo of the pleasure she'd felt before returning already. "Perhaps we'll
have time to do it again," she said, hopeful.

"I like the way that beautiful mind of yours works,"
he said, but his smile was dim. Almost forlorn. He stood,
picking her up as he did, and carefully laid her down in
the grass. "I wish we could stay here forever, like this.
In our own perfect paradise."

She wrapped her legs around his hips and pulled him
closer, deeper. A fine sheen covered his sinewy muscles,
and the moonlight illuminated every exquisitely masculine contour. His hair hung low over one brow; his eyes
glowed with a passion so fierce it left her breathless. He
held her bottom as he thrust, faster and harder, until she
couldn't speak or think or feel anything but him.

"Yes, Sophie," he growled. "Let go."

The words were barely out of his mouth before pleasure

whirled and pounded through her body with all the raw, wondrous power of a tempest. He stayed with her through the initial onslaught, but then abruptly withdrew, turned away, and moaned as he spent himself on the grass.

A sense of loneliness squeezed her heart, like wild vines choking the life out of a fledgling tree. She understood why he'd left her in that moment and knew it had been an entirely selfless act. But it still made her sad. Still made her long for something that could never be.

She ran a hand over his shoulder and pressed her lips to his skin, loving the salty, virile taste of him. "Look at me," she whispered.

He rolled toward her, his expression tender but weary.

"I love you," she said. Partly because she needed him to know, and partly because she longed to hear him say it too.

He swallowed and cupped her cheek in his palm. "I love you with all my heart, Sophie Kendall . . . and I'm sorry that it's not enough."

When she would have protested, he stood, grabbed the quilt from the swing, and draped it over her body. Then he reached for his trousers and slipped them on.

She sat up, holding the blanket to her chest. "I don't need to rush home," she said. "We can stay here for a while."

"We're only delaying the inevitable," he said, pulling on his boots. "Prolonging the misery."

Her stomach dropped. "So you want me to go?"

"Of course not." He scooped up his shirt and stuffed an arm in one sleeve. "But I already know that you *will*—and that I can't change your mind."

Sophie's eyes stung, and she blinked back tears.

"I've been brushing up on my mythology recently," he said, his voice chillingly hollow. "Did you know that the wretched souls who were condemned to an eternity of torture were able to see into the beautiful land of Elysium? While they endured their excruciating punishments, they were taunted with the beauty of a paradise that they'd never enjoy."

"Reese," she breathed, a single drop rolling down her cheek. "Don't do this."

"That's how it is for me. I've seen the life I want—a future with you—and it will never be mine." He sank to the ground beside her and dropped his head in his hands. "I don't want that heaven dangled in front of me like some precious fruit that will always be just beyond my reach."

She shivered despite the warmth of the night. "I think I understand. It's the same for me. But I have no wish to inflict pain on you—that is, more than I already have." She reached for her corset and gown, trying to ignore the hurt blossoming in her chest. "I will go."

"I'm sorry, Soph. But I do think it's for the best." He helped her to her feet, and she tried to dress herself in spite of her shaky legs and her bruised heart. He gathered up her stockings and slippers and handed them to her, regret plain in his eyes. "I can drive you home in my curricle, if you'd like, but if you'd prefer that my driver take you in the coach, I can guarantee his discretion."

"The coach is fine." She was beyond caring about her reputation. All she wanted now was the privacy of her guest bedchamber at Fiona's house, so that she could release the sobs that threatened to bubble up in her throat.

She turned her back to him, and he slowly, gently laced up her gown—as though, in spite of his apparent determination to say goodbye, he was truly reluctant to let go.

When she spun around to face him, lines marred his brow. "You said there were two things you wanted to tell me," he said. "But you only told me one."

Oh God. She'd forgotten about Violet and Reese's brother and the baby. "The second thing might be difficult to hear," she said. "But if I were in your shoes, I'd want to know."

He gave a curt nod. "Please."

"It concerns a maid that worked here at Warshire Manor—up until a few months ago. Her name is Miss Violet Darby, and she's with child. She should deliver the baby in another month or so."

"I don't recall meeting her. She must have left before I returned." Reese frowned. "Is she ill?"

"No. She's doing quite well, physically, but I thought you should know that the father . . ." Sophie hesitated, unable to make her mouth form the words.

Reese searched her face, confused. "Is he one of my staff? If he's harmed her in any way, or if he's refusing to do right by her or the child, I swear he'll answer to me."

"It's not one of the staff," she said soberly. "The babe's father is . . . Edmund."

Chapter 29

"Edmund?" Reese repeated, incredulous. There was no way on God's green earth that his brother—his honorable, principled, upstanding brother—had fathered a child out of wedlock. "Impossible. There must be some misunderstanding."

Sophie placed a hand on his forearm. "I'm afraid not, Reese. It's the truth."

He raked his fingers through his hair, beyond agitated. The serenity of the garden where they stood was no match for the anger that simmered in his chest. "This woman," he spat, "Miss Darby, was it?—has no right to spread salacious rumors about my brother. She's sullying his name, knowing full well he's unable to defend himself."

Sophie swallowed. "I realize this must come as shock, but Violet is a trusted friend. I don't believe she'd lie about something like this. In fact, she was reluctant to say who the father was until . . ."

"Until what?" he prodded.

"Until she realized I had a connection to you."

"What a coincidence." He didn't bother to mask his sarcasm. "It sounds like your friend saw an opportunity and is trying to take full advantage."

Sophie's pretty eyes clouded with confusion—and hurt. "What are you suggesting?"

"Isn't it obvious?" he snapped. "Miss Darby is trying to profit off of my brother's untimely demise. She intends to blackmail me."

"No," Sophie said, clearly horrified. "She's never asked for anything. That is, I know her family doesn't have much and would be grateful for assistance, but she's not the sort of person who'd falsely accuse another for financial gain."

"Then why are you here, telling me this right now?" he challenged.

Her chin trembled, but she quickly composed herself. "I thought you'd want to know."

Damn it, none of this made any sense. Edmund had *not* been the type of man who'd dally with a woman in his employ. He'd been a gentleman of the highest order—upstanding, moral, and true. And now, Miss Darby was attempting to smear his good name by making an allegation that was impossible to disprove.

Reese looked away from Sophie—and the undisguised disappointment in her eyes. "Your friend has made a miscalculation," he said, his voice harsh and cold to his own ears.

"Violet thought that Edmund cared for her," Sophie said, insistent. "But when she told him she was with child, he fired her."

"My brother would *never* do that," he said. He'd known Edmund better than anyone. He'd been the rule follower—the one who'd studied Latin all summer instead of going fishing, the one who'd ensured his sotted friends made it home after a wild night of carousing, the one who'd never cheated at cards. Edmund would never take advantage of a pretty young maid. He couldn't have.

Because if he had, everything Reese thought he knew

about the world was wrong. Completely upside-down. Edmund had been the constant, his compass, the guiding presence in his life.

Shit. Reese felt like he was backsliding. All the strides he'd made over the last couple of weeks, with Sophie's help, were being swallowed up by anger. And now it seemed that the huge boulder he'd been pushing up the hill was on the verge of rolling backward, threatening to crush him under its immense weight.

"I will not allow Miss Darby to malign my brother or extort money from me," he said coldly. "Feel free to pass that message along to her."

"Reese," Sophie whispered hoarsely. "I didn't mean for the evening to go like this. I'm sorry that the news about Edmund upset you, but Violet doesn't deserve your anger . . . nor do I."

Guilt, sharp and fierce, stabbed him like a bayonet, and some of his fury bled out. He stalked to the reflecting pool and stared into the water. Darkness stared back. "You're right."

The rage and hurt still swirled inside him, but the truth was that neither Sophie nor Violet was to blame.

He reached down in the flowerbed near the water and plucked a purple flower with daisy-like petals. His heart in his throat, he handed it to her. "Forgive me, Soph."

With trembling fingers she took the flower by the stem and lifted it to her nose. "An aster," she said.

"A peace offering," he replied, forcing a smile. "I will think about all you've said." Just not now. He was fighting the urge to flee even as he spoke. He couldn't remain there and hear one more word against his brother. Not when he was already reeling from losing Sophie.

"I understand," she said calmly. She stood in the garden against a backdrop of lush greenery, colorful blossoms, and sparkling water, but none of it could compare to her beauty, strength, and goodness. "I know you, Reese. And I believe in you. I always have."

"I need to go," he choked out. "Would you like to come inside to wait for the coach?"

"No. I'll stay here for a little while and meet the coach out front." She sighed wistfully. "I'm going to miss this place. But mostly I'm going to miss you."

Not trusting himself to speak, Reese slipped the aster from her fingers and tucked it behind her ear, where the violet petals shimmered like amethysts in her pale blond hair. Slowly, he brushed his thumb across her lower lip, and when she opened her mouth slightly, he kissed her—slowly, madly, passionately—until he couldn't bear it any longer.

Gasping, he broke off the kiss, turned, and strode away.

"How are plans for the ball coming along?" Fiona asked.

"Hmm?" Sophie looked up from the stack of sketches she'd been sifting through, hoping to find one suitable for next week's column.

Lily set down her pen and glided across her sister's studio, her green eyes narrowed shrewdly. "Your engagement ball," she said, arching a dark brow. "In case you've forgotten, it's only a week away."

Sophie pretended to study a lovely drawing of a couple picnicking in the countryside in order to avoid looking directly at either Lily or Fiona, who were both far too perceptive. "I haven't forgotten. Lord Singleton—er, Charles—is attending to the details. I think he wishes to surprise me."

"How romantic," Fiona said kindly, clearly trying to summon enthusiasm for the event and, moreover, Sophie's impending betrothal.

"It's very thoughtful of him," she agreed. Turning to Lily, she said, "Tell me again—what do you plan to write about this week?"

Lily wrinkled her nose as if Sophie's blatant attempt to change the subject carried a distinctly foul odor. "We don't have to discuss the ball if you'd rather not," she said smoothly. "But I hope you've at least given some thought as to what you'll wear."

"I'll find something in my armoire, I'm sure," Sophie said, nonchalant. Her emotions were scraped raw after her meeting with Reese last night, and despite her friends' attempts to cheer her, she couldn't forget the haunted look in his eyes just before he'd kissed her—and walked away. "I don't think my gown will change the course of the evening, in any event," Sophie mused.

Lily gasped as if the offhand comment had been blasphemy of the first order. "A pretty gown can work small miracles, Soph. Perhaps *that* should be the subject of this week's column," she said, smirking. "We could have a bit of fun with that."

"We certainly could," Fiona said. "But I think perhaps we should use this week's column to respond to some of the column's detractors."

"Oh no," said Sophie. "Has there been another letter to the editor?" There had been two rather incendiary letters printed in the past week, both written by gentlemen who objected to the content of The Debutante's Revenge.

Fiona placed a folded newspaper on the desk in front of Sophie. "I'm afraid so. In this one, a gentleman asserts that since his wife began reading the column she has become 'considerably less docile and submissive.'"

"Heaven forfend," Lily said dryly.

Fiona winced. "He also blames the column for her

tendency to 'whisper with her lady friends and make jokes at his expense.'"

Lily clucked her tongue blithely. "Goodness, he sounds as delicate as a flower."

Sophie quickly scanned the letter, raising her brows at the final jab. "He concludes by calling The Debutante's Revenge 'the work of a devious and deranged witch who wishes to cast her wicked spell over London's most impressionable and fragile population.'"

"What? That's absurd and insulting!" Lily crossed her arms, clearly incensed. "If you ask me, the author of that letter—I shan't call him a *gentleman*—doesn't deserve to be acknowledged with a response."

"Normally, I would agree with you," Sophie said, "but there *has* been a rising tide of malice directed at the column lately. Several members of the Debutante Underground have mentioned that their fathers, brothers, or husbands have recently forbid them to read it. Maybe it's time we directly addressed the hatred."

For several seconds, Lily paced, clearly fuming. Then she stopped abruptly, turning to her sister and Sophie. "Yes," she said, with a sudden, chilling calm. "We will respond forcefully and unapologetically. This week's column will produce one of two outcomes. It will either silence the opposition to our column, or . . ."

"Or?" Sophie asked as gooseflesh rose on her arms.

Lily rubbed her palms together. "*Or* it will whip them into such a frenzy that they'll expose themselves as the small, hypocritical, unenlightened heathens they are."

Sophie and Fiona glanced at each other and shrugged. Sophie almost felt sorry for the poor saps who were about to face the wrath of Lily's pen—*almost*.

"What sort of drawing would be appropriate to accompany the column you intend to write?" Fiona asked.

Lily pressed a finger to her lips, thoughtful.

"I have an idea," Sophie ventured, rising to her feet. When her friends looked at her expectantly, she said. "What if we were to embrace the label of *witch*? Why not claim it and make it our own?"

Fiona's blue eyes turned distant and dreamy—as though she were picturing the sketch in her mind's eye. "Yes," she said softly. "I believe I *can* work with that."

Lily joined Sophie and Fiona and took one of their hands in each of hers, forming an intimate circle. "I think it's very fitting that we're doing something special for our last column with Sophie."

"As do I," said Fiona. "Do you remember the day we first toasted to the debutante diaries? We joined hands just like this and vowed we'd write down our most intimate thoughts about our first seasons. It wasn't that long ago . . . but look at how our lives have changed since then."

Sophie remembered that day—the headiness of setting out on a bold new adventure, the naïve confidence that love would prevail in the end. For Fiona and Lily, love *had* prevailed.

Two out of three wasn't bad, she supposed.

As though privy to her thoughts, Lily gazed at Sophie, her gorgeous green eyes flashing like she was . . . well, a witch. "Never underestimate the power of the diaries," she said solemnly. "There may be a little magic left in them yet."

Chapter 30

Reese bolted upright in bed, sweating and shivering at the same time. His blood pounded in his ears, and his chest heaved like he'd sprinted up twenty flights of stairs.

Christ. He dragged his hands down his face, scrubbing his eyes as if that could erase the remnants of his nightmare—one that had been different from the usual terrifying visions, but equally as haunting.

He'd seen Sophie's beautiful face reflected in the pool at the base of the waterfall, her eyes so full of sadness that his throat ached. But then the water rippled, she vanished into the depths, and Edmund's face appeared in her place.

Memories of his brother flashed on the pool's surface: holding the reins as he drove his curricle, laughing each time he hit a bump on the rutted road. Making a toast at the head of the dinner table, charming everyone in the room with his wit. Embracing Reese and slapping his shoulders on the morning he'd left for the army, keeping a stiff upper lip as they said goodbye.

But then the water darkened. Edmund was riding his horse toward the woods, a hunting rifle strapped to his hip. Reese tried to call out to him, but the words wouldn't come. Oblivious, Edmund charged into the forest, and the menacing trees wrapped their gnarled branches around him, sucking him in like a tentacled sea monster. Reese plunged his hand into the pool, reaching for his brother, desperate to pull him out.

But the ground beneath him started to shake, and the sky turned blood red.

A sinister *crack*, a deafening shot, rang through the air.

And Reese cried out, knowing he was too late.

He'd woken in a panic, the sheets tangled around his waist and his heart thumping with the force of a blacksmith's hammer.

Groaning, he freed himself from the bedclothes, padded to the window, and shoved open the curtains. The late-afternoon sun slanted across the garden, creating harsh shadows everywhere he looked. It was hard to believe that only the night before, he and Sophie had lain together by the waterfall, as close as two people could be.

But everything had unraveled after that.

Reese couldn't stop thinking about his brother and what Sophie had said about him. That he'd seduced a maid and gotten her with child. The idea that his honorable, upstanding brother would have done such a thing was inconceivable.

But the sinking, sickening feeling in Reese's gut wouldn't go away. And it whispered to him that maybe—just maybe—he hadn't known his brother as well as he thought he did.

He hastily pulled on trousers and a shirt, then went to the washbasin and splashed cool water on his face. Though he was tempted to ring for Gordon and request a glass of whiskey, he resisted. Instead, he walked to his dresser and picked up the brass key.

The one he'd found on his pillow on the night he'd returned home from Portugal. His valet hadn't been able to say who had left the key on Reese's bed or what it might unlock; neither had any of the staff.

But Reese *did* have an inkling—and he couldn't ignore it any longer.

Taking a deep breath, he strode out of his bedchamber and down the hall to the master suite that still held Edmund's things. He slowly swung the door open, bracing himself for an onslaught of memories, emotion, and pain.

He swallowed and entered, half expecting his brother to strut out of the adjoining dressing room, shoot him a sardonic grin, and ask Reese how his cravat looked. But the room was unnaturally still and the memories were . . . oddly comforting.

Reese stood in the center of the room for a minute or so, giving himself time to breathe and appreciate the mementos strewn about the room—his brother's favorite beaver hat sitting on the bureau, an Egyptian vase that he'd brought back from his Grand Tour on the nightstand, a stilted but nonetheless cherished family portrait hanging on one wall.

Reese turned the key over and over till it was warm in his palm.

And then he went to the large trunk at the foot of Edmund's bed. He lifted the lid, which was unlocked, and pushed aside a folded velvet quilt, a heavy wool greatcoat, and two gleaming pairs of Hessian boots. There, at the bottom, he spotted what he'd been looking for—a small mahogany chest with a brass lock.

He pulled it out, closed the trunk, and sat on top of it, placing the wooden box on his lap. Edmund had used it to store his most prized possessions. Not the most valuable things, which were secured in the safe downstairs, but the most precious. He'd once opened the chest and shown Reese a few of the items inside: a handkerchief their mother had embroidered, a single cuff link that had belonged to their father, and an old snuffbox he'd won in a wager at Eton.

Before Reese could lose his nerve, he tried the key in the lock. A chill skittered up his spine as the lock clicked, then turned.

His heart racing, he pushed back the hinged lid and peered inside. As expected, the chest contained an odd assortment of keepsakes, but Reese's eyes went directly to a folded note sitting on top—with his name written on the outside in his brother's hand.

Panic clawed at Reese's spine and raised the hairs on the back of his neck. Every instinct yelled for him to slam the chest shut, lock it, and throw the key in the moat surrounding the garden.

But then he thought about Sophie and the faith she had in him. He thought about the way she looked at him, so calm and trusting, like she believed he was capable of overcoming anything.

Swallowing, he set the chest aside, picked up the note, and opened it.

Dear Reese,
Forgive me for leaving without saying goodbye
in person. I've done something reprehensible
and am beyond ashamed. I can't bring myself to
transcribe my sins in pen and ink, so I will simply
say this: if Miss Violet Darby should seek you out,
please tell her that I'm sorry. Provide her what-
ever assistance she needs. And, above all, be kind
to her, because—to my everlasting shame—I was
not.
    I leave our estate and family name in your

*capable hands. I wish that our finances were not
in such disarray, but I know you will soon right
matters. Do not doubt yourself, brother, for the
strength of your character has always surpassed
mine. You are braver, more resilient, and more
compassionate than I have ever been.*

*I regret I must leave you, but I know that you
will lead a long, happy, and meaningful life. That
is my wish for you, Reese—that you'll stop running
from your demons. That you'll find the peace I
could not.*

Your loving and remorseful brother,

Edmund

Reese's stomach clenched and his hands trembled as
he read the letter again, trying to come to grips with the
words Edmund had written. He hadn't died in a hunting
accident.

Jesus, Reese should have known. The details of the day
Edmund died had been sketchy at best, but the staff said
his brother had ridden out that morning alone. Given that
he'd been an experienced hunter and excellent marksman,
an accident was highly unlikely.

But maybe Reese hadn't really wanted to know the
truth. He hated to think of how much Edmund must have
suffered in his final days—and, moreover, of how much
suffering he must have caused Violet. He hated that his
brother had been so alone and ashamed and closed-minded
that he hadn't believed there was any way out of his predicament. That he hadn't felt that he had any choice but to
take his own life.

Reese dropped his head in his hands and cried—for
Edmund, for Violet, and the babe that his brother would
never meet.

Raw sobs racked his body, but for once, he didn't bother trying to hold them back. He let the pain crash over and flow through him till some of its power diminished and all that was left was sadness.

And an unexpected, newfound sense of purpose.

Because Edmund had been wrong. His brother, for all his intellect, had failed to see the truth of his situation. He hadn't realized that he *did* have another choice. That there was *always* another choice. And Reese knew exactly what he needed to do.

He returned to his bedchamber and rang for Gordon. When the valet appeared in the doorway, Reese gestured to the armchair across from his own. "Will you join me for a moment?"

Gordon frowned, but sat. "Is everything all right, my lord?"

"Not really." Reese heaved a sigh and steepled his fingers beneath his chin. "I'd like you to tell me everything you know about Miss Violet Darby, who, I understand, once worked here."

"Violet?" The valet's spine snapped straight, as though he was instantly on guard. "Why would you want to know about her?"

"I've recently learned that she's with child and might be in need of assistance. I'm hoping you can give me her address because . . . I want to help."

Next Friday morning at breakfast, Mary casually opened the *London Hearsay*, and Sophie's heart began to trip. She hadn't seen the final version of the column Lily wrote and delivered to the paper, nor had she seen Fiona's sketch.

But she did know that both women had intended to make a statement in this week's edition.

She resisted the urge to snatch the paper from her

sister's hands, and, instead, asked, "What's the topic of today's Debutante Revenge?"

Mary raised a fair brow. "Oh, I'd quite forgotten that a new column appears in the paper today. I was looking for the fashion pages."

Sophie refrained from rolling her eyes—barely. She knew that Mary enjoyed the column as much as anyone. Her sister simply refused to admit it.

"Give the column to Sophie, then, so she can read it to us," Mama instructed, briskly stirring cream into her tea. "Her engagement ball tomorrow night is a particularly momentous event; perhaps this week's edition will have some pertinent advice."

Sophie cast Mama a skeptical glance as Mary sullenly handed over the paper. She opened it to the column expecting one of Fiona's gorgeously romantic drawings.

But the image was strikingly different. The sketch, much larger than usual, took up half of the newspaper page. In it, three barefoot women wearing half masks and long, flowing gowns danced around a bubbling cauldron. The first woman held an artist's palette in one hand and paintbrush in the other, pointing it like a rapier. The second wielded a large feather quill near her shoulder as though it were a dueling pistol and she was about to pace off. The third outstretched her palm to reveal a seed that had sprouted into a lovely flowering vine.

Dear Lord. Fiona had skillfully hidden their identities, and yet, Sophie had never felt so exposed.

"Goodness." She looked up at her mother's and sister's expectant faces. "Today's sketch is quite different from the usual fare," she said, hoping she sounded nonchalant.

"Just read the column," Mary said, slightly annoyed. "Mama and I shall look at the illustration later."

"Very well." Sophie cleared her throat and began.

Dear Debutantes,
When a gentleman accuses you of being a witch,
he is unwittingly acknowledging the considerable
power that you possess.

Sadly, some men will feel threatened by that
power and attempt to undermine you with dubious
claims about your character. Some may try to
sabotage your efforts to gain knowledge. Some
may forbid you to discuss and share your ideas.

Do not be intimidated.

A man who disparages you does so because of
his own insecurities and because—oh, how shall I
put this delicately, dear readers?—because he may
not measure up in other regards.

It gives me no pleasure to say this. Indeed, I
think it safe to say that it gives no one pleasure.
However, you should know that a gentleman's
derogatory comments have much less to do with
your faults than they do with his own—pray,
forgive me again, dear readers!—rather sensitive
shortcomings.

But all hope is not lost. There are plenty of
confident, strong, and capable men who will
encourage you in your pursuits and celebrate
your triumphs. Seek a partner who will not be
threatened by your power, but instead, be in awe
of it . . . and of you.

In the meantime, embrace your power. Cast
your spells. Follow your dreams.

And never, ever apologize for who you are.

Sophie's cheeks were burning by the time she read the last sentence. She looked up from the paper to see Mama's eyes had grown wide as saucers. Mary stared blankly.

"Nothing very instructive in there," she said, biting into her toast. "Why on earth are you blushing, Sophie?"

"I'm not certain," she lied.

"Perhaps it's best if you don't show us the accompanying drawing," Mama said, before taking a fortifying sip of tea. "Now then. I'm sure I don't need to remind you girls how important tomorrow night's ball shall be. Come Sunday morning, everyone will be talking about Lord Singleton's ball—and his betrothal to Sophie. We must not give the gossips any reason to ridicule us."

Sophie reached over and patted her mother's thin, pale hand. "Forgive me for saying so, Mama, but the gossips are likely to find fault in *something* we do. Even if our manners are flawless, they will misconstrue a word or gesture and invent a faux pas in their imaginations."

"Perhaps," Mama said, frown lines creasing her forehead. "But I'd prefer that we not make it too easy for them. I, for one, will ensure that your father is well rested and in good form."

Sophie nodded gratefully, for she knew the task of keeping Papa relatively sober would require a great deal of time and effort, including hiding some spirits and watering down the rest.

"Mary," Mama continued, her tone uncharacteristically stern, "you shall wear your prettiest gown, pretend to enjoy yourself, and dance at least three sets."

Mary gasped as though their mother's request was on par with one of Hercules' labors. "But Mama," she said, "what if no gentleman asks me to dance?"

"If you keep your distance from the potted palms and manage to smile once or twice, you'll have your choice of dance partners. I'm sure of it."

When Mary gave a pathetic cough and opened her mouth to protest, Mama cut her off at the pass. "You haven't been ill in a long time, Mary. Your sister is marrying Lord Singleton so that your father will not go to debtors' prison and so that you and I do not become destitute. Considering the sacrifice Sophie's making for us, I don't think it's too much to ask that you fill your dance card at the ball."

Sophie and Mary sat there, momentarily stunned. Never before had Sophie heard her mother speak to her sister so sharply. And she'd never heard Mama explicitly acknowledge what the marriage would cost Sophie.

She supposed that hearing her sister finally being held to account should have been satisfying, but instead the conversation left Sophie feeling unbearably sad and bereft.

She couldn't help thinking about Reese and the life that might have been theirs. Couldn't help remembering how safe and happy she'd felt in his arms.

Her eyes stung as she glanced at the folded newspaper on the table, open to Fiona's clever depiction of their intrepid trio. She'd drawn Sophie with her hip cocked and a wicked, self-assured gleam in her eyes. Unapologetically bold, confident, and powerful, the woman on the paper staring back at her could have been the goddess of nature, and the mistress of all that grew and bloomed.

Sophie was humbled to think that her friend had imagined her that way.

But the truth was that Sophie barely recognized the woman in the drawing—and with every day that passed, she became more of a stranger.

Chapter 31

Later that evening, Sophie maintained a cheerful façade as she welcomed the women to what would be her last meeting as chair of the Debutante Underground. The room buzzed with nervous chatter, for it seemed that the latest edition of The Debutante's Revenge had rocked London like an earthquake, and the aftershocks had been rolling through town all day long.

"My older brother was incensed," one young woman confessed. "He said the authoress of such vile advice should be placed in stocks in the middle of St. James's Square."

"My father intends to take up the matter with the authorities," another chimed in. "He said today's column is proof that the authoress has poisoned impressionable female minds."

The members rolled their eyes and erupted in a collective disgusted groan.

"Both your male relatives seem to have missed the underlying message of today's column," commented Adelaide, a razor-witted grandmother. "In expressing their disdain for the authoress, they expose themselves as both intolerant and ignorant, making them look very *small* indeed."

The women chuckled with mirth, but tension in the room still stretched as tight as strained corset laces.

Sophie stood at the front of the circle and—for her very last time—called the meeting to order. She'd promised herself she wouldn't allow her emotions to bubble up, but there was a catch in her voice as she recited the rules, and a heaviness in her chest as she handed a copy of the newspaper to Sarah so she could read the column.

When Sarah finished, a lively discussion ensued. Many women expressed anger and concern that harm might come to the authoress. Others worried that the Debutante Underground would be exposed and that they'd all be publicly humiliated, bringing shame—however unjust it might be—upon their families. Still others argued that they must not cower from the attacks, and that it was more important than ever to stand strong.

Sophie stood next to the shop's counter, listening intently. Shortly before it was time for the meeting to conclude, she walked to the front and addressed the group again.

"There's no denying that The Debutante's Revenge has been on everyone's lips this week and that it's facing a rising tide of opposition. But perhaps this is because it's influencing more women than ever."

The group murmured in agreement.

"Whatever the reason," Sophie continued, "there are many who wish to silence the authoress—and her followers. I would urge all of you to listen to your instincts and act accordingly. If you sense that a family member or acquaintance is becoming suspicious, take the precautions you must in order to protect yourself and all of the women here."

"Hear, hear," the women responded.

Sophie smiled at the faces she'd come to know so well.

These women were more than friends. They were her family. And the time had come to say goodbye.

"It's been my honor to serve as chair of this amazing group. But, as you know, this is my last night in the role. I'm very pleased to announce that Sarah has graciously volunteered to take over my duties, and I leave you in her capable hands." With that, she gestured toward the auburn-haired widow and invited her to the front.

Sarah slipped an arm around Sophie's shoulders and presented her with a journal. "This is from all of us. We each took turns writing down what the Debutante Underground means to us and some of the ways it's made a difference in our lives."

Sophie ran her hands over the buttery-smooth leather cover, briefly flipped through the pages filled with heartfelt notes, and squeezed the journal to her chest. "Thank you. I'll treasure this."

Sarah pulled her into a warm embrace, then waved over Violet, who gave Sophie a lovely bouquet of tulips. "We'll miss having you at the helm," the younger woman said with a sniffle. "But even more than that, we'll miss your calm, kind, generous presence. Thank you for bringing us all together."

Sophie swiped at her eyes and addressed the assembly again. "I've loved being a part of this group and am so proud of the knowledge you've shared and of the relationships we've forged. If any of you is ever in a bind, I won't be far away. Sarah knows how to reach me, and I promise I will help if I can. Once a member of the Debutante Underground, forever a member." Since she was on the verge of dissolving into a puddle of tears, she concluded with a curtsy. "Farewell, my friends, and thank you for all you've taught me about courting, desire, intimacy, and, most of all, love."

The room erupted in heartfelt applause and appreciative cheers. And when the din died down, the women approached Sophie one at a time, showering her with effusive hugs before reluctantly bidding her goodbye.

When the tailor's shop had mostly emptied and only Sarah and Violet remained, Sophie invited them to sit in the pair of old leather armchairs and perched on an ottoman opposite them. To Sarah, she said, "Thank you for volunteering to chair the meetings. Especially since I know you already have so many responsibilities, not the least of which are your two precious girls. You must let me know if it becomes too much, and we will seek someone else to step in, if necessary."

Sarah smiled, her blue eyes twinkling. "My sainted sister has agreed to watch Rose and Julia every Friday evening, and I'm beyond grateful for the chance to leave the nappies behind for a few hours and talk with other adults. Besides, I'm no longer worried about keeping a roof over our heads or food on the kitchen table. Now that Lord Warshire is paying our rent and providing a generous allowance, I can focus on the important things—like ensuring the girls never forget their father . . . and trying to fill the hole he left in their hearts."

"You must look after your own heart as well," Sophie said softly. Ironically, the mention of Reese had left hers aching too. God, she missed him. "Has Lord Warshire visited you again?" she asked, trying not to reveal how desperate she was for any scrap of information about him.

"No." Sarah smoothed an auburn strand behind her ear, thoughtful. "Rose keeps asking me when the man with the sad eyes will return, but I'm not certain that he will. He must be frightfully busy," she said diplomatically.

Violet cleared her throat. "I have some news concerning Lord Warshire."

Sophie and Sarah both turned to the young pregnant woman, expectant.

"Several days ago, I received a polite letter from the earl asking me to call on him at Warshire Manor," Violet continued, absently rubbing her belly. "He sent his coach and his valet, Gordon, to fetch me, and I went."

Sophie's chest felt unbearably tight. She trusted Reese to treat Violet with respect, but she hated to think of how painful the meeting must have been for both of them and all the sorrow that it must have dredged up. "What did Lord Warshire want?"

"To apologize on behalf of his older brother. Edmund knew the babe was his and asked that the new earl provide for both of us, if I wished." Violet sniffled. "It was such a relief to hear him acknowledge the babe as Edmund's. I know that the two of you believed me, but I didn't realize how much I also needed someone from his family to know and accept that this little one is a part of them too."

Sarah dabbed a handkerchief at the corners of her eyes. "That's wonderful."

The young woman nodded, saying, "But there's more. The earl asked if he might be permitted to meet the babe and visit occasionally . . . as any uncle would."

"Lord Warshire is a good man," Sophie breathed, wondering why he'd tried to hide that side of himself for so long. Why he hadn't even believed it existed.

Violet smiled. "When he asked what assistance he could provide, I told him that all I really wanted was my old job back after the babe is born. Warshire Manor is a strange old house with an even odder garden, but I have friends there, and it's where I belong."

"What did the earl say?" Sophie asked, stunned.

"He readily agreed. But he insisted on giving me an allowance in addition to my salary."

"Who will care for your baby while you're working?" Sarah asked, frowning. "Where will you live?"

"Lord Warshire said he should be able to provide suitable quarters for us—and that he might know someone to help with the child." Violet shrugged. "He's going to contact me again soon."

Sophie blinked back tears. She'd known in her heart that Reese would do the right thing, and he hadn't let her down.

She was ridiculously proud of him. Not only because of what he was doing for Violet, but because of what he was doing for himself. He was slaying his demons, dragging them out into the light. It wasn't going to be easy, fighting all the guilt and grief and pain he felt about losing his brother and Conroy. He'd have to manage those emotions for the rest of his life . . . but he'd taken the first steps.

He wasn't the same man she'd met a couple of months ago in that very spot in the tailor's shop. He was climbing out of his dark, gloomy underworld, doing his best to leave the shadows behind.

For the first time since she'd said goodbye to him, Sophie breathed a little easier. She still longed to see his warm, brown eyes, to hear his deep, gruff voice, and to lay her head against his hard, muscled chest. But at least she knew he was going to be all right—and she took some comfort from knowing she might have played a small part in initiating his healing.

"You must let me know when the babe arrives," Sophie said to Violet. "I can hardly wait to find out if you shall have a boy or a girl."

"Will you visit us?" Violet asked, her dark eyes pleading.

"I'll try," Sophie said, but she knew it would be difficult. Especially if Violet was living at Warshire Manor.

"In the meantime, I've gathered a few things I thought might come in handy."

She stood, retrieved a basket from behind the counter, and handed it to the young pregnant woman. Sophie had used the last of her money from the newspaper to buy some swaddling blankets, baby booties, bonnets, and a rattle. Violet thanked her profusely, then hugged her and Sarah before waddling out of the shop.

Sarah remained behind, helping Sophie wash a few dishes, straighten the furniture, and set the tailor's shop to rights. But when the young widow glanced at the clock and realized it was almost eleven o'clock, she clucked her tongue and scooped up her shawl. "I had better go before my sister thinks I've left London on a holiday."

"Take care of yourself and your sweet girls." Sophie handed her a few wrapped packages that contained dolls for the girls and a pretty hair comb that she'd known would look lovely in Sarah's auburn curls.

They clung to each other for a few seconds, and then Sarah pressed a kiss to her cheek and dashed out the door, into the night.

Sophie took one last turn about the deserted shop, so full of memories. It was where she'd prepared valerian-root tea for Reese and where they'd wagered buttons on a game of vingt-et-un. It was where she'd watched him sleep and where she'd started to give him her heart.

And she was never coming back.

She swallowed the walnut-sized lump in her throat and gathered all her things—her reticule and bonnet, the tu-lips, and the journal Sarah had given her. She turned down all the lanterns and was about to blow out the last candle on the counter—then paused.

Next to the candlestick sat the little potted ivy plant that had been brown and sickly on her first visit to the shop.

Now boasting four-foot trailing stems and thick green foliage, it made her think of Reese's transformation. And she wanted it.

Deciding he wouldn't mind, she grabbed the clay pot, juggling it with the other items in her arms, and blew out the candle. She made her way to the door, locked it behind her, and slipped into the dark alley, walking briskly toward the spot one block over where she normally hailed a hackney to Fiona's house. Only, tonight, she was going home so that she'd be well rested for her engagement ball tomorrow night.

She was thinking of the ball and all she needed to do the next day as she rounded the corner—and ran directly into a tall man walking in the opposite direction. She slammed into his chest, and the impact momentarily knocked the wind out of her, but she managed to remain upright. She blinked up at the man, irrationally hopeful that she'd see Reese's chiseled cheekbones and full lips.

But the man was a stranger—an older gentleman with graying hair and distinct scowl lines bracketing his mouth. "Forgive me," he said with a haughty glare. "Are you all right?"

Not trusting herself to speak, Sophie nodded vigorously and averted her gaze. "Mmm-hmm," she mumbled, before striding away as fast as her legs would carry her.

"Wait, miss!" the man shouted behind her, but Sophie kept her head down and refused to stop running, even when she heard him call out a second time. She didn't think that the stranger had gotten a good look at her face, and she certainly didn't want to provide him with another opportunity to identify her or, worse, inquire as to what she'd been doing. So she sprinted two blocks before hailing a cab. Her chest heaved as she scrambled into the coach and slammed the door. She told herself she was safe, but all the way home, her heart pounded as though Cerberus was chasing her, his huge canines gnashing at her heels.

She didn't breathe easy again until she'd reached her bedchamber and closed the door behind her. She washed her face, dressed in her nightgown and climbed into her bed, thinking back on the evening. Despite the frightening encounter in the alley, all had gone well.

Closing her eyes and nestling her cheek against her pillow, she tried to soothe herself with thoughts of the waterfall and the swing and the feel of Reese's lips on hers. She'd almost drifted off when an icy-cold finger traced a terrifyingly chilling path down her spine.

Sweet Jesus. The journal.

She bolted upright and leaped out of her bed, praying her suspicion was wrong. She grasped at each of the items she'd left on top of her bureau. Her reticule, bonnet, the potted ivy plant, and the tulips that she'd popped into a vase were all there.

But the journal that Sarah had given her was *not*.

Oh no. *No, no, no.* Her gut sank and she started yanking open drawers, rifling through gloves and petticoats and stockings. Maybe she'd stowed the book among her clothes earlier, worried that her mother or sister might discover it. But the journal wasn't in her bureau.

Panic rising in her chest, she dashed to her desk and then to her armoire, searching every corner of her bedchamber.

God help her. The journal—the very sweet, thoughtful, and *highly* incriminating journal—was nowhere to be found.

A scream began to rise in her throat, and she clamped a hand over her mouth to stifle it.

She must have dropped the book when she'd collided with the stranger.

And now, the most closely held secrets of the Debutante Underground—including the names of every one of its members—had been exposed for all of London to see.

Chapter 32

Reese swiped a sleeve across his brow as he walked up his drive. He'd spent the morning inspecting a large cottage on the edge of his property. His great-aunt had once lived in the charming but now-neglected house, which had been shuttered two decades ago when she'd died.

In his pocket, he had a list of improvements needed to make the cottage habitable, including repairs to the thatched roof, a fresh coat of paint inside and out, and a thorough top-to-bottom scrubbing. But the house had good bones—plenty of windows, spacious rooms, a yard with plenty of sturdy trees for climbing and lots of open space for running.

Perfect for what he had in mind.

Besides, he needed another project. Now that the garden had been restored to its former glory, he required something to occupy him. Something all-consuming, so that he wouldn't think about Sophie and the gaping hole she'd left in his heart.

He trudged along the gravel drive, squinting at the manor house as it came into view. It almost looked as though there were a coach-and-four parked in front of the entrance. He held a hand to his brow, shielding his eyes from the sun's glare, and sure enough, it appeared he had a visitor.

He immediately thought of Sophie. Maybe she'd decided to call off the engagement and cancel tonight's ball. Maybe she was upset and needed someone to talk to.

He started walking faster and faster until he was jogging, and he didn't stop until he was sprinting up the steps to his front door, where his butler, Thomas, was waiting. "There you are, my lord," he said, jowls wagging nervously. Clearly, the staff had become unaccustomed to visitors of any sort.

"Who's here?" Reese said, handing his hat to the older man. "I didn't recognize the coach." But he still hoped against hope it was Sophie's.

"It's a gentleman."

Reese deflated. He was on the verge of asking Thomas to send the visitor away when the butler added, "Lord Singleton."

Shit. Reese froze. He couldn't think of a single reason that the marquess would want to see him. They'd never even been formally introduced, and, as far as Reese knew, the only thing that they had in common was . . . well, Sophie.

"Where is he?" Reese asked.

"In the drawing room," Thomas intoned. "I informed him that you were out and asked if he'd like to leave his card, but he insisted on waiting." The butler shuffled his feet nervously. "He seemed rather agitated."

"Did he?" Reese said, his jaw twitching. If Singleton had somehow found out about him and Sophie, he might have come to Warshire Manor to challenge Reese to a duel. If so, Reese was more than happy to meet him at dawn.

As long as Sophie was not the object of the marquess's anger. As long as she was safe.

"Shall I send for tea?" Thomas asked.

"Thank you, but that's not necessary," Reese said. "The marquess and I don't have much to say to each other. He won't be staying long."

Reese strode up the stairs and into the drawing room, where he found his guest sitting on a long sofa, tapping his knee, and scowling at nothing in particular.

"Singleton," Reese said, keeping his tone low and even, "to what do I owe the pleasure?"

The marquess stood and faced Reese, chest to chest, while each man silently took the measure of the other. Reese had to concede that Singleton was an inch taller and twice as polished, from the obviously coiffed hair on his head to the unnatural shine of his boots. "Warshire," the marquess said at last, extending a hand. "How do you do?"

Reese tried to hide his surprise. Singleton wasn't stewing with the fury of a man looking for a fight. He was acting rather . . . civil. Reese decided to play along. "Well enough. Can I interest you in a brandy?"

The marquess gave a grateful nod, so Reese strolled to the sideboard and poured a snifter for each of them while Singleton started to pace. When Reese handed him a glass, the marquess tossed it back, emptying it in one swallow. He carefully set the snifter on a table and pulled on the sleeves of his jacket before speaking. "I've recently learned that some distasteful business is being conducted out of a building that you own."

Reese arched a brow. "And what building might that be?" he drawled.

"I believe it used to be a gentleman's shop of some sort. I checked the property records earlier, and apparently it belongs to you."

The hairs on Reese's arms stood on end. "I'm vaguely

aware of the vacant building," he lied. "I can assure you that no one is currently using it."

"I have reason to believe otherwise," Singleton said. "My uncle was fond of the old shop and happened to be walking by it late last night when he saw a light coming from the windows. He thought it was odd, so he stopped to investigate."

Holy hell. Reese didn't know exactly what Sophie did at the tailor's shop on Friday nights, but he did know two things. First, it was important to her. And second, it was imperative that no one discovered what she was doing.

Reese flashed a cajoling, conspiratorial grin. "By any chance was your uncle coming from the pub after a long night of drinking?"

The marquess frowned. "No."

"My building is empty," Reese said firmly. "But then, many of the shop fronts look similar. I'm sorry to inform you that your uncle is mistaken."

Singleton pursed his lips and slowly shook his head. "I'm sorry to inform *you*," he countered, "that your property is being used—perhaps without your knowledge—for nefarious purposes."

Reese chuckled, couldn't help it. The thought of Sophie involved with anything nefarious was ludicrous. Still, he'd have to warn her at the first available opportunity that the shop was no longer a safe place for her to conduct her meetings.

"This is no laughing matter, I assure you," Singleton said, clearly affronted. "I have good cause to believe that your building is the headquarters of a highly radical, subversive group—an organization known as the Debutante Underground."

Reese spewed his mouthful of brandy halfway across the drawing room. "I beg your pardon," he said, cocking one ear toward the marquess. "Did you say the *Debutante Underground*?"

Singleton lifted his impeccably clean-shaven chin. "I did," he said imperiously. "Apparently, that's the name given to devotees of The Debutante's Revenge."

Reese arched a sardonic brow. "And what, exactly, is The Debutante's Revenge?"

The marquess clucked his tongue. "Been living under a rock, have you?"

"Something like that," Reese said, unapologetic.

"It's a weekly column in the *London Hearsay*," Singleton explained. "And the authoress's latest installment is her most controversial yet."

"How so?" Reese asked, not bothering to hide his skepticism.

"It encourages the use of witchcraft to shrink a man's . . ."—the marquess swallowed, clearly uncomfortable—". . . manly parts."

Reese barked a laugh, grateful he hadn't been drinking this time. "Don't tell me you're worried, Singleton."

"Laugh all you want," the marquess said. "But the authoress and her followers grow bolder and more devious by the day." With that, he tossed a folded copy of the *London Hearsay* onto Reese's lap.

Deciding he'd humor Singleton, Reese picked up the newspaper and glanced at the large sketch accompanying the column. His eyes were immediately drawn to the mask-wearing woman who held the flowering vine in her palm. Though most of her face was hidden, he knew deep in his bones that the woman was Sophie. Somehow, the artist had managed to capture her natural grace, innate kindness, and quiet confidence—all the things he loved about her.

He took a minute to read the accompanying column,

doing his best not to smile. When he'd finished, he glared at Singleton. "I don't think the author presents a danger to society. And this column doesn't say anything about casting spells or shrinking cocks."

"Not explicitly," the marquess conceded. "But I think it's fair to say that the threat is implied."

"Personally, I see nothing objectionable here." Reese crisply slapped the paper on the table, hoping to signal the end of the conversation. "Even if I did, I don't know what you expect me to do. I've already told you that no illicit meetings are taking place in my building."

"I wouldn't be so sure," Singleton said ominously. He reached into his jacket and pulled out a small, leather-bound book. "My uncle bumped into a woman outside of your abandoned shop, and she dropped this in the alley."

Reese shrugged and leaned back in his chair. "It looks like a journal. Don't tell me you object to women keeping journals."

"Not as a rule, no," Singleton said, oblivious to Reese's sarcasm. "But there's one name that is written in here again and again, and it may refer to someone who is . . . rather close to me."

An odd tingling stole across Reese's neck. "Perhaps you should take the matter up with that person."

"I am hoping it's merely a coincidence," the marquess confessed. "Only given names are written in the journal, and this one is not terribly uncommon."

Reese stared at the book in Singleton's hand, fairly certain that it belonged to Sophie—and that she would *not* want her fiancé to have it. Reese was tempted to snatch it away from the marquess and light it on fire, but even he could tell the situation called for subtlety.

And a little finesse.

"I'll tell you what," Reese began, pretending concern.

"I will stop by the shop myself later today and check that the locks are secure. If there's any sign that the property has been disturbed or any clues that would lead me to believe a clandestine meeting has taken place there, I shall inform you at once. Perhaps we can uncover the mastermind behind this plot to emasculate the men of London."

"I would appreciate that." Singleton exhaled as though he was relieved to have finally found an ally. "I'm hosting a ball tonight," he said. "You should put in an appearance."

At Sophie's engagement ball? He'd rather be chained to a rock and have his liver eaten by an irate eagle. "Thanks, but I do my best to avoid balls and social engagements in general." Reese leaned forward, propping his elbows on his knees. "May be so bold as to make a suggestion?"

The marquess nodded warily. "Of course."

"I would not discuss your suspicions or share the contents of the journal with anyone else—not until we're able to gather conclusive evidence. If the women realize that we're close to uncovering their scheme, they'll simply go, well, farther underground. Besides, we don't want to falsely charge anyone—especially the person who is close to you."

"True, true," Singleton said, frowning. "Although time is of the essence."

"I feel certain we'll get to the bottom of the matter quickly," Reese assured him. "Maybe even before tonight."

"That would be helpful." The marquess cast a distasteful look at the journal, then tucked it back into his jacket pocket. He stood and shook Reese's hand. "Thank you, Warshire."

Reese nodded and walked with him as he shuffled out of the room. "Glad to be of assistance."

Halfway to the door, the marquess froze, his boots

nailed to the floor. "One more thing," he said, turning to Reese. "Would you happen to know a woman with the first name Sophie? A cousin or other family member, perhaps? Maybe even a member of your staff?"

Reese kept his face impassive, paused for several seconds, then shook his head. "It's hardly an unusual name, but no. I'm afraid I don't have much family, and I'm not aware of anyone on my staff who goes by Sophie. Why do you ask?"

Singleton pressed his lips into a thin line. "Let's just say that the name appears quite often in here." He tapped the journal in his chest pocket. "I'd wager that finding this particular Sophie is the key to unlocking all the secrets of the Debutante Underground—and putting an end to its twisted sorcery."

Shit. Reese scrambled for something, anything, to plant a seed of doubt in Singleton's feeble mind. Shrugging, he said, "I suspect that an organization as devious as this one could use code names to protect their identities."

"Perhaps," the marquess mused, his expression grim. "I truly hope that is the case."

As the marquess stalked from the room, Reese dragged a hand down his face. He needed to warn Sophie before her engagement ball. And, if at all possible, he needed to get her journal back.

Chapter 33

"We're going to your engagement ball, not a funeral." Mary tugged on her pale yellow kidskin gloves and checked her reflection in the mirror of Sophie's vanity. "You might at least pretend to be happy."

"I know," Sophie said, tamping down an unseemly but potent wave of resentment. "It's been a rather trying day." Since most of the staff were gone, Sophie and Mary had taken on many of the household chores. They were exhausted before they even began ironing their gowns, styling their hair, and dressing each other.

Besides, Sophie was saving all her pretending for tonight's ball. When Lord Singleton—that is, Charles—announced their engagement at midnight, she would have to play the part of a delighted bride-to-be. And that was going to be exceedingly difficult, considering she was still grieving over losing Reese *and* desperately worried that her journal would fall into the wrong hands. Or any hands. Blast.

Sophie was fastening the clasp of her aquamarine necklace when Mrs. Pettigrew, their sweet and loyal housekeeper, appeared in the doorway. Upon seeing Sophie and Mary, she pressed a thin hand to her chest and gasped. "Goodness me," she said. "You two look like a pair of princesses."

It was true—they *had* turned out rather well. Mary's thick blond hair was piled on top of her head with loose ringlets framing her face. Dressed in white silk shot through with gold thread, she looked as though she should have been the belle of the ball.

Sophie had pulled her hair to one side, letting the long curls spill over her shoulder. She'd settled on a pale green silk gown embroidered with dark green vines because Fiona and Lily had once said it made her resemble the goddess of spring, and if ever she'd needed the courage and confidence of a goddess, tonight was the time.

But her favorite accessory was the crown of white silk flowers she'd woven into her hair. They weren't asphodels, but they made her feel as though Reese was with her. And they reminded her of the night when he'd pronounced her the queen of all she surveyed.

Sophie cast the housekeeper a grateful smile. "Thank you, Mrs. Pettigrew. And thank you for all your help today."

"It's my pleasure, Miss Sophie." The housekeeper beamed. "To think you'll soon be a marchioness!"

"Yes," Sophie replied, feeling herself wilt.

"Well, then," Mrs. Pettigrew said, "there's no time to dally. I just left your mother and father downstairs; they said they'll wait for you in the coach."

"We should go," Mary said forlornly—as though *she* were the lamb that had been sacrificed on the family altar, when in truth, the only thing she'd lost was a night at home reading her beloved books.

Sophie grabbed her reticule and shrugged to herself. She'd already made her choices, and wishing things were different couldn't make it so. Neither could blaming her sister, for it wasn't Mary's fault that she'd been so sheltered. "I'm ready," she said, striding out of the bedchamber.

Mary followed on her heels as they glided through the hallway, down the staircase, and into the foyer, where Sophie stopped in her tracks. The silver tray on the side table held a single envelope—and it was addressed to her.

"I wonder when this arrived," Sophie said. A shiver skittered down her spine as she picked it up and examined the outside, which simply read: *Miss S. Kendall.*

Mary winced guiltily. "I'm sorry, Soph. A footman dropped it off a couple of hours ago. I happened to answer the door and, in the rush to prepare for the ball, I forgot to mention it."

"That's all right," Sophie said breezily. "It's probably from Fiona or Lily. Why don't you head out to the coach and tell Mama and Papa I'll be along momentarily?"

Mary bobbed her head and hurried outside, leaving Sophie alone in the foyer. She had a sinking feeling that the letter had something to do with her journal, and the possibility that someone might use it to expose and eviscerate the Debutante Underground made her gut clench. Hands trembling, she opened the letter.

> *Dear Sophie,*
> *I must talk with you. I'll be at the shop between*
> *four and seven o'clock. Meet me there if you can.*
> *Make certain no one follows you.*
>
> *R.*

Oh no. Reese needed her, had waited for her. She detected the urgency in his words, but she'd missed the chance to see him, and now she didn't even have time to pen him a quick note.

She wished she had some inkling of what he wished to

discuss. He'd known that her engagement was going to be announced at the ball tonight, and she couldn't help but wonder if he wanted to try and dissuade her from going forward with it.

If that was the case, it was best that she hadn't met him. Because where Reese was concerned, she was weak. She'd thought that once she'd said goodbye to him, she'd feel a sense of finality and peace. Instead, she missed everything about him, from his dark allure to his quiet thoughtfulness to his gruff charm. If she'd met him earlier that afternoon, and he'd begged her to run away with him to Gretna Green, well . . . she wouldn't have been able to resist him.

She tucked the letter into her reticule and pressed a palm to her unsettled belly. As she walked out of the house and strode down the pavement to the coach, she decided there was no way she could contact Reese tonight. Tomorrow, she'd write to him and apologize for not meeting him. By then, the news of her engagement would be on everyone's lips, and her stubborn heart might finally give up on its hopelessly naïve notions.

The fairy tales had been wrong.

Love *didn't* always win.

Sophie, Mary, Mama, and Papa glided into Lord Singleton's ballroom, carried along with a stream of animated guests who exclaimed over the ballroom's shimmering silk wall hangings, the abundant, fragrant white roses, and the brilliantly lit crystal chandeliers. Music floated up to the high coffered ceilings, and bubbly champagne flowed freely on the silver trays of efficient footmen.

Clearly, Lord Singleton had spared no expense, and the crowd already buzzed with whispers that the marquess would make a special announcement at midnight. Sophie painted on a smile as she approached him, extending her hand. He let his gaze wash over her, his expression appreciative . . . but also slightly wary.

"You're looking positively lovely, Miss Kendall," he said, bowing over her hand.

"Thank you, my lord." Looking around the dazzling ballroom, she said, "You've outdone yourself. It's beautiful." She couldn't shake the feeling that they were two strangers—mere acquaintances who were about to bind themselves together for eternity.

"I'm pleased you like it." Leaning closer to her ear, he whispered, "Forgive me for not claiming you for the first set. If I did, I'm afraid everyone would guess our exciting news—and I would rather prolong the suspense."

"I understand," Sophie said, grateful that she wouldn't be the subject of speculation all night long. Perhaps she'd even have the chance to talk privately with Fiona and Lily—and tell them the troubling news about her lost journal.

Charles proceeded to greet Mama with a polite bow, Papa with a bracing slap on the shoulder, and Mary with a kiss to her hand. Mary blushed furiously, and as they moved toward the refreshment table, Mama clucked her tongue. "If you attended more balls, Mary, you would not become so easily flustered."

Papa grunted his agreement and reached for a glass of champagne, but Mama deftly steered him in the opposite direction. "Ah, I see the Hartleys are here. I haven't spoken to them in an age. Let us go and pay our respects."

Sophie walked behind her parents, nodding greetings to various acquaintances and craning her neck in search of Fiona's fiery auburn hair or Lily's gleaming dark curls. She didn't see either of her friends or their dashing husbands, but one gentleman in the crowd *did* catch her eye.

He was older—perhaps sixty years or so—and his halting, uneven gait was oddly familiar. She waited for him to turn, so she'd have a better view of his face, and when he did, her blood turned to ice. The thin, drawn lips, the deep crevices in his cheeks—they belonged to the man she'd collided with in the alley. The man who must have her journal.

Terrified that he'd recognize her, she quickly spun, then swayed on her feet. "Sophie," Mama said, her voice laced with worry. "Are you feeling well?"

"Just a little dizzy. I think I'll head to the terrace for some fresh air."

Before her mother could object—or worse, send Mary with her—Sophie made a dash for the French doors at the back of the ballroom. She didn't think the man had seen her, but she intended to stay as far away from him as possible.

She rushed onto the empty flagstone terrace, leaned her back against a brick pillar, and closed her eyes, inhaling lungfuls of air. It felt as though her carefully constructed plan to save her family from financial ruin was teetering, on the brink of crumbling around her. If her involvement in the Debutante Underground became known, Charles would no longer wish to marry her. He'd demand that Papa repay his loans, and her father would go to debtors' prison, leaving Mama distraught and all of them destitute.

To make matters worse, her role in the scandal of the season would ensure that they were barred from proper drawing rooms and cast out of polite society. Because if there was one thing the ton loved more than reading The Debutante's Revenge, it was having the front-row seat at a spectacularly disastrous fall from grace.

Oh God. She snapped open her fan and waved it vigorously, as if her problems were persistent puffs of smoke that could be carried away with a good, stiff breeze.

"Sophie." The voice, gravelly and deep, stopped her fan midwave. Unless she was now hearing things—which was quite possible given her current state—she knew that voice. She knew that *man*.

She turned and looked out at the small garden beyond the terrace. "Reese?" she whispered.

He emerged from behind a tall boxwood several yards away. Dressed in a dark evening jacket and buckskin trousers, he stood in the moonlight like a mysterious and powerful god who'd decided to spend an evening in the amusing world of mortals.

"What are you doing here?" she asked.

"There's something you need to know," he said. "But we can't discuss it here. Will you come with me?"

She wanted to say that she'd go with him anywhere. Anytime. "I can't disappear for long," she said regretfully. "I'll be missed."

He nodded, his expression unreadable. "This way."

She walked toward him, and he reached for her hand, lacing his fingers through hers as though it were the most natural thing in the world. He led her down a pebbled path and behind a row of hedges, seemingly unaware that the simple pressure of his palm on hers made her belly turn cartwheels.

They sat on a secluded stone bench, their hands still joined and their knees a scant inch apart. Even in the relative darkness, she could see the heat and longing in his eyes.

"You're beautiful," he said reverently. With a knee-weakening smile he added, "You should wear flower crowns every day."

Swallowing the lump in her throat, she said, "I'm sorry

that I didn't meet you earlier. I received your message too late."

"It's all right. I wouldn't have written to you if it wasn't urgent." His handsome face turned serious, and an ominous chill stole over her skin. "Singleton visited me at the manor house this morning."

Panic swirled in her chest like a freshly spawned tornado. "What? Why would he do that?"

"His uncle found a journal outside the tailor's shop. Singleton thought I might know who it belonged to."

"Oh no," she said, shaking her head. "Please tell me that he doesn't have my journal."

Reese winced. "I'm afraid he does. He said that it contains the first names of all the women who are part of a secret society called the Debutante Underground."

"Dear God." Her whole body started to shake, and he gave her hand a reassuring squeeze.

"He suspects that the journal may be yours, but he has no proof. If he asks you about it tonight, I suggest you deny any knowledge of it. In the meantime, I'm going to steal it back."

A seed of hope sprouted in the arid, cracked earth of her heart. "You'd do that?"

He looked at her as if she was mad. "I'd do anything for you."

Warmth flooded her limbs. "But . . . how? Do you even know where it is?"

"No," he said, frowning. "But I'm going to try his study first. If it's not there, I'll sneak into his bedchamber. If necessary, I'll search the house, room by room, until I find it."

"What if someone discovers you sneaking around?" she said. "It would look very bad."

"I don't plan to get caught," he said with a shrug. "Even if I did, I would never implicate you."

"Oh, Reese," she said, touched by his desire to protect her. "I got myself into this dilemma. It's not fair that you should risk everything to get me out of it."

"This isn't about blame or fairness." He flashed a grin that melted her insides. "I love you. If you're in trouble, then I'm always going to want to help."

"Even if I'm engaged or married to someone else?" she asked weakly.

He flinched at that, then looked earnestly into her eyes. "Always means always. I know I can't have you and that, after tonight, I might never see you again. But that won't change the way I feel about you, Soph."

"I . . ." She wanted to blurt out everything in her heart. To tell him she loved him too and that she'd forever treasure the nights they'd spent together. But Reese was already gutted, and revealing her feelings at this point would only be twisting the knife. "I don't deserve such kindness."

"I disagree." He lifted her hand and pressed a tender, lingering kiss to the back. "You deserve the world."

Before she could properly catch her breath, he released her hand and stood. "I should go. Remember, you don't need to admit anything to Singleton." He paused for a moment, then added, "He thinks that the Debutante Underground is a radical, subversive organization that threatens the fabric of society."

"He said that?" Her blood heated with a mix of rage and fear.

"Something like that." He shoved his hands in his pockets and took a step toward the house, his dark eyes full of regret. "Good luck tonight."

"You too," she breathed. "And thank you."

He nodded, turned, and started up the path, but she called out, "Reese, wait."

When he spun to face her, she hesitated, then voiced the question she couldn't resist asking. "What do *you* think of the Debutante Underground?"

He tilted his head, thoughtful, then said, "I don't know much about it, obviously, but if priggish, narrow-minded people take offense, I'd say that's a sure sign you're doing something important and worthwhile."

With that, he strode off, leaving her alone and more certain than ever that she'd given up the one man who could have been her true partner—and true love.

Chapter 34

At the sound of the doorknob jiggling, Reese dove behind the sofa in Singleton's drawing room and held his breath.

The door creaked as it swung on its hinges, and footsteps shuffled across the hardwood floor. If he had to guess, the utilitarian, brown shoes belonged to a maid, and she hummed softly to herself as she moved about the room.

Reese hoped she didn't walk to his side of the sofa, but if she did, he was prepared to play the part of a ball guest who'd drunk too much and gone in search of a quiet spot where he could sleep off his excesses.

He'd spent the last hour furtively searching Singleton's study and bedchamber, but after scouring every shelf, drawer, and closet in both rooms, he still hadn't found the journal. He'd reasoned that the marquess might have spent time in the drawing room before the ball—and that he might have left the journal out on a table or even stowed it in the desk drawer.

But a thorough check of the room had yielded no sign of it, and now doubts were creeping into Reese's mind. What if Singleton had hidden the journal in a locked drawer or safe? What if he'd decided to keep it with him, and it was tucked inside the pocket of his bloody evening jacket right now?

Frustrated, he grabbed a fistful of hair and cursed under his breath.

"Is someone there?" the maid called out, her voice threaded with alarm.

Damn it. He quickly debated whether to reveal himself now or to pretend to be passed out. Heaving a sigh, he rose on his haunches and—

"Where have you been, lass?" asked an older female in a scolding tone. "The mistress has been asking for her lorgnette. Can ye not find it?"

"Ah, here it is," the young maid replied, "hiding beneath a cushion."

Reese went still as a statue as she leaned over the sofa.

"Hurry along, then." The older woman clucked her tongue. "Lady S. isn't a patient sort."

He waited until he heard the door click shut behind them, then sprang to his feet. The diary wasn't there in the drawing room—and he was running out of time. To make good on his promise to Sophie, he needed to find out exactly where Singleton had hidden her journal, and soon.

Which meant Reese would have to put in an appearance at the ball—his first in approximately three years. Even worse, he'd have to dance.

For several minutes after Reese left Sophie in the garden, she remained sitting on the bench, perilously close to tears. She'd thought she could set aside her own feelings and desires to help her family. Moreover, she'd thought that she *should*—that it was the noble and selfless thing to do.

But now she knew differently. Binding herself to Lord Singleton wouldn't save her family. Only love could do that.

Papa needed to find the strength and support necessary to curb his drinking.

Mama needed to find the backbone to hold Papa accountable for his behavior.

And Mary—well, Mary needed to find a reason to occasionally leave her bedchamber.

Sophie loved her family dearly, but she was not going to fix all their problems by marrying Lord Singleton. They might be granted a temporary reprieve, but, eventually, Papa would accrue more debt, Mama would continue to make excuses for him, and Mary would remain cloistered in her safe, sheltered world.

Meanwhile, Sophie would find herself chained to a man who thought that the wonderful sisterhood she'd created was dangerous and subversive. She'd wake up every morning feeling miserable, knowing she'd thrown away the rare and precious gift that Reese had given her—his unwavering love.

She stood and paced the wide pebbled garden path, trying to imagine that she was in the tailor's shop with all the familiar faces of her friends circled around her. If she could explain her dilemma to the members of the Debutante Underground and seek their advice, what would they say?

She pictured Sarah and Ivy, Violet and Abigail, and all the others . . . and she knew *precisely* what they'd tell her. To be fearless, and to follow her heart.

She knew, because it was the same advice she'd offer anyone else who asked. And now she had to find the fortitude to act upon it. She had to walk back into that ballroom and tell Lord Singleton that she couldn't marry him.

Feeling more sure of herself than she had in days, she picked up her skirts and ran toward the house. It would be difficult to tell Charles that she'd changed her mind, but she'd be doing both of them a favor in the end. And once she'd officially called off their betrothal, she couldn't wait to seek out Reese.

She dashed across the terrace, through the French doors, and into the ballroom, breathlessly searching the room for the marquess—and, almost immediately, he appeared at her side.

"There you are, Miss Kendall," he said slyly. "Would you care to dance?"

"Actually, I hoped we could talk," she said.

Lord Singleton chuckled and glanced nervously at the small group of people gathered around them. "I'm sure we can converse on the dance floor," he said.

Sophie hesitated. Now that she'd made her decision, it felt rather hypocritical to waltz with him. But she didn't wish to humiliate him either.

"Very well," she said, accepting the arm he'd offered. "But I'd like to talk with you afterward."

He gave her hand a patronizing pat and escorted her to the dance floor, where he swept her into a line of couples twirling in time to the music.

"What was it you wished to talk about, my dear?" he asked smoothly.

Sophie raised her chin so that she could meet his eyes. "I think it best to broach the subject after this set—in private."

"That could be rather difficult. I am the host of this ball, after all," he said, deftly spinning her underneath his raised arm. "And it's less than an hour till midnight, when we shall toast our engagement. Perhaps I could call on you tomorrow morning and we could have a proper conversation then."

Her heart kicked into a gallop. "This cannot wait," she said firmly.

He narrowed his eyes as, hands raised above their

heads, they moved toward each other, then apart. "I do hope you're not having second thoughts."

Blast. She hadn't wanted to tell him like this . . . but there was no help for it. "I'm afraid I am. I cannot marry you, Charles."

For several beats of the music, he said nothing; then he shrugged. "I suspect it's perfectly normal to feel anxious prior to announcing one's engagement. I'll fetch you a glass of champagne after this set. It will calm your nerves."

"I'm not suffering from a case of nerves," she whispered. "And I'm truly sorry I didn't tell you how I felt before now. I thought I could be a dutiful wife, that I could make our relationship work . . . but I can't." She glanced around to make sure no one could overhear them and blinked at a new couple on the dance floor. The woman looked like Lily and the man looked like . . . heavens, Sophie clearly needed spectacles because the man looked like *Reese*.

Charles steered her away to a less crowded spot and leaned toward her ear. "I think I know what this is about."

Sophie gulped. "You do?"

"You've had strange ideas put into your head by that awful column. And the Debutante Underground."

Sweet Jesus. She looked directly into his eyes. "I don't know what you're talking about."

"I think you do," he said, his tone menacing. "And I have the proof right here." He released her waist so that he could tap his chest—where she could make out the rectangular outline of her journal.

"You're speaking in riddles, Charles," she countered, even as heat rose up her chest and neck.

"Then allow me to make myself very clear. I have invested a great deal of time, effort, and money into this arrangement—an arrangement that obviously benefits your father. We *will* announce our engagement tonight. And if you are foolish enough to cry off, not only will you be throwing your family to the lions, but you will force me to expose this secret society of yours. I'll publish the name of every last member in the *London Hearsay.*"

Oh God. The women of the Debutante Underground had placed their trust in her, and now she was letting them down. The room started to tilt and her ears began to buzz. The silk-lined walls closed in on her like the cold stone of a Newgate jail cell. The corners of her vision turned gray, and her knees wobbled.

"Please . . . let me explain," she mumbled, but her tongue was thick and uncooperative. "I—"

Bam. Before she could finish her sentence *or* properly swoon, another couple slammed into her and Charles, knocking her off her feet with a teeth-jarring jolt.

"Sophie!" called a familiar feminine voice. A soft but surprisingly strong arm circled her waist. Green eyes gazed down at her with concern. Lily propped Sophie against her side while Charles and Reese gained their footing.

"Forgive my clumsiness," Reese was saying, giving Charles a good-natured slap on the shoulder. "My dancing skills are sorely out of practice."

"I'll say." Charles scowled as he straightened his cravat.

Turning to Lily, Reese said, "Are you all right, Your Grace?"

"I am fine," Lily replied, her shrewd eyes assessing. "But I am concerned about my friend. I'm going to escort Sophie to the terrace so she can take a bit of fresh air."

"Thank you," Charles said stiffly. Turning to Sophie, he said, "Miss Kendall, I trust that you'll be feeling much improved in time for our midnight toast."

Sophie blinked back tears of frustration and rage. "I doubt that I shall, my lord."

"Please, accept my apologies," Reese said. He placed a hand over his heart as the women left the dance floor and cast Sophie a furtive, reassuring smile.

She tried to smile back but faltered. Nothing was all right. Charles had the means to destroy the reputations and lives of dozens of her friends. And the only way Sophie could protect them was to deny her own heart and marry him.

Chapter 35

Lily whisked Sophie outside and ordered her to sit on the half wall that surrounded the terrace. "Are you hurt, Soph?"

"No," she assured her friend. "I'm fine, physically."

"Good," Lily said, smiling sweetly. "Because I want to know what the bloody hell is going on, and *you* had better tell me."

"It's awful," Sophie said, hardly knowing where to begin.

"Lord Warshire is in love with you, isn't he?"

Sophie nodded. "How did you know?"

"From the moment he entered the ballroom, he couldn't take his eyes off you. It's clear he's smitten, Soph."

She felt herself blush. "I love him too. I tried to call off the engagement, but Charles found out about the Debutante Underground and is threatening to publish a list of all its members . . . unless we are married."

Lily gasped and clenched her fists. "What a cold-hearted, self-righteous, narrow-minded little—"

"There you are!" Sophie and Lily turned to see Fiona anxiously gliding across the flagstones toward them, her auburn hair gleaming in the moonlight. "I saw what happened on the dance floor. Are you both all right?"

"Yes, yes," Lily said, not bothering to hide her agitation. "But it turns out Lord Singleton is a malicious prig."

"Oh no," Fiona said. "I must admit, I much prefer Lord Warshire—even if he is a bit rough around the edges."

Sophie sniffled. "He's *all* edges. But he's also the most honorable, selfless, decent man I know."

"Speaking of Lord Warshire," Fiona drawled. "He asked me to give you a message."

Sophie leaped off the wall and clasped Fiona's hand. "What did he say?"

Fiona gave her a knowing smile. "He asked you to meet him in the library."

"When?" Her heart squeezed.

"As soon as you can slip away, I imagine."

Sophie frowned. "If my parents or sister ask where I've gone . . ."

"We'll cover for you," Lily said, making shooing motions with her hands. "Go on, now."

Sophie pressed a kiss to Lily's cheek and gave Fiona a quick, fierce hug. "I'm afraid that Charles will still be announcing our engagement tonight—but at least I'll have a chance to explain myself to Reese . . . and to say one final goodbye." She smoothed her hair behind her ears and took a fortifying breath. "Wish me luck."

Sophie skulked down the dimly lit corridor, boldly peeking into various rooms as she searched for the library. The first door opened into a masculine-looking study that smelled faintly of tobacco and leather. The second was a small parlor that emanated the scents of rosewater and tea.

The realization that this grand townhouse would soon be her home made her throat thick with sadness. There was no denying that the house was elegantly appointed and impeccably maintained, but somehow, it still felt dry and inhospitable, like arid soil where nothing beautiful could grow or flourish.

She was carefully closing the door to the parlor when she heard voices behind her, whispering. *Blast.*

She hurried to the next door, opened it, and ducked inside the dark room, relieved to see the walls were lined with shelves of books. There was no sign of Reese, however, so she moved toward one of the tall mullioned windows where moonlight shimmered between the heavy drapes.

And felt a strong, warm hand on the small of her back. "Soph."

She turned in to his chest, threw her arms around his neck, and touched her forehead to his. She wanted to tell him that she needed him like a wildflower needs rain. That she'd miss him more than sunshine in December. That she loved him with her whole heart.

But his eyes were dark and heavy lidded with desire, his hard body was pressed against hers, and his wicked mouth was tantalizingly close, making him quite difficult to resist. Impossible, really.

So she brushed her lips across his, savoring every touch, every taste. His racing heart beat against her chest, and he moaned softly into her mouth. It was a heady feeling, knowing she could affect him so. A lovely, sweet pulsing began in her core, and she melted into him. Deepened the kiss into something raw and sensual and hot.

He kissed a path down the column of her neck. Greedily caressed the curves of her breasts and bottom. Their tongues tangled, and their bodies melded.

When he grasped her hips and moved against her, she clung to his shoulders so that she wouldn't dissolve into a puddle. "Reese," she breathed. "I . . ."

"Wait," he whispered close to her ear. "I hear something."

They froze, their senses on high alert. Muffled voices came from behind the door, and the knob rattled.

Reese whisked Sophie toward a waist-high table where a large atlas was displayed. "Under here," he mouthed, swiftly pulling her beneath the table. He held her close to his side as the couple they'd heard shuffled into the room and drifted toward the far wall.

Oh God. Sophie covered her mouth with her hand. The night had started out badly and somehow turned even worse. She'd known that meeting Reese would be risky—and it seemed she'd tempted fate one time too many. She looked longingly at the library door, wondering if it was possible to make a dash for it.

As though he'd guessed the direction of her thoughts, Reese flicked a glance at the door and shook his head. He was right; leaving their hiding spot was far too dangerous at the moment.

Her stomach sank, but then he squeezed her hand and gave her an encouraging smile. If she had to be trapped under a table with someone, terrified that her family's reputation would be dashed to bits, there was no one she'd rather be trapped with than Reese. She rested her head on his shoulder and huddled close to him while they listened, waiting for their chance to escape.

She desperately hoped that the opportunity presented itself before midnight, for if she wasn't there when Lord Singleton, her family and friends, and every guest at the ball gathered to toast her engagement, it would look very bad. Indeed, everything she'd sacrificed—her happiness, her future, her one true love—would have been for naught.

"There's no need for tears," crooned a male voice across

the room—and her skin prickled with recognition. The man was *Charles*. "Come and have a drink," he said smoothly.

Sophie heard the clink of glass and the splash of liquid. "That's Lord Singleton," she whispered in Reese's ear, and he arched a dark brow in response.

"If I am honest," Charles said to his female companion, "I find your reticence quite appealing . . . and undeniably attractive. But I did not realize that you returned my feelings."

Sophie supposed that she should have felt a smidge of jealousy or anger, but all she could summon was sympathy for the poor young woman, who sobbed and mumbled incoherently.

"You mustn't despair," Charles was saying. "We shall still see each other, after all."

Sophie's body went numb—but, in truth, she was more shocked than sad.

"I chose Sophie because she'll make an excellent marchioness," Charles said—almost regretfully. "But there's no reason that you and I should deny the passion that simmers between us, even after I say my wedding vows. *Yours* are the lips I shall dream of kissing. *Yours* is the body I shall long to hold."

Charles's confession was followed by sounds of sloppy slurping, heavy breathing, and passionate grunting. Sophie valiantly fought back a wave of nausea.

Reese slipped an arm around her shoulders and pressed a kiss to her temple. "Singleton's a bastard," he said earnestly. "Break off your engagement. Marry me."

"You don't know how badly I want to," Sophie whispered. "But he's blackmailing me. My journal contains the names of every member of the Debutante Underground, and he's threatened to publish the complete list. I simply can't expose my friends. I must protect them—even if it means binding myself to him."

Reese laced his fingers through hers. "Soph, you don't need to do that."

A tear slipped down her cheek as she thought of Violet, Sarah, Ivy, and all her dear friends. "You don't understand—"

"It's a quarter to midnight," Charles said to his companion. "We must return to the ballroom for the toast. But I will be thinking of you . . . and I'll see you again soon."

"Promise me," murmured a female voice—a voice that was also disturbingly familiar. But . . . it *couldn't* be. Surely not. "Promise that you'll arrange for us to meet within the week."

"You know that I will try," he said huskily.

"Yes," the familiar voice replied. "And I suspect it is because I am willing to give you the affection that my sister does not."

What the *devil*? Sophie scrambled out from under the table, needing to witness the scene with her own eyes. There, across the room from her, her sister sat on a desk while Lord Singleton stood between her legs, which were hitched around his hips. Mary's fingers clutched the lapels of his jacket, and his hands were around her waist.

Sophie blinked to make sure that her eyes and the room's shadows hadn't conspired to play tricks on her mind, but no. Finding her voice at last, she choked out, "*Mary*?"

Chapter 36

"Bloody hell," Lord Singleton spat.

Sophie watched, dumbfounded, as he released her sister, turned, and grabbed a fistful of his hair. Meanwhile, Mary frantically pulled at the hem of her gown so that it covered her legs. Her cheeks turned red as strawberries.

Reese had emerged from beneath the table and stood behind Sophie, placing a reassuring hand at the small of her back. She searched her sister's face. "You and Lord Singleton?"

"I'm sorry," Mary said, her voice cracking. "It only happened once."

Sophie arched a brow. She'd always been able to tell when Mary was lying.

Her sister swallowed and glanced at the carpet. "Twice."

"You should have told me you cared for him," Sophie said. Then she turned to Charles. "I should think it goes without saying, but the engagement is off."

"Let's not be so hasty," he said. "Your sister and I had a dalliance. By the looks of it, you've had one with Warshire as well."

Sophie raised her chin, refusing to apologize. "Your affections are engaged elsewhere, as are mine. That's no way to begin a marriage."

Lord Singleton began to pace, rubbing his chin in agitation. "You forget, Sophie, that this was never about sentimentality or love. Besides, I've already invested quite a bit in this bargain."

"I'll find a way to repay Papa's debts," she said.

Lord Singleton snorted. "I don't see how you possibly could. He owes me a small fortune."

Reese took a step forward and folded his arms across his chest. "Send me a detailed accounting of his debts. I'll figure out a way to pay them—even if it means selling all my personal possessions."

Singleton's brows shot up. "Ah, you fancy yourself Miss Kendall's knight in shining armor," he said dryly. "How noble. But I'm afraid this arrangement is about more than money. I've spent the whole damned season courting Sophie and haven't any more time to waste. I'm eager to establish myself in society and proceed with the business of producing an heir."

Sophie shuddered. "I will not marry you. And I most certainly will not be your broodmare."

"Oh, but I think you will," Singleton drawled. "You forget that I have the means to ruin you and your friends."

Sophie's heart dropped like a stone tossed into the Thames.

Over by the desk, Mary sniffled. "What's he talking about, Sophie?"

Before she could respond, Singleton said, "I have, in my possession, a journal that details the inner workings of a radical secret society of women and list the names of all its members—some of whom may be witches."

Mary inhaled sharply. "You're connected to The Debutante's Revenge?"

Sophie's fingers went numb. "I . . . I . . ."

Reese strode toward Charles, stood toe to toe with him, and clenched his fists. "I'm afraid you're mistaken, Singleton. Miss Kendall does not own a journal."

"Your loyalty would be impressive"—Charles flashed Reese a smug smile—"if it weren't so pathetic. You've seen the journal with your own eyes, Warshire. In fact, I have it right—"

Sophie clutched the edge of the table beside her so that she wouldn't launch herself at Charles and pummel him.

The marquess patted his chest with one hand, then the other, and his pompous expression turned to panic. "What the devil? How did you—" His eyes narrowed and his nostrils flared. "The collision on the dance floor? Damn it, Warshire. You're no better than a St. Giles pickpocket."

Reese shrugged.

"I demand that you return the journal to me at once." Lord Singleton's mottled red nose was almost touching Reese's, but he didn't retreat an inch.

"I thought I was clear. There *is* no journal. And if there ever was . . ." Reese's voice trailed off, and his gaze flicked to the fireplace.

"You. Bastard." Singleton spun on his boot heel, punched the plaster wall, and moaned, cradling his limp hand against his abdomen. Mary rushed to his side, eager to play nursemaid, while Sophie did her very best to refrain from rolling her eyes.

"As luck would have it," Reese said, nonchalant, "there's an obvious solution to this dilemma—one that should be satisfactory to all of us."

"Damn it, man," Singleton cried, "it's two minutes to midnight."

Reese grinned. "Then we'd better not waste any more time."

As the grandfather clock outside the ballroom began to chime, footmen weaved through the crowd, flourishing trays of fizzy champagne. Sophie slipped into the room through the main entrance, with Mary by her side. The air buzzed with speculation about the marquess's impending toast. Most guests predicted that Lord Singleton would announce his engagement, but there was endless speculation as to who his fiancée would be.

Behind Sophie, a group of rowdy gentlemen placed wagers. Apparently, a fresh-faced debutante named Lady Arabella was the favorite, with odds of five to one. Sophie was mentioned as the dark horse; it seemed the dance floor spectacle she'd been involved in earlier had made her even more of a long shot.

"I'm so sorry, Sophie," Mary whispered.

"I know. But the blame isn't all yours. I've been keeping secrets too."

Mary nodded soberly. "Are you nervous?"

"Yes," Sophie admitted. "My heart's beating so loudly, it's a wonder you can't hear it." She craned her neck, looking for Charles and Reese, whom they'd left in the library only minutes ago.

Mary lifted her chin in the direction of the doors leading to the terrace. "There they are now." The men sauntered into the ballroom as though they'd simply stepped outside to sneak a cigar. Reese hung back while Charles smoothed his jacket and headed toward the dais where the orchestra sat, resting their instruments and awaiting the toast.

Sophie swallowed a knot the size of a goose egg. "We'd better make our way to the front." As they did, she spotted their parents near the refreshment table. Papa's glazed, bloodshot eyes could have been from too much drink, or not enough. Mama's thin, drawn lips and creased forehead betrayed her anxiousness. They all knew this was the final round of a high-stakes game, where a win would give their family peace of mind and prosperity, but a loss would mean complete ruin.

But Sophie had gambled even more—her heart, happiness, and soul.

Across the room, standing beside their dashing husbands on the perimeter of the dance floor, Fiona and Lily smiled encouragingly at Sophie. She adored them for their valiant attempts to support her, but she could see the underlying sadness in their eyes as they watched Charles step onto the dais. They'd wanted more for Sophie.

They'd wanted her to have passion and respect and love. The kind she could have had with Reese.

"If I may interrupt the festivities for a moment," Charles announced loudly, "I'd like to make a toast."

The room immediately quieted, and every head swiveled toward the handsome marquess.

"I apologize for keeping you in suspense all evening," he said with the sort of self-deprecating charm that made several ladies titter. "But I do hope you'll agree with me when I say that the happy news will have been well worth the wait. It is with great pride and pleasure that, at long last, I can officially announce my engagement to my lovely fiancée . . . Miss Kendall."

Dear God. A chorus of cheers and a smattering of applause rose above the crowd as every person in the room turned to stare at Sophie. Her limbs froze and her body turned to ice so brittle that one tap would have left her in shards on the parquet floor.

Charles cleared his throat and continued, "Miss *Mary* Kendall."

The ballroom erupted in a mix of disbelieving gasps and shocked exclamations.

Sophie thawed and gave her sister's clammy hand a reassuring squeeze. "Go to him," she whispered. "All will be well."

Mary sheepishly joined Charles and accepted the arm he offered. Her demure smile and timid behavior created a stark contrast to the passionate scene in the library, but Sophie was delighted to know that her normally reserved sister had a wild side. Who knew? Perhaps she'd even join the Debutante Underground one day.

All around Sophie, the ballroom exploded in a cacophony of clinking glasses, effusive cheers, and excited murmurs. As well-wishers swarmed the dais, she hurried to her parents, who stood just outside the throng, each wearing the distinctly confused expression of one who bit into a tart thinking it was raspberry only to discover that it was, in fact, marmalade.

Mama reached for Sophie's hand, patting it consolingly. "I don't understand what's happened, my dear, but I'm certain your father will set it to rights."

Papa grunted. "I'll not let Singleton toss you aside like this," he said firmly. "Even if it *is* for my other daughter. It isn't right."

Sophie hugged each of her parents in turn, warmed by their devotion. "Everything is exactly as it should be," she assured them. "Mary cares for Lord Singleton and is delighted by the arrangement. He's warmed to the idea as well. I think they're going to be very happy together."

"But what about you?" Mama asked. "This must have come as quite a shock. I do hope you're not heartbroken."

"Not at all," Sophie said. She glanced about the room, hoping to catch a glimpse of Reese, but he seemed to have disappeared. "Indeed, my heart is more hopeful than it's been in a very long time. Mary and I will explain more tomorrow. For now, I suggest you celebrate the engagement as though you'd expected this pairing all along."

Mama cast an assessing gaze at Mary and Charles as they stood on the dais, graciously accepting congratulations from well-wishers. "I didn't think our Mary had it in her," Mama mused, tilting her head. "But now that I see them together, I must admit they make a rather striking couple."

"They do," Sophie agreed.

"Ah, Fiona and Lily are coming this way," Mama said. "They'll know just how to cheer you up."

Sophie opened her mouth to say that she wasn't sad in the least, but thought better of it and simply nodded. "Will you both excuse me?" she asked her parents, heading toward her friends. Lily and Fiona each grabbed one of her elbows and whisked her to a quiet corner of the ballroom.

"Would you like to tell us what is going on?" Lily asked in a stage whisper, her green eyes flashing with curiosity. "How did Mary . . . ?"

"It's a rather long story, but suffice it to say that Mary's pleased with the outcome."

Fiona rubbed Sophie's arm soothingly. "What about you?"

"I'm delighted that I no longer have to marry Charles," she admitted. "In fact, I'd turn cartwheels across the room right now if it wouldn't make me look quite mad."

Lily chuckled, then bit her lower lip. "What about the journal? Is Charles still threatening to expose the Debutante Underground?"

Sophie shook her head. "When we collided on the dance floor earlier, Reese managed to reach into Charles's jacket and recover my journal. He destroyed it before Charles realized it was missing from his pocket."

"Thank heaven," Fiona said, sweeping an auburn curl behind one ear. "Although I'm sad to hear your journal is gone."

"It is a shame. But considering the alternative . . ." Sophie suppressed a shudder.

Lily shot her a saucy smile. "So, after tonight's events we can conclude that your Reese is devastatingly handsome, terribly heroic, *and* wickedly good with his hands. I wonder where the mysterious earl is now?"

Sophie wondered the same thing. "To say that he's not particularly fond of balls would be a gross understatement. Now that disaster has been averted, I suspect he's on his way back to Warshire Manor," she said, trying to mask her disappointment.

"Good evening, ladies."

Reese's voice, deep and gravelly, sent a delightful shiver over her skin, and she whirled to face him. She wanted to throw her arms around his neck and kiss him till the world around them faded away. But instead, she properly introduced him to her friends, who smiled warmly, immediately accepting him into their tight circle.

"Gray introduced us a bit earlier," Fiona said. "We're so happy that all has ended well."

Reese surreptitiously reached for Sophie's hand and laced his fingers through hers. "There are still a few matters to be resolved," he said. To Sophie, "Is there any chance you could slip away tonight?"

The moment Sophie gazed into his heavy-lidded eyes, she felt herself drowning in a sea of longing and love. "I might be able to arrange that," she breathed.

"Good." His voice vibrated through her, and every nerve ending in her body came alive. "I'll be outside in my coach, waiting for you." He pressed a lingering, sensual kiss to the back of her hand, then bowed and strode away, leaving all three women fanning themselves. Vigorously.

"Well," Lily said, a bit breathless. "I can't imagine what you're waiting for, Soph."

She watched Reese walk away, and the sight of his broad shoulders and taut backside made her insides flutter. "Neither can I." She shot her friends a mischievous grin. "But I might need a bit of help."

Chapter 37

Reese sat in his coach, rapidly tapping the heel of his boot against the floor in an effort to expel his excess energy. While he waited for Sophie, he mentally rehearsed all the things he wanted to say to her. Wondered if she'd ever realize just how much his chest ached every time he looked at her.

She emerged from Singleton's house a few minutes later, the starlight gilding her blond hair and illuminating her delicate features. His heart pounded with anticipation as he hopped out of the cab, met her on the pavement, and quickly helped her step into the coach.

He closed the door and turned to drink in the sight of her face. "Thank God you're here," he breathed, and before the words were even out of his mouth, she'd climbed onto his lap, her knees straddling him.

As the coach began rolling over the cobblestone streets, their mouths collided in a raw, ravenous kiss. His teeth tugged at her bottom lip, her nails dug into his shoulders. He speared his fingers into her hair and grabbed a fistful of silken strands. She ground her hips against his cock, and he thrust back.

"Reese," she murmured against his neck, "I need you. I need this."

Sweet Jesus. He'd never made love in a moving coach before. Or a stationary one, for that matter. But he was *definitely* up for the challenge—as soon as they resolved one small matter.

Cupping her cheeks in his hands, he looked deep into her eyes. "I need you too," he said raggedly. "I was trapped in a prison of grief and guilt, sentenced to reliving the torture over and over again. But you walked into my godforsaken life, lighting it up like fireworks. Challenging everything I thought I knew. Reminding me of how it feels to be happy."

She licked her plump, kiss-swollen lips. "You've changed me too. I've been living so much of my life in secret—the Debutante Underground, all the nights I spent with you—and I don't want to hide those parts of myself anymore. I don't want to apologize for what I believe in or who I love."

"I'm glad to hear that." He tipped his forehead to hers and ran his hands over the curves of her hips, pulling her closer. "Because I love you, Sophie Kendall. I love your tender heart and your bold spirit. I love the way you nurture and heal everything you touch. And I love that one smile from you can make the darkest night feel like Christmas morning."

"Oh, Reese," she breathed. "I love you too."

"Good," he said, brushing his lips over hers. "Because I have something to ask you, and I'm desperately hoping that the third time will be the charm."

"What do you mean?" She leisurely raked a hand through his hair, making him want to purr like a cat.

"I asked you once when we were sitting on the swing in my garden and another time when we were hiding beneath a table." He traced the low neckline of her gown with a fingertip. "Both times I was refused."

"Let me guess," she teased. "You'd like me to make a list of improvements to your garden?"

He tugged one sleeve off her shoulder. "No."

"Hmm," she mused. "You'd like me to brew you a pot of tea."

He slid off the other sleeve. "No."

She lightly caressed the back of his neck, driving him wild. "Then what do you wish to ask me?"

"I want to know if you'll marry me," he said earnestly. "If you'll let me spend the rest of my days loving you and caring for you. Doing my damnedest to make you smile."

"Yes." Her eyes welled as she nodded. "Yes, I'll marry you. Nothing in the world would make me happier, Reese."

"Nothing?" He grinned and tugged on the laces at the back of her ball gown.

Her gaze turned soft and sultry. "Well, maybe *some-thing*."

He loosened her gown and corset and freed her breasts, staring shamelessly as they bounced each time the coach hit a bump in the road. He teased the rosy tips with his tongue, alternately nibbling and suckling her till she arched her back and moaned with pleasure.

He slid a hand beneath her gown and up the back of her thighs. Squeezed her luscious bottom. Caressed the slick heat between her legs. The temperature rose and the coach windows fogged over. Only the two of them existed, and they were both panting, dizzy with desire.

With nimble fingers, she unbuttoned his trousers and stroked the long, hard length of him. "I have missed you," she said. "I have dreamed of this—of you—every night."

He gasped as she positioned his cock at her entrance and writhed against him. "You're amazing, Soph. I can't believe you're here . . . with me like this."

"I'm here," she repeated, taking him inside her tight, hot body. "And I'm not going anywhere."

He eased in slowly, letting her adjust to the size of him. Her knees on either side of his hips, she placed her palms on the ceiling of the cab and began moving up and down, slow and fast, measured and frenzied. The swaying of the coach and the vibration of the seat felt wickedly erotic. Every time she lowered herself, sheathing him completely, he went a little mad. In the best bloody way.

He grasped her hips and nibbled the taut peak of one breast until she whimpered. Clenched her muscles around him. Cried out in ecstasy.

"Oh God, Reese." Her eyes fluttered shut, her back arched, and her body pulsed as release shimmered through her, carrying him right along.

Head buzzing, muscles coiling, he came with the raw force and power of a hurricane. Pleasure, pure and potent, roared through his body, mind, and soul, obliterating the grief and guilt inside of him. Washing it out to sea.

He and Sophie floated above the storm, clinging to each other and savoring every surge, until, at last, she collapsed on top of him. Resting her head on his shoulder, she murmured, "I love you."

He trailed his fingertips over her bare back, soothing her heated skin. "I love you."

But as she slid her hand from the side of his neck down his chest, she sat up, frowning. "What's this?"

"Hmm?" His mind was still pleasantly dazed, his body completely sated.

She patted the outside of his jacket. "There's something hard in here."

"Oh." Grinning, he sat up, pulled the object out of his pocket, and presented it to her. "For you."

"My journal," she breathed. Once again, her expression

turned rapturous as she clutched the book to her gloriously naked breasts.

"I didn't think it possible to be jealous of a journal," he said. "But I've proven myself wrong."

"I thought you'd burned this!" she exclaimed.

He shook his head. "I only wanted Singleton to believe I had."

"Thank you." She leaned forward and kissed him, warming his chest and completely thawing the frozen center of his heart.

Reluctantly, he pulled away. "We'll be at Warshire Manor soon. Let me help you straighten your gown."

He did his best, but it turned out he was far more adept at *un*lacing than lacing, and after a few failed attempts, all he'd succeeded in doing was making Sophie giggle. Which, he decided, was definitely not a bad thing.

"Stop," she chuckled, wiping her eyes. "I've laughed so much my belly hurts."

"I never claimed to be a lady's maid," he grumbled, even though his heart felt lighter than ever before.

"I should say not," she teased, circling her arms around his neck. "My gown is falling off, my hair is a disaster, and I'm in an utter state of dishabille."

He gazed into her bottomless blue eyes. "If it makes you feel any better, I can state with absolute authority that you have never, ever looked more beautiful." He shrugged off his jacket and slipped it around her shoulders.

She gratefully snuggled into it and pressed a tender kiss to his cheek.

As the coach rolled to a stop in front of the manor house, he took her hand and laced his fingers through hers, marveling at the rightness of it. "How long can you stay?"

"I told my parents I'd be spending the night with Fiona

and Gray," she said, leaping out of the coach and into his arms. "Which means we have all night."

"In that case," he drawled, "would you like to go for a walk in the garden?"

"I would." She flashed him a smile so bright it lit up the evening sky. "How did you guess?"

After stopping in the house briefly to drop off the journal and pick up a couple of lanterns and a quilt, Sophie and Reese slipped out of the back door, joined hands, and strolled toward the garden.

As they crossed the quaint footbridge over the sparkling moat, all the happiness inside her bubbled up and escaped in a blissful sigh. "I'll never tire of spending time here," she said. "Especially at night, when everything from the rustling leaves to the fragrant flowers feels otherworldly and magical."

"This place never felt magical to me," Reese said. "Not until you came here. You've changed the way I look at everything."

She gazed at his handsome profile, wondering at the physical differences in him. The hollows had disappeared from his cheeks; the haunted look had vanished from his eyes. "How have you been sleeping?" she asked.

"I still wake up in a cold sweat occasionally, but not as often as before." They stepped up onto the pavilion and paused by the railing to take in the view. Twisted black poplars to one side, pale grey asphodels to the other, and a glimpse of paradise beckoning in between.

"That's good." She leaned her head on his shoulder, drinking in his sturdy, solid comfort. "Maybe the nightmares will continue to lessen over time."

"Maybe," he mused. "Maybe not. But I think the best way I can honor Conroy and the others we lost is to live each day to the fullest—and to take care of the families they left behind."

She slid a hand over his muscled biceps. "Have you seen Sarah and the girls recently?"

"I have." He turned toward her and circled his arms around her waist. "She, Rose, and Julia were here a couple of days ago."

"Here?" Sophie tipped up her chin so she could meet his eyes. "In the garden?"

"Not exactly. I was showing them a cottage on the edge of my property. I've spent the last couple of weeks improving it. The girls seemed to like it."

Sophie blinked, stunned. "Did they?"

"They ran around the house like heathens." Reese's mouth quirked, softening the harsh angles of his face. "Sarah had a difficult time prying them away from the rope swing I hung in the yard."

"You hung a . . ." She shook her head, wondering if she'd heard him correctly. "Are Sarah and the girls going to live in the cottage?"

He nodded slowly. "Along with Violet and the babe, once it's born. Violet wants to return to her old position in a few months, and Sarah was thrilled at the prospect of watching the little one while Violet is working at the manor house. And, selfishly, I'm looking forward to watching my niece or nephew grow up. Conroy's girls too."

"That's wonderful," Sophie breathed. It felt as though her heart would burst with happiness. "I'm so proud of you, Reese."

He shrugged. "It took me a while to realize that Edmund wasn't perfect. That none of us is. I can't change decisions I've made in the past, but I can try to do the right thing now." He gazed at her, his dark eyes unexpectedly shy. "I was thinking that, since you have a talent for bringing people together, maybe you could help me with a new project."

"Of course I'm willing to help," she said, humbled by his trust in her. "What did you have in mind?"

"A regular gathering for soldiers who've returned from war—and their families too. A place where they can talk if they want to . . . and not feel so alone."

Sophie found herself on the verge of tears again. She placed her palms on either side of his face and beamed at him. "That is a beautiful idea. I'd be honored to play a part in bringing it to life." Grinning, she added, "I happen to know of an excellent meeting location. It's booked on Friday evenings, but available any other day of the week."

"Is that so?" he asked, flashing a wry grin of his own.

"I've been thinking about making some changes too," she said.

"Oh?"

"I've been keeping secrets from my family, my friends, even you. Maybe it's time for the Debutante Underground to come out of the shadows."

"I understand why you've kept the meetings a secret up until now," he said earnestly. "But I can also see how that would create its own set of problems. Sometimes revealing your secrets releases you from their power . . . and frees you. Whatever you decide, I'll stand by you."

"I'll have to ponder it for a bit, and speak with all the other members," Sophie said, but she was already warming to the idea. "In the meantime, I think we should head to the garden."

He picked up the quilt and one of the lanterns, then handed the other to her. "Let's go."

They strolled down a winding walkway, past lushly blooming flower beds populated with charming stone statues of woodland animals, sprites, and nymphs. They heard the cheerful splash of the waterfall before they saw it, and when they reached the clearing, Reese set their lanterns near the reflecting pool and spread the quilt on the grass.

"It's so warm," Sophie said, frowning at the skirt of her gown, which stuck to her legs like a gauzy cobweb.

"I know how we can cool off," Reese said. He was already shrugging out of his jacket and pulling off his boots. Sophie gleefully attacked the laces of her gown, and before long, they had both stripped off every stitch of their clothing.

His eyes turned dark with desire, and something like a growl escaped his throat. "You're gorgeous, Soph."

"So are you." To be precise, he looked like a god. Her very own Prince of Darkness. And she never, ever wanted to leave him again.

He moved behind her and slowly removed the handful of pins left in her hair, running his fingers through the honey-colored strands as he kissed the column of her neck. "You're mine," he murmured, sending a shiver through her limbs. "Always and forever."

His wicked hands cruised up her sides, beneath her swollen breasts, and over the curves of her hips. When her knees wobbled, she leaned into him, and he easily scooped her into his arms. "I have another special place to show you."

He carried her toward the edge of the pool and behind the fall, where they were surrounded by cool rock on one side and clear water on the other. She snuggled against his hard, warm chest as she stuck a toe through the chilly, wet curtain.

He arched a dark brow. "How does it feel?"

"Perfect."

He shot her a grin that made her belly flutter. "Want to walk through with me?" he asked.

"Of course," she said, holding on a little tighter. "I want to go everywhere with you."

Deliberately, he eased his back below the sheet of water, and it sluiced over his tanned, chiseled body, splashing on his broad shoulders and spraying cool droplets on her head. She held her breath as he carried her under the smooth, rushing water. Savored the way it slid over her breasts, down her belly, and between her legs. Sighed when he set her on her feet and pulled her against him.

They moved in and out of the falling water, kissing, laughing, and clinging to each other. And when they both were dizzy with desire, they ran, dripping, back to the quilt and made love so slowly, so sensuously, that hot tears trickled down Sophie's cheeks.

Afterward, as they lay on their backs, gazing contentedly at the starlit sky above, Reese plucked a daisy, placed it on her belly, and kissed her forehead.

When she giggled, he propped himself on an elbow and looked down at her, love shining in his eyes. "Miss Kendall," he said, his voice husky and low, "why are you laughing?"

She picked up the daisy, twirled the stem between her fingers, and playfully brushed the petals beneath his chin. "I was just thinking of all the flowers you've given me. And now I have one more for the collection in my diary."

"Your diary?" He shot her a rakish grin and lazily trailed a fingertip between her breasts. "You're going to write about this?"

"I've written about all our nights together," she admitted. "And I've dried and pressed the flowers from each encounter. I have the yellow rose from Lady Rufflebum's garden and the crown of asphodels. I have the peony bouquet from our night at the lake and the violet aster you tucked behind my ear. They're all precious to me because they remind me of the way you made me feel. I never want to forget those feelings."

"I won't let you forget," he said earnestly, brushing a kiss across her lips. "I hope your diary has a lot more pages, because we have a lifetime together. A lifetime of feelings . . . and more flowers than you'll know what to do with."

She swept the daisy's soft petals across the planes of his chest and lower, over the ridges of his abdomen, then shot him a sultry smile. "I feel certain I'll think of something."